Asda Tickled Pink

45p from the sale of this book will be donated to Tickled Pink.

Asda Tickled Pink want to ensure all breast cancers are diagnosed early and help improve people's many different experiences of the disease. Working with our charity partners, Breast Cancer Now and CoppaFeel!, we're on a mission to make checking your boobs, pecs and chests, whoever you are, as normal as your Asda shop. And with your help, we're raising funds for new treatments, vital education and life-changing support, for anyone who needs it. Together, we're putting breast cancer awareness on everyone's list.

Since the partnership began in 1996, Asda Tickled Pink has raised over £100 million to help its charity partners. Through the campaign Asda Tickled Pink has been committed to raising vital funds and awareness through fun and engaging in-store activities and via our exclusive range of Tickled Pink products which support our charity partners with on pack breast checking messaging and donations. The funds have been vital for Breast Cancer Now's world-class research and life-changing support services, such as their Helpline, there to help anyone affected by breast cancer cope with the emotional impact of the disease. Asda Tickled Pink's educational and outreach work with CoppaFeel! aims to empower one million 18-24 year olds to adopt regular checking checking behaviour by 2025. Together we will continue to make a tangible difference to breast cancer in the UK.

Asda Tickled Pink and the Penguin Random House have teamed up to bring you Tickled Pink Books. By buying this book and supporting the partnership, you ensure that 45p goes directly to the Breast Cancer Now and CoppaFeel! This donation will be split 70/30 to Breast Cancer Now and CoppaFeel! respectively.

Breast Cancer is the most common cancer in women in the UK, with one in seven women being affected by it in their lifetime. (Cancer Research UK 2021. Breast cancer incidence [invasive] statistics.) (Cancer registration statistics, England: 2021)

Around 55,000 women and nearly 400 men are diagnosed with breast cancer every year in the UK and nearly 1,000 people still lose their life to the disease each month. This is one person every 45 minutes and this is why your support and the support from Asda Tickled Pink is so important.

A new Tickled Pink Book will go on sale in Asda stores every two weeks – we aim to bring you the best stories of friendship, love, heartbreak and laughter.

To find out more about the Tickled Pink partnership
https://corporate.asda.com/asda-tickled-pink

ASDA Tickled *Pink*

CHECK YOUR BOOBS, PECS OR CHEST REGULARLY

One in seven women in the UK will be diagnosed with breast cancer in their lifetime

'TOUCH, LOOK, KNOW YOUR NORMAL, REPEAT REGULARLY'

Make sure you stay breast aware

- Get to know what's normal for you
- Look and feel to notice any unusual changes early
- The earlier breast cancer is diagnosed, the better the chance of successful treatment
- Check your boobs regularly and see a GP if you notice a change

Jo Thomas worked for many years as a reporter and producer, including time at Radio 4's *Woman's Hour* and Radio 2's Steve Wright show.

Jo's debut novel, *The Oyster Catcher*, was a runaway bestseller and won both the RNA Joan Hessayon Award and the Festival of Romance Best EBook Award. Her book *Escape to the French Farmhouse* was a No. 1 bestselling ebook. In every one of her novels Jo loves to explore new countries and discover the food produced there, both of which she thoroughly enjoys researching. Jo lives in Pembrokeshire with her husband and three children, where cooking and gathering around the kitchen table are a hugely important and fun part of their family life.

Visit Jo's website: jothomasauthor.com
or follow her on:
𝕏 Jo_Thomas01
❤️ JoThomasAuthor
📷 JoThomasAuthor

Sign up for Jo's newsletter at:
www.penguin.co.uk/jo-thomas-newsletter

Also by Jo Thomas

THE OYSTER CATCHER
THE OLIVE BRANCH
LATE SUMMER IN THE VINEYARD
THE HONEY FARM ON THE HILL
SUNSET OVER THE CHERRY ORCHARD
A WINTER BENEATH THE STARS
MY LEMON GROVE SUMMER
COMING HOME TO WINTER ISLAND
ESCAPE TO THE FRENCH FARMHOUSE
FINDING LOVE AT THE CHRISTMAS MARKET
CHASING THE ITALIAN DREAM
CELEBRATIONS AT THE CHÂTEAU
RETREAT TO THE SPANISH SUN
KEEPING A CHRISTMAS PROMISE
SUMMER AT THE ICE CREAM CAFE
COUNTDOWN TO CHRISTMAS
LOVE IN PROVENCE
A RECIPE FOR CHRISTMAS
A PLACE IN THE SUN

Ebook short stories:
THE CHESTNUT TREE
THE RED SKY AT NIGHT
NOTES FROM THE NORTHERN LIGHTS

Jo Thomas

Christmas at Hollybush Farm

PENGUIN BOOKS

TRANSWORLD PUBLISHERS

UK | USA | Canada | Ireland | Australia
India | New Zealand | South Africa

Transworld is part of the Penguin Random House group of companies
whose addresses can be found at global.penguinrandomhouse.com.

Penguin Random House UK, One Embassy Gardens,
8 Viaduct Gardens, London SW11 7BW

penguin.co.uk

Penguin
Random House
UK

First published in Great Britain in 2025 by Penguin Books
an imprint of Transworld Publishers

001

Typeset in 11/14pt ITC Giovanni Std by Six Red Marbles UK,
Thetford, Norfolk
Printed and bound in Great Britain by Clays Ltd, Elcograf S.p.A.

The authorized representative in the EEA is Penguin Random House
Ireland, Morrison Chambers, 32 Nassau Street, Dublin D02 YH68.

A CIP catalogue record for this book is available from the British Library

ISBN: 9781804993873

Penguin Random House is committed to a sustainable future
for our business, our readers and our planet. This book is made
from Forest Stewardship Council® certified paper.

For the young farmers who have chosen agriculture as their career and go out to work come rain or shine, to put the food on our tables.

1

November: six weeks until Christmas

'They look as if they want to eat me!'

They sound like a pack of hungry wolves demanding to be fed. I can see that, if you don't know the farm dogs and how friendly they really are, you could be mistaken for thinking they're after your blood.

I turn to Matthew and smile. Despite the rain hammering against the windscreen, it feels so familiar and I'm happy to be here. I place a reassuring hand on his knee. 'They're just pleased to see us.' I engage the handbrake on Matthew's new electric car – he's finally let me drive it so we can share the couple of hours' journey from our Cardiff base to west Wales on the dark evening. I took over when we left the main road to do the last few miles along narrow lanes stretching from the coast over windswept common land on the mountain, then lush green fields and eventually the small town where I grew up. We're making for my family's farm on its outskirts.

Matthew looks out of the windscreen through the rivulets of rain and the smooth swish of the windscreen wipers, distinctly unsure. I find it quite endearing: I haven't seen him like this before, out of his comfort zone. In the corporate world he and I work seamlessly together. He manages a hotel in the Catref Group, and I'm the area manager, over-seeing all our hotels in the east of the principality. We know what we're doing, what the other is think-ing. We've worked alongside each other for two years now, understanding the hotel brand, its emphasis on luxury and fine dining.

Now I know him well enough to understand why he wanted to make this trip to meet my father. It's his first time here, even though I come home every November for an early Christmas before I get mad busy in work. I'm hoping this Christmas is going to put Matthew's and my relationship on the next level. We've made all the right moves. We've climbed the career ladder, even had a conversation about pen-sion plans and retiring somewhere hot, but that's a little way in the future. But it *is* in the plans. We may not have much time off at Christmas, what with the influx of hotel guests and seasonal gala dinners, but

Matthew has asked to meet my father for a particular reason. I've always been very independent, but there's something touching about Matthew's idea to ask Dad for my hand in marriage this weekend.

'Just open the gate. I promise they won't hurt you,' I say, looking down at his clean, polished brogues. 'Actually,' I say, 'I can go.' I know these puddles so well.

My hand is on the door when he reaches over and smiles tightly. 'No, no, it's fine, Jem. I can do it. Got to get used to this if I'm going to be with a farmer's daughter.'

Sweet, I think. It's not that I forget I'm a farmer's daughter, but I've been in hospitality for so many years that farming is a long way in the past. A past I left behind when I moved away, and especially since I met Matthew on the company team-bonding weekend. We eat and sleep work. Pillow talk is often about how the rotas are looking, a new chef in the kitchen or plans for the following year's summer bookings. Yet when I'm back here, like now, I feel like I've been away no time at all.

'Okay. Just watch out for the puddle by the gatepost.' I point. 'It's deeper than you think.'

I see him swallow as he opens the door tentatively. He pushes and the wind sweeps in, the rain rushing to meet him through the crack. I glance at his feet again. When I said bring suitable shoes I didn't expect him to be in his best brogues.

'They don't look pleased to see us, if you ask me.' Matthew has one hand on the passenger door, but isn't making a move to get out and open the gate.

I look at the three dogs barking furiously. The ever-feisty, energetic Jack Russell, named after Dolly Parton, Dad's favourite singer; Dad's older hardworking collie Ffion; and the younger pup I haven't even met. Dixie or . . . I can't remember what he said. He was the last in Ffion's litter. I look at the pup, leaping at the gate.

'I can't believe I haven't met him yet!' It's been a whole year since I was home. It's not for want of trying, but Dad keeps insisting that I get on with life where I am. Enjoy myself while I can. Life has been so busy since I got the promotion, travelling to each of the different hotels, overseeing their activities, staffing and service. But now, there's another promotion on the horizon, and the possibility of a move abroad for Matthew and me. I can't wait to introduce Matthew to Dad. I'm bubbling over with excitement, like a twenty-year-old not the forty-year-old I am, and hoping that this Christmas Matthew wants to make things more permanent. Why else would he have suggested the trip when work is so busy for both of us? We're about to start preparing for our big annual events at Christmas and a trip to the States straight afterwards. New year, new adventures.

I look towards the farmhouse at the top of the

drive. I know Dad will have a pot of cawl on the go for when we arrive. It was always a favourite when I was growing up. He had to step up to be Mum and Dad after Mum went off to live her 'best life' in Mallorca with a man she'd met on a girls' holiday, getting away from the winter grey of the farm. Since she left, it's been just me and Dad, with Gramps and Nan, until they died. In Mallorca Mum had set up a B-and-B. I've been there, but it didn't feel like home. The farm-house, especially the kitchen, was always home. Then Mum moved on to Australia, got a job as an air stewardess. We stay in touch, birthdays and Christmases. She has a new husband, and a much-cherished child with him. She has a new life without me or Dad in it. I hated the thought of Dad being on his own at the farm, but he insisted I shouldn't stay. He didn't want me to feel trapped, as my mum obviously had.

The sign over the farm gate is swinging in the wind. Older and creakier than I remember. How can it have weathered so much in the time I've been away? I peer at the familiar fields around me in the dark afternoon. I know every dip, curve and run on them, every tree on the skyline, bending in the wind. And I'm right back to being a child, coming home from school into the warm kitchen where there was a pot of tea on the table. Dad would stride in from the yard in his boots and overalls and try to hug me, making me squeal with delight. I'd dump my bag and tell him about my day, then head out into the yard with him to help feed the animals. Despite Mum leaving, this was always my happy place.

I look again at the cream sign with black writing: Fferm llwyn Celyn, Hollybush Farm. It has always been there, and Dad has always given it an annual spruce. Maybe he'll still do it before Christmas. He liked to push the boat out for Christmas, when it was the four of us, and even when it was just him and me. Christmas always felt special at Hollybush Farm, with carols in the church and the Christmas fair in town. Other farmers would drop in, making the effort to be with each other and not on their own in their farmhouses. I'm surprised Dad's not outside to greet us, wearing a Santa hat or maybe just one from the eclectic mix that has accumulated over the years by the back door.

The dogs seem particularly worked up. I push my door open and step out into the rain. 'I'll go,' I say, dodging the deep puddle, which is definitely wider than it used to be, and put out my hands to the dogs. 'Hey, come on, settle down,' I say, as Dad would. But they keep up their noisy greeting, barking loudly. I hear the sign squeak on its hinges as I step forward to the gate, feeling the rain on my face. After a long drive with the heating on, it's cold, but refreshing and familiar. I'd forgotten how wet dark afternoons could feel on the farm.

When I was a teenager, Dad couldn't wait to encourage me out into the world, to see what was there. Hospitality was a great way to enjoy the lights and fun of city life. He wanted me to live away from the farm. He didn't want me to resent it, like Mum had. She'd found a way out with bar work and followed her dream of living in the sun. But right now, as I breathe in the cold, wet air, it feels good to be home. Even if a few jobs around the place have been missed. I'll need to speak to Owen, Dad's assistant. If Dad's paying him to help, these things should be done, I muse, with a flash of irritation. I'm not having him take advantage of Dad, being paid and not putting in the work. He's always relied on his cheeky smile and sparkling eyes to get him whatever he wants in life. I push open the gate, which promptly falls off its hinges to a cacophony of dogs barking even louder.

2

'Dad?' I shout, getting out of the car, which I've parked in the yard, next to his old Land Rover.

The dogs don't give up their incessant barking, circling me, despite my best efforts at being strict. Matthew hasn't even got out of the car yet.

'Dad! We're here!' I call again, hauling my well-travelled case from the back seat, and the bag of Christmas presents. A new jumper and socks. 'What's Christmas without new socks?' he would always say, when I asked him what he wanted. I've brought festive food and drink for him too, to enjoy after we've gone.

Usually he'd be standing on the front-door step, in the open-sided wooden porch, under the lantern light, his smile as wide as his open arms, waiting to hug me. I may be all grown-up now, but I still want my hug. The sort of hug that tells you, whatever is going on in your life, it's all going to be okay.

'Dad? Where are you? We're here!' I call into the rain that's sliding sideways across the front of the farmhouse, exposed but with a clear view over the fields below and the stock. There isn't even a light on outside. Or in the kitchen. Don't tell me he's forgotten what time we're due and nipped into town. I say, 'nipped': it's down the drive, then the twisty lane, which holidaymakers attempt to drive along as a shortcut when they're towing caravans and boats, and onto the main road that finally leads to town. But the Land Rover is there, so he must be too.

'Dad?' I hurry towards the front door, which is part-open, as it often is, the dogs coming in and out. 'We're here!' I call, carrying my case and the festive treats for Dad. A bottle of his favourite Welsh whisky, a tin of shortbread, some local cheese, a bottle of red from our suppliers, some posh dog treats for the gang, who are still running around barking like they're possessed, and a jar of spicy, pickled onions with a real kick. They're made just down the road and I stopped off to buy them, as I always do when I come home.

'Matthew, grab your case and the onions and bring them in,' I call over the rain. 'And the wine from the boot. This way!' I point towards the door and run on ahead.

In the kitchen, it's cold. Despite the front door

being open it's usually warm in here. The range is always on. I look around. No sign of dinner waiting. No cawl on the go – he'll make a batch that lasts him for days. It's that or fried eggs on toast when the hens are laying. I frown. I touch the range as I pass it on the way to put my bags down. It's stone cold.

Ffion is running to and from the living room barking, as if she's telling Dad I'm here . . . or, and I go cold, even colder than I was, telling me that Dad is there.

'Dad?' I run into the living room and he's in his chair. The fire in the grate is dead.

He looks at me, his eyes wide and confused. 'IshnososurchIfeelingwoof . . .'

I stare at him in shock. Is he drunk?

No. He's not drunk, but he is in shock. 'It's okay, Dad. I'm here. You're going to be fine.'

The dogs stop barking. I reach for the landline phone, which is on the table beside him, a letter underneath it. Yes, he still has a landline: the mobile reception around here is generally dreadful.

'Jem!' I hear Matthew call my name as I'm dialling 999.

'In here,' I call back. 'It's Dad. I think he's had a stroke or something.' Then to Dad, 'It's going to be okay,' I say. 'I'm here . . . Hello? Ambulance, please!' I put my hand on Dad's. 'They're on their way, Dad,' I tell him, as I hang up, feeling his cold hands.

Blankets. I need to keep him warm. Like we'd do with the lambs that struggle when they're first born.

I run into the kitchen, grab the latch and pull back the internal wooden door to run upstairs for blankets.

My old bedroom is as I remember it – it always is. But Dad has put on fresh bedding and laid out towels, clearly getting ready for our stay. I toss the towels onto the floor, yank the duvet off my bed and run back downstairs with it in my arms, my nose in its folds, smelling the comfort of home as I do.

'There you are,' I say.

Matthew is standing in the doorway, holding his case, a box of wine and a jar of pickled onions, rain dripping from his neatly cut short hair.

'Did you hear me calling you?' I ask.

'No, sorry, I was in the car, just waiting for the rain to pass. But it didn't. God, it's wet out there! Did you say you were calling me? What did you say?'

I take a deep breath. 'It's Dad!'

'Oh, yes? Where is he? Looking forward to saying hello.' He looks left then right, sniffs and looks down at the sole of his smart brogue. The corners of his mouth turn down. 'But I think I may have stepped in something . . . unpleasant,' he says.

But Matthew's brogues are the last thing on my mind right now.

3

'Sepsis,' the doctor tells me at the hospital. 'Good job you brought him in when you did. Left for much longer it would have been a lot more serious. We're lucky to have caught it in time.'

I'm in shock, what-ifs racing round my head like a rollercoaster ride. *What if I hadn't got there when I did? What if I hadn't come down this weekend? What if no one had found him?*

'He shouldn't try to rush his recovery. It'll take a while to build up his strength again. His appetite may not be good, but you should encourage him to eat.'

I nod.

'We'll keep him in for the next day or so to see how things are looking. Once he starts to pick up, we'll send him home.'

'Hear that, Dad?' I put my hand on his. 'You'll be home in no time. Back on the farm.'

He opens his eyes and nods wearily. I turn back to the doctor. 'Just one question, how did he get sepsis? Is it likely to come back?'

The doctor gestures at the bandage around Dad's hand. 'Probably from that. A cut. Anything could have done it, a rusty knife, a bit of fencing. We see it a lot in farmers – they're used to small injuries and tend not to get them looked at. If a cut isn't cleaned properly, it can lead to sepsis.'

I can just imagine Dad not really noticing a cut when he's working in the yard, just carrying on. I lean in and kiss his forehead. He's hot, like he's got a fever.

'His temperature should come down once the antibiotics kick in.'

'Thank you. Thank you so much,' I say to the young doctor.

'No problem. It's what we're here for,' he says. His eyes are tired. Maybe he's coming to the end of a long shift.

After an evening at the hospital, I'm stiff from sitting in uncomfortable waiting room chairs. I leave Dad tucked up in bed, under the thin blankets in the warm ward, sleeping, with reassurance from the nurses that they'll call if there's any change. I thank them and head out towards Reception, where a nurse is smiling as she wheels a patient through the big double doors. I hold the door open for her and she thanks me. I recognize her from school, I think, but I don't say anything. All I can think about is Dad, and I replay what the doctor said: Lucky to have caught it in time.

What if I hadn't been there? The thought runs round and round in my head.

I slide into the car, where Matthew has been napping most of the evening. Everything seems a bit surreal. He puts out a hand and rubs my knee.

We drive back to the farm in silence. All I can think about is how pale and helpless Dad looked in the hospital. So different from the big, strong farmer who usually comes to mind when I picture him.

I get out of the car and lift the listing gate open for Matthew to drive through, then prop it shut and jump back in. He drives us up to the yard in front of the farmhouse, with the familiar red front door.

Matthew looks up at the house from behind the windscreen. 'You know, we could get a hotel for the night. Somewhere . . . a little more luxurious. You deserve to be pampered, what with the shock of finding your dad like that. We don't want to put any extra strain on him by having guests.'

I stare at him, wondering if I've heard all the words in the right order. 'I'm not a guest, Matthew.

This is my home, and my dad has sepsis. I need to be here for him once he's been discharged from the hospital.'

'Yes, of course. I can always find somewhere else. Just to stay out of the way.'

'There's only one pub in town with accommodation, and I'd hardly call it luxurious. To be honest, I'm not even sure they offer the rooms any more.' I pause, thinking about everything that needs to be done. 'I need to stay on for a night or two. Check all the animals. Find out where Owen is. After all, he's supposed to be the farm manager. Why didn't he find Dad?'

'Of course you need to get everything sorted. I can always come back once your dad's better. Like I say, maybe this isn't the best time. Don't want to add to any stress' – he gives a gentle laugh – 'by asking for his daughter's hand in marriage!'

I smile at him, but right now, there's no excitement. I'm tired and I'm worried. I look up at the farmhouse again, in need of attention, like the rest of the place. 'That's kind of you . . . Maybe we should just hold off telling him all our news right now. About the new job and everything else going on, the move across the Pond.' I lay a hand on his forearm. 'You understand?' I ask gently. 'Just until things are a little more settled. Until he's feeling better.'

I have an urge not to overwhelm Dad with all

the changes I've been talking about – new job, new country, engagement – to protect him. I'm feeling apprehensive about it all and if it's me who's strangely overwhelmed by everything. But why? This is all Dad has ever wished for me. To get out, see the world and find someone special to share my life with. And I have, in Matthew. He's the perfect fit, and just the person for me to be making this new leap with.

He nods a lot.

'Of course, I totally get it,' he says warmly, and then, 'I can shoot off whenever. Like I say, I don't want to be in the way.'

'I need to know he's going to be okay, when or if . . .'

'When,' he says, with a firm smile.

'. . . if I accept the job and move stateside. Part of me wishes he could come too,' I say. 'But I know he won't leave this place. He loves it.'

And just for a moment I wonder if I hear Matthew sigh. I snap my head round to him and half laugh, half frown. 'Was that a sigh of relief?'

'No, no . . . God, no,' he says. 'Just tired. You must be shattered. Let's get you inside,' he says, pushing open the car door into the familiar rain.

In the chilly kitchen, the dogs are quieter, much quieter. I pat them and thank them for their good work and hand out the Christmas dog treats, handfuls at a time.

'Could you light a fire in the living room, Matthew, while I get the range going?' I ask, pulling open the door with the temperature control in it.

'Sure,' he says, sounding doubtful.

I stare at the button, but it's already on. I pull open the front door and march to the oil tank in the yard.

'Out of oil!' I stare at the gauge on the oil tank in dismay. I hurry back into the kitchen and go to ring the number on the wall. The calendar has this day circled, many times, and my heart twists.

Suddenly the phone rings, before I have a chance to dial the number. 'Hello?'

'Oh . . . hi. I was looking for Mr Edwin Jones. It's Llew, Llew Griffiths, tell him.'

'It's not a good time,' I say, quickly and efficiently. 'He's been taken ill. I need the phone. I'm sorry. Please call back later.'

'Oh, yes, of course, sorry. I hope—' I cut him off before he has a chance to finish and surprise myself with my curtness, but I'm really worried about Dad. And why on earth he's been left without oil and heating.

I ring the oil man quickly from the landline phone, with its long curly cable.

'Unpaid bill?' I repeat, and look over at Matthew, who is standing in the kitchen in a dark blue blazer,

17

looking very over- or perhaps under-dressed. I point to my handbag and he hands it to me. 'I can pay that now. It must have slipped Dad's mind,' I lie.

He never lets bills slide. He always pays straight away because he knows how tough it is to be kept waiting. For a self-employed farmer, getting a payment can be the difference between the weekly grocery shop or not.

I pull out my credit card and pay the bill, which makes my eyes water. 'And you'll have a delivery here as soon as possible?' I say. 'Dad's in hospital. I need to get the house warm for him coming home.'

'Sorry to hear that. We'll get it there tomorrow. Your dad's a good customer. No idea why he didn't order before he ran out. He knows we'd cut him some slack on the payment,' says Alun the oil man.

'Like I say, it must've . . . slipped his mind. He has sepsis,' I say. 'Sorry about that. And *diolch*, thank you,' I say, slipping into Welsh without thinking about it, unable to imagine Dad needing to have any slack cut. His finances were always well organized.

I hang up, then go through my phone and find Owen's number. I ring it, but it goes to voicemail. I look around the cold farmhouse kitchen. I open the cupboards. There are eggs from the hens, I'm guessing, which are clearly still laying. Some bread, that is past its best and will need toasting.

'Looks like it's eggs on toast,' I say to Matthew, who

is shivering. 'And red wine and cheese.' I reach for the treats I've brought with us for Dad. 'How's the fire coming on?'

Matthew grimaces. 'Not so good,' he says. 'I'm not a real-fires man. More used to the fake ones at the hotel.'

I put down the eggs and bread, and head into the living room to get the little fire blazing in next to no time. I sit back on my haunches and smile, staring into the flames. Everything about sitting here like this says I'm home.

I turn back to Matthew, who doesn't look as pleased as I am to have the fire blazing and looks frozen. 'Let's get some jumpers and blankets. The oil will be here tomorrow and it'll be much cosier after that.'

He nods, turning a shade of designer blue to match his blazer.

'Now, how do you like your scrambled eggs?' I ask. 'I can microwave them or microwave them.'

He looks at me as if I've gone mad.

'It'll be fun, I promise. But first we need to head for the pub. I need to find Owen and ask him what's been going on around here. Or not. I should be able to track him down, find out where he's living now, if we ask behind the bar.'

4

Stepping into the pub is like stepping back to my youth. The wave of warmth from the fire, stoked up and burning brightly, greets us. The Shepherd's Rest was always the hub of the town, especially when there was something to celebrate – Halloween, Bonfire Night, and Christmas Eve after carols in the little church.

Although it all looks the same, something's missing. I look around. People.

'Gosh, it's quiet,' I say to Matthew.

He shrugs. 'It's the industry all over. People aren't going out like they used to. You know that better than anyone. You have to pull them in. That's why your gala nights and weekday getaway specials are so good. You give people a reason to want to come to the hotels. Make it an affordable treat, while offering something a little extra.'

'Yes,' I agree. 'But the margins are still slim. We have to make savings wherever we can.'

'And that's why you're so good at your job. Buy in bulk for the lowest price. Running the same menus in all the hotels at the same time means you're making it work when the small businesses can't.'

I look around the quiet pub. 'It's hard out there right now. Unless you're a big company like us, it's pretty brutal for independents. But that's enough shop talk. This weekend was supposed to be a break from work.'

'You'll never be able to stop talking shop.' He grins. 'You live and breathe it. It's one of the things I love about you, your commitment to the job. And that you're so good at it.'

Right now, I need to be committed to sorting out Dad and finding Owen. Unless I give Owen a piece of my mind and get him to pull his weight at the farm, I won't be able to go back to work with peace of mind . . . and I need to be able to do that, with the busiest time of the year coming up. I want to know that Dad has all the help he needs.

'Jemima,' says a small man, sitting at the bar, using my full name, reminding me that I'm home again, with half a pint cradled in his gnarled hands. 'I heard about your dad.' It's Twm Bach. He was always a little man, hence his name – twm means 'small' in English – fit as a fiddle. Now he's much smaller and not looking as fit as usual. His family had a big dairy farm once upon a time, but none of the children wanted to take it on, so it was sold, Dad told me. 'My grandson Pedr works at the hospital. Said he'd been taken in. How is he?'

'He's okay,' I say, feeling a sense of relief as I say it and slightly tearful at the same time. 'I mean, he's been better but he's in the right place. It's sepsis. Probably from a cut in the palm of his hand. Hoping to bring him home soon.' I attempt to smile again, like I would to reassure hotel guests that there's nothing that can't be sorted, but with all sorts of worries at the back of my mind about how he'll be when he comes home. Will he be able to manage the stairs? Make his own food? Should I look at getting someone in to look after him? I guess I won't know anything until he's home.

'Sepsis. Can be nasty if they don't catch it early enough! Give him my best. Haven't seen him in a while. None of us seems to get out like we used to,' says Twm Bach. 'Years ago, we'd have been meeting up on one another's farms. Nowadays we only see each other at funerals, it seems like.'

'Actually I'm looking for Owen,' I say to Twm. 'Owen Rhys.'

'I know who you mean.' He scoffs. 'You two used to be inseparable! Back to look him up, are you?'

'No, no, nothing like that. This is my partner.' I

introduce Matthew, standing beside me at the bar. 'But I need to find Owen.'

'Pleased to meet you,' says Matthew, holding out a hand for Twm to shake, which Twm does, warily, without returning the sentiment. 'Yes, I'm the lucky fella,' he tries to joke to Twm, who still gives nothing back, like a tennis ball hitting a wet blanket and falling to the floor.

Twm turns back to me. 'I'll give him a text message,' he says. 'Tell him there's a pint waiting for him. Although he may not get it. His phone's been cut off for a while.'

Twm pulls out an old brick phone and types. 'Marvellous technology, isn't it? When it works. I reckon he'll be here in a bit anyway. He'll be glad to see a friendly face. Mind you . . . I think technology's stopped us all talking to each other face to face. I should have called up on your dad a long time ago, like we used to.'

'Maybe you could, when he's home,' I say hopefully. It can't hurt to have people dropping in and checking on him. 'Can I get you a drink, Twm?' I ask.

'Half of dark, if you're sure,' he says, pushing his glass across the bar. '*Diolch*, and good health to your dad.'

I turn back to Matthew, who evidently needs something to make this whole experience a little more enjoyable. 'What would you like?'

'A Sauvignon blanc?' he asks the bar person, who looks at him blankly. I don't know her. She's young. I wonder where Sali, the landlady, is. 'Wine?' he adds.

'White or red?' she asks warily.

'Let's have gin and tonic,' I answer quickly.

Matthew looks at me as if he's arrived on another planet. He leans forward. 'Do you have Tanqueray?'

'Gordon's is fine,' I cut in, and the barmaid looks at me as if it's Matthew who's from another planet. 'Where's Sali? She hasn't sold up, has she?' I ask.

'She's on a cruise,' says the barmaid. 'Says she's had enough of this weather. But the Bay of Biscay was a nightmare! Ice and a slice?'

We take our drinks to a table and chairs by the fire, and Matthew seems finally to be thawing a little. We sip the gin and tonic, with melting ice cubes, and wait.

The door opens and I recognize him straight away. Owen doesn't change. Still the same crop of blond hair, as thick and plentiful as a field of corn. 'Owen!' I say, standing from the table.

'Oh, hi, Jem. What's happening? I just heard about the ambulance up at your dad's place.'

I step out from the table and walk towards him. 'I should be asking you the same question,' I say crossly.

Owen puts up his hands and takes a step back. 'Whoa!'

Matthew stands too, behind me. 'She's upset. Her father's unwell. I'm Matthew,' he says, putting out his hand. 'Jem's partner. We work together. Met on our first week with the company on a team bonding weekend. Didn't realize a weekend of role play and murder mystery in a country house would lead to finding my future wife,' he tries to joke. 'Been together for a couple of years now. I'm here to meet her father.' But before Owen has a chance to take his hand I step in.

'She is upset, yes,' I say, turning and glaring at Matthew, who seems to lean away as I do. 'And I can speak for myself,' I say quietly. Then slowly I turn back to Owen. 'Owen, I've just come from the farm.'

'What's happened to your dad?' he asks, looking concerned.

'He's in hospital with sepsis.'

'Oh, God – will he be all right?'

I take a deep breath. 'Yes. No thanks to you.'

He frowns. 'What? What do you mean by that?'

'He's paying you to work on the farm and the place has gone to ruin! And you couldn't check in on him and see how he's doing? Not work out that he hasn't had any heating on there for God knows how long? Or even contact me? It's not like you don't know my number. I haven't changed it!'

'Whoa,' he says again, holding up his hands. 'Of course I could've checked in on him. I haven't seen him for a while. I've been . . . had things on my mind. But, yes, I should have, I'm sorry. And I've been to get credit on my phone. Only just got your message.'

'We all have things on our minds, Owen, but Dad's paying you to look after the farm and from where I'm standing, you're not doing it very well.'

He takes a deep breath and puts his hands on his hips, on his worn leather belt, running through the belt loops on his soft, worn jeans, over his dark brown scuffed boots. He looks at me, his face as familiar now as it was when we were in school. Round, with a dimple in the middle of his chin. Only the laughter from his blue eyes has disappeared. His eyes always had laughter in them, right up until the day I told him I was leaving, going to see the world, taking a job on a cruise ship, and finished with him. Of course I've seen him since but we've both moved on. He has a partner and two children. I now have Matthew and the chance of a new life in America on the horizon.

'There's clearly things you need to catch up on around here, Jem,' he says, biting at the corner of his lip, as he always did when things were on his mind. Like when he'd spotted one of the younger kids getting bullied by some of the rugby boys. He couldn't stand back and waded in with a couple of well-placed punches and some stiff words of warning. What

Owen lacked in academic qualifications he made up for in heart and respect from his peers.

I frown. 'What's that supposed to mean? Things I need to catch up on.'

He takes another deep breath. 'It means I don't work for your dad, not any more.'

'What? But you've been there for years! You've left? Owen! How could you? No wonder he's not coping.'

'I didn't want to go. In fact, I kept turning up until he told me to get off his land.'

'Dad did?' I frown. 'Well, he must have been fed up with you taking another job.'

He shakes his thick blond hair again. 'I didn't find another job, Jem. He laid me off. He couldn't afford to keep me on, not with the way things were going, lamb prices and wool. Fleeces are worthless these days. He's been working the farm on his own.'

'On his own? For how long?' I turn back to Matthew. 'Why wouldn't he tell me that?'

'You know your dad. He wouldn't have wanted to worry you.'

Tears spring to my eyes, hot and angry. I nod and press my lips together. That's Dad all over.

'I'm sorry,' I say, looking up at the ceiling, to stop the tears falling. 'I had no idea.' I give a wry laugh. 'That says a lot about how good a daughter I've been, doesn't it? Didn't even know he'd laid you off and come home to find him practically in a coma, without heating.'

'He was happy for you, Jem. He was glad you'd found your own path. He wouldn't have wanted you rushing back here.'

'And what about you?' I say, concerned. 'Did you find another job?'

He shakes his head. 'Things are . . . difficult around here at the moment. Plenty of work still to be done, but no money to pay farm hands.'

'I'm sorry,' I say again. 'I shouldn't have—'

'It's fine. You're upset. Give your Dad my best and just call me if you need anything, anything at all. I have credit now. You can get hold of me and I'm happy to help, you know that.'

'I do,' I say, feeling utterly wretched.

'Now, I'm going to have my pint that Twm's promised me for cutting his grass.' He nods at Matthew. 'Nice to meet you, Matthew.'

'At least let me get you one,' I offer.

'I don't need charity. Not yet . . .' He gives a little smile but the laughter isn't there.

He walks to the bar and orders a pint of cider.

'How are your heifers?' asks Twm Bach.

Owen shakes his head. 'Got a buyer coming to look at them this week. I can't keep them going over the winter so I have to give them up. And the land.'

'Solar panels, that's what you want. Everyone's doing it. Don't cost to feed them.'

'And ruins the countryside for everyone, while sending the power to other parts of the UK so the locals don't even benefit from it.'

I sit in silence with Matthew, desperate to get back to the farm.

At the farmhouse I find more blankets, stoke the fire.

'I'm going to check the sheep. Then we'll eat,' I say to Matthew. 'Do you want to come with me, or wait here and open the wine?'

'I'll open the wine. At least I know what I'm doing there!' he says.

'I won't be long,' I say, kissing him, then grabbing Dad's wax jacket, with its torn pockets and worn collar, from the hook by the door. I breathe in its familiar scent.

'Come on, girl,' I say to Ffion. She's looking at me as if she knows she needs to step up now and help. 'We can do this together. I've just got to remember what I'm doing!'

'See, I told you it would be cosy,' I say, as we sit in front of the crackling fire, blankets over our knees, the dogs curled up at our feet. Our empty plates are stacked on the coffee-table, and I've just refreshed our glasses from the bottle of red I brought. Matthew looks around the small but cosy living room, with big windows looking out over the fields that drop away from the house. In daylight, you can see the sheep gathering under the big oak tree, like office workers at the coffee machine, passing on the gossip. And I'm remembering those early mornings in the lambing shed with Dad. We'd be knee-deep in straw and smiling at each other every time a new one was born and safely on its legs with its mum.

'With the rain lashing so hard you can't see a thing' – I point to the window – 'but when the snow comes, it's really special.'

'Is this how it was for you growing up?'

'Pretty much.'

'No telly?'

'Oh, yes, we had telly! Colour too!' I laugh. 'It wasn't the land that time forgot. But we were outside most of the time. I'd be helping Dad with the sheep, or with the dogs.'

'And you didn't miss other things? Cinemas, bars, shops?'

I smile. 'Not back then, no.'

I gaze into the fire, remembering when here was the only place I wanted to be. Safe, with Dad and the animals. Until life moved on . . . I moved on. 'It's what Dad always wanted me to do, see the world.' I smile at the memories. 'He didn't want me to end up resenting this place, like Mum had done. Feeling trapped here. For him this place was everything but he knew it wasn't for everyone. This was my grand-parents' place before it was my parents',' I explain, and start to tell him how things were before we had heating and electricity. What Christmas was like when the new range cooker was put in. I turn, beaming at the memory, but Matthew's head is on my shoulder, his eyes shut, fast asleep. Like I say, this place isn't for everyone, but it'll always be home to me.

5

The next morning, Sunday, when I wake up in my old bedroom in the big brass bed with the thick eiderdown, it's still freezing. Under the covers, it's warm as toast, but beyond the warmth of my bed, I can feel the cold nipping at the tip of my nose, making it itch. I remember these mornings only too well. Sometimes there would be ice on the inside of the glass. Today it's just cold and dark.

I steel myself, push back the covers quickly and dive straight to my case, pulling on as many layers as I can. Matthew seems to have gone to bed in all his clothes, including a smart grey beanie hat, and is still in them, fast asleep.

I take a look at his sleeping face. Dad may not be here, but I really do want to show Matthew where I grew up and why I love this place so much. Hopefully, after breakfast, I can take him out and introduce him to the land, particularly Gramps's field. It's the big one just below the house. That field made Gramps want to come to this farm. The views are amazing, and there is a wooden bench where he would sit to look out over the sheep and feel that all was well. It's always been a special place. It's the perfect spot.

Now, though, my head turns to hospitality. Breakfast. The last of the bread, and maybe more eggs.

I consider the café in town. Beti's. That was the place to go around here. She always did a brilliant breakfast. I remember Dad telling me that Beti had died, but her son had taken it over. I hope it's still as good as it was.

Downstairs, I'm shivering as I pull on Dad's coat, my old wellingtons, pink with flowers, that have seen better days, a woollen hat, and a head torch that's hanging on the hooks. I go to check the flock and deliver hay to them from the back of the old Land Rover, which is as reluctant as I am to get going this morning. The rain is back and relentless. I do a tour of the fields, checking for any fences down in the wind last night, and prop them up as best I can. Others will need new stakes and stock fencing and I'll tackle them when it's light. I check the water butts, but they're running clear, no ice yet.

After I've fed the ewes, Bertie the ram, his field mate Harriet, a small Welsh mountain pony, and the three chickens that Dad still has, I drive back to the farmhouse with the dogs. When I was growing up, Dad had lots of chickens and Dad did an egg round.

In the kitchen, it's still cold. Not like the early mornings I remember as a child, when I would run downstairs and the range would be on, opening its arms and giving me a great big hug. There's no fancy coffee machine here, I think, with a smile, remembering the joy of the one Matthew bought me for my last birthday that now sits pride of place in our small apartment at the hotel. I love turning it on in the mornings. Now I stand with my back to the range, wishing it would warm my backside, while waiting for the electric kettle to boil. I watch the clock, wondering what would be a reasonable time to ring the hospital to ask how Dad is. The puppy is chasing Ffion's tail, playfully tapping at it and biting it but she doesn't mind or even notice, just looks at me as if waiting for news. His energy is boundless, running in and out of the living room, pulling blankets and cushions onto the floor and tossing them around with carefree abandon.

I stare out of the window overlooking the yard, as it starts to slip from darkness to daylight, wondering what today will bring. Wondering if Dad has had a good night, if and how he's going to recover from this . . . and where to start trying to help while I'm here. The fallen gate, the swinging sign, checking the flock. And what happens to Dad when I leave? I look down at the puppy playing. How's Dad going to cope with all of this when he needs to take it easy and recover? I decide to go and keep an eye out for the oil tanker. I slip into my boots, pull on Dad's jacket and a woolly hat from the hooks beside the back door. There's always an odd selection there. I've no idea which belongs to whom, but I pull one over my ears, grab the head torch and go to open the door.

There's a knock and the dogs jump up, barking. I'm hoping it's the oil delivery.

'Hi!' I say, looking at a man in an expensive countryside coat, thick gloves and polished yard boots. He's fully prepared for the weather by the look of it.

'Hi,' he says, raising a hand, and smiling. It's actually an alarmingly good-looking smile.

'Er, the tank's over there. You know it, right?' I point at the oil tank. He glances over his shoulder. 'Hang on, I'll show you,' I say, glad of the distraction right now.

'Er, actually, I came to see how Edwin is. Are you his daughter? Jemima?'

That stops me in my tracks. I've no idea who he is.

'Oh, he's . . .' I look at the clock. It's nine. 'I'm about to phone the hospital.' I note the lack of signal on my phone – it'll have to be the land line. Then I look back at the stranger. 'Sorry, who are you?'

'I'm Llew. Llewelyn Griffiths. Your dad and I are talking through some options . . . for the farm.'

I stare at him blankly. 'With an oil delivery?' I look around for the delivery truck.

'Sorry, no. Erm . . . Just came to see how he was.'

The dogs give a bark but quickly settle and sniff around his feet, around his clean but well-worn ridgeback ankle boots. Clearly a man used to being outdoors, just not working in it.

'Oh, no news yet, but I can give you my number if that helps.'

'Sure.' He pulls out his phone and types as I say my name and reel off my number. And then, as he's confirming the details, he says, 'Actually, sorry, but did you know that your ram is out?' He points over his shoulder.

I frown. 'The ram?'

'Yes, big bugger. Seems to be having a fine old time in with the ewes. I'm thinking he's not supposed to be there, but I wasn't sure.'

'The ram's in with the ewes? But how? The gates were shut!' I must have missed a fallen fence in the dark. 'The ram's in with the ewes!' I realize what this means. 'He can get in . . . and they could get out! Quick!'

The man on the doorstep doesn't need asking

twice. He throws his phone onto the work surface, with a bag of something that smells warm and delicious. I pull the door open and run down the drive, with him in step beside me.

As we reach the field – I'm wearing the head torch – I call instructions.

'You go left,' I say 'I'll go right.'

Ffion is beside me. There are sheep all over the drive and, clearly having a fine old time, so is Bertie the ram.

At last, with Bertie back in his field, the ewes in theirs, we click the final gate shut, breathing heavily.

'Well, it's been a while since I've rounded up any stock,' I say, panting.

'And a first for me!' he says, leaning on the gate.

'Thank you. You were good. Fast.'

'No problem. But maybe make sure your gate gets fixed at the end of the drive and check for any fallen fences.'

'Can I make you a cup of tea?'

His breathing calms quicker than mine does. 'That would be very welcome,' he says, and again gives me his very attractive smile.

I can't help but smile back as we turn to walk towards the farmhouse. It's cold now, and the wind is biting.

'So, you're here visiting your dad?' he asks.

'Well, I was. But then he had this turn. Not really sure how long I'll be here.'

'It's a lot for him to manage on his own.'

'It is,' I say, worry creeping into my voice.

We head for the farmhouse, where the light is on over the door, as it always was. Not like when we arrived the other night.

I pull off my boots and hat. 'Thank you again for spotting Bertie and helping,' I say.

'No problem. I may not be a farmer, but I've worked with a few.'

'Intriguing.'

'I expect your dad's told you about me.'

I frown and shake my head, blowing on the tea and wrapping my hands around the cup.

'We've been in conversation. I was due to meet with him over these couple of days. It's why I'm in the area.'

I frown again. 'Sorry, what did you say your name was?'

'Llew. Llewelyn. Your dad doesn't really do things by email, so I thought I'd visit in person. Let me know if there's anything I can do to help.'

'Well, how are you with a hammer and screws to fix a fallen gate?'

He laughs. 'Not as handy as I'd like to be!'

I laugh with him.

'Sorry, you said you and Dad were talking through some options for the farm?'

'Yes, I'm' – he corrects himself – 'we're working with him, as you probably know.'

'Working with him? What do you mean?'

'Well, maybe you'd better speak to your dad.'

'Okay,' I say, confused. 'I'm just waiting to call the hospital. Find out how he's doing. I'm hoping they won't keep him in too long. But I do need oil so I can get the heating on before he comes home,' I say. Heat will make things a lot better.

'Tell him I sent my best.' He raises a hand and turns to leave. 'I brought these,' he says, handing over the bag and the tray of cups from a big-brand coffee shop he had been carrying when he arrived.

I take them from him. 'I didn't even know they had a store here!'

'Just outside town,' he says. 'Drive-through. Quite a few of them popping up nowadays. People like the convenience.'

'Wow! That's progress here,' I say. How different things are since I was growing up: drive-through coffees compared to Beti's, where the fire would be lit and there'd be the hubbub of chatter, the steamed-up front window and no need for social media because nothing got past Beti: she knew everything that was going on.

He turns to leave, holding up a hand. 'As I said, let me know if there's anything I can do.'

'Sure. Okay, thank you,' I say, thinking again how attractive he is. I'm not at all sure what he's talking about, but if Dad is getting some help around the place that's good. I smile. 'We'll be in touch.' I raise a hand back and watch him go, as he gets into his smart, clean car. Not the sort of vehicle I'd expect a farm hand to drive, that's for sure.

I breathe in the scent of the coffee and croissants.

'Nice to meet you. Bye,' he says, as he clicks the car open and steps in.

I can't help feeling as if I may just have been flirted with, bringing a little glow to my cheeks.

'*Hwyl*, bye.' I find myself slipping into Welsh again as I watch him go, smiling and still glowing from our short meeting. A handsome, polite man bringing coffee and croissants to my door and enquiring after my dad. This could be exactly what Dad needs. Someone to help and 'work together' on the farm. Excellent news! I feel my spirits lifting. I grab one of the coffees, step out of the back door and into the yard, pulling the door closed behind me. The dogs are at my feet, Ffion not leaving my side and her pup darting about but not going far. The old Jack Russell, Dolly, has gone back to her bed in front of the range, clearly not happy that it's so cold.

As the oil men fill the tank, I shove my hands into my pockets and head up to the feed shed, one of the many old barns that stand just above the farmhouse. My phone pings into life, letting me know I've got signal there. Inside, I sit on a bale and ring the hospital to ask about Dad's condition. They tell me he's had a comfortable night. They'll know more after the doctor has done his rounds later.

'Thank God,' I say to Ffion, who is sitting at my feet, looking up at me, as I come off the phone. I hold my forehead to hers and let a few tears fall into her soft fur. I take a few moments, then sit up, looking out of the dirty window. I lean forward and rub a pane with the sleeve of my coat, as the rain begins to clear and a big fat rainbow appears.

I sip the coffee, although somehow it doesn't have the same taste or make me feel like it would if I was at home, in my office, getting ready for a day's work, approving menus, schedules and plans for events, staffing and suppliers. Right now, I want a pot of tea and a thick doorstep of toast, with lots of butter, at the kitchen table.

I pull out my phone and take a picture, through the small square panes of glass in the feed shed, to take with me when I'm back in the office . . . and even to the States. I think about the meeting I had to discuss the job, the new hotel in Seattle, a flagship hotel, broadening the company's horizons, with me at the head, if I decide to take it. But I need to talk to Dad about it. Although I know what he'll say. He'll tell me to take it.

41

I shove the phone into my pocket as I watch the oil tanker leave.

Back in the kitchen, I get the range turned on and wait for it to start warming up, then take some coffee, heated again in the microwave, and a croissant up to Matthew.

'Morning, sleepy head,' I say.

'God, it's freezing,' he says. 'Ooh, is that coffee I can smell?' He opens his eyes and spots the cup I put beside him and the croissant, then pulls himself onto his elbows. 'Hey, this is looking better!'

'Dad's had a comfortable night,' I tell him, without waiting for him to ask. 'We'll know more when the doctor has done his rounds.'

'Good, good.' He sips the coffee.

'Yes. And it looks like Dad's got some kind of new work colleague he hasn't told me about yet. Some guy coming to help on the farm. He turned up earlier with the coffee and croissants. Apparently there's a drive-through just out of town now.'

'Well, that sounds good. Looks like you and your dad have things to catch up on. You, the job . . . us.' He reaches out a hand from under the covers and entwines his fingers in mine. 'It's great there'll be someone here working with him when you go back.'

When I go back, a voice says in my head. *The new job . . . us.* It seems a long way from here, from Dad and Hollybush Farm. I just need to be sure he's going to be okay and maybe Llew Griffiths is the answer. I kiss Matthew lightly and go back downstairs, where the pup has shredded the delivery note the oil man had pushed through the letterbox. I pick up the pieces and put them into the bin, to the puppy's perplexity.

'That's better!' I say, heat emanating from the range. I stand with my bum to it as I always did when I came in from school, hands on the rail, leaning into the warmth, and this time it starts to give me something back.

When I've warmed a little, I pull the kettle onto the hotplate. Matthew comes downstairs, shivering and seemingly wearing all the bedclothes. 'This place is freezing.'

'It'll soon warm up,' I say. 'You'll see.'

'So, what's the plan? I mean, your dad isn't going to be in the mood for guests when he comes out,' says Matthew.

I stare at him. 'I'm still waiting to hear if he's definitely allowed home today.'

'Yes, yes, of course. Once he's home, I mean,' he says. 'Get him settled. Then we should get back. Great the heating's on.'

'Matthew . . .' I turn from the range feeling mildly irritated, which is new for me: Matthew and I never argue. We just don't. And this isn't an argument, but he's not seeing what's going on here. 'I can't leave him. He'll be just out of hospital.'

43

Matthew looks out of the front window onto the yard. 'Is there anyone else who can drop in on him, make sure he's got what he needs?'

'There's Myfanwy next door. But she and Dad haven't spoken in years. All to do with a ram sale, I think . . . when Dad bought Bertie at the mart and Myfanwy had had her eye on him.'

The landline rings, making me jump.

'Hi, I'm Evie, the nurse from the GP practice. I was just ringing to see how Edwin is.'

'Oh, um, I'm waiting for news. Hoping he'll be home soon.'

'Okay, great. I'll drop by over the next day or two.'

'Really? Oh, that's fantastic!'

'No problem. I'll add him to my list.'

I put down the phone.

'Looks like solutions are often closer than you think,' says Matthew. 'I'll get dressed,' he says, hurrying upstairs. I hope I'll have time to take him out to Gramps's field before we go to the hospital to pick Dad up.

There's another knock at the door. The dogs bark and I stand away from the warming range.

6

'Myfanwy!' I say, surprised to see her on the doorstep. She hasn't changed a bit.

'What's the old bugger gone and done now, then?' she asks gruffly. 'Heard he'd landed himself in hospital. Won't stay. Just came to check on the ewes, but you're here now. I saw the light on, so I know they're being looked after. Wouldn't want them going without.'

'He's in hospital . . . sepsis.'

'Ooh, nasty.' Behind her I can see she's driven herself here on an old Massey Ferguson tractor that looks older than me. 'Bloody farmers, see, they think they're invincible.'

The landline rings again. 'Excuse me, I must get that! Come in,' I wave to her as I dive to the phone and listen. I hang up and Myfanwy is still in the kitchen, waiting.

'That was the hospital. Dad's asking to come home. They've said they'll only let him if there's someone to look after him and there's a medical professional on hand to check on him. If so, I can pick Dad up this afternoon . . .' I say, as a wave of relief rushes over me. 'I need to tell the nurse. As long as she's on hand, and I'm here, he can come home. As long as we phone the hospital if there is any change at all!' I look at Myfanwy, feeling that we've just dodged a bullet.

'That is good news. I'll bring some Welsh cakes. They might go with a cup of tea,' she says matter-of-factly.

'That's really good of you, Myfanwy.'

'No, not good of me. Your dad and I can't stand each other. Haven't seen the bugger since he outbid me on that ram at the mart. But we're neighbouring farmers and it's what we do. If we don't look out for the stock, who else will? Besides,' she says, a little quieter, the wind going out of her sails, 'it's very scary thinking he was alone here – anything might have happened. Could have been any one of us.'

She looks around the kitchen again. 'We may not see eye to eye on lots of things, me and your dad. But I'd hate to think of another person being in trouble. Here, in case you need anything.' She hands me a used envelope with her phone number on the back.

'For when you go home, like, to . . .' Her forehead wrinkles. 'Where is it you are?'

'All over the place at the moment. Mostly Cardiff, but I'm an area manager for the west of the country, mostly the hotels in the east of Wales. But Bristol too. Oh, this is Matthew, my partner,' I say, as he appears dressed, in his jacket, carrying his overnight bag. He comes to stand beside me.

I can feel him wanting to say something about me becoming an overseas manager too and, for some reason, I pray he doesn't. I don't want anyone else to know before I've told Dad.

'*Diolch*, thank you, Myfanwy. This means a lot. I know you and Dad have had your differences.'

'I'd like to think the old fool would be there if I needed him. Not that I intend to be in that situation.' She sniffs and pushes her clasped hands up under her bosom. 'Now, who have you got to look after the flock?'

'I . . .'

'You could ask that Owen chap to come back. He seemed to know how things run.' Matthew nudges me.

Myfanwy nods her approval.

'Actually,' I lift my chin, 'Dad may have someone else in mind. I'll be here to do it until things are more sorted.'

Matthew frowns. 'But we have to get back, Jem.

There's a lot to organize. It's our busiest time of the year.'

I lower my voice and say calmly, 'I can't leave yet, Matthew. Dad is coming out of hospital. There's the farm to see to.' Then, a little louder with a smile, 'You go. I'll catch you up. I'll let head office know I'm staying on for a few days. Compassionate leave. About time I took some of the advice I hand out to staff.'

'But you've spoken to the nurse. And Owen could help out,' he says, and I know he's frustrated and itching to get back.

'Not if there isn't enough money to pay him, he can't,' I say quietly. 'Everyone needs to make a living. He can't work for nothing.'

Matthew looks at me as if I've lost my mind. 'But it's only just over a month until Christmas.'

'I'll be back as soon as I can,' I snap, wishing I hadn't in front of Myfanwy, who doesn't seem to be moving. 'Like I say, I'll let HR know I need some compassionate leave.'

I see him take a breath. 'Well, don't stay away too long. There's a lot of people out there who'd kill for the job they're offering you.'

I feel myself flushing and glance at Myfanwy. 'I know,' I say quietly.

Myfanwy is studying me with interest, her head on one side.

'But today,' I lift my voice, 'Dad is coming home

from hospital. There are animals out there. A farm that needs running. Farmers don't get days off. Dad can't even get himself to the loo now, let alone run the farm single-handed.'

'So, you mean it? You're going to stay on and run the farm?'

I can hardly believe we're having this conversation. 'Yes, of course. I have to.'

'But for how long?'

'Just until Dad is on his feet. And this new guy is here to help out. You go back. I'll get the train when things are sorted.'

'When will that be?'

I laugh. 'Matthew, I have no idea. He isn't even home yet!'

'But you'll be back for the Christmas gala dinners and then New Year?'

'Of course! Keep me in the loop!'

'And you'll be okay, will you? On your own? I mean, I would offer to stay . . .'

'I'll be fine,' I say. 'I've done this before. I may be a bit rusty, but I'm sure I'll remember how it all works soon enough. And I can always ask Owen if I can't.'

'Owen, yes . . . Your ex, according to the man in the pub last night.'

'It was a long time ago. He's settled with children now. Really, there's nothing between me and Owen.' I mean it. We were close as youngsters and it was lovely to see his familiar face, but there was no leap of excitement. I didn't wonder if he was the one who got away. He wasn't.

I can still feel Myfanwy staring at us, as if she's watching an episode of *EastEnders*. I look around the kitchen. 'This place could do with cleaning. And I need to get some food sorted. And check what time I can collect Dad.'

'Okay.' He picks up the weekend bag he's brought from upstairs, ready to leave as soon as he can. 'What will you do for a car?'

'I'll use Dad's Land Rover. It's still going – just!' I look out of the window at it on the drive. 'Or there's always the cattle lorry.' I chuckle. 'I've still got my licence to drive it.'

'Well, this is certainly a side of you I haven't seen before. Jem, the sheep farmer.'

'You'll be fine.' Myfanwy waves a hand. 'It'll come back to you in no time,' she says.

'And you'll definitely be back in time for Christmas and then' – he looks at Myfanwy and back at me – 'the trip! Our new adventure.'

'Of course. I wouldn't miss it for the world. Back for Christmas and everything it entails at the hotels.'

'Then on to January in Seattle! A week of being wined and dined by the bosses before we—'

'Can't wait!' I smile uncomfortably, wishing Matthew hadn't said anything before I've spoken to Dad.

Yes, we'll go for a week to get to know the place before I finally agree to take the post and start in February.

'Quite the jetset lifestyle!' Myfanwy gives a little laugh and looks out of the window over the sink onto the yard, as the rain comes down again. 'Well, I'm sure your dad's very proud,' she adds.

'He is,' I say.

'And your mum?'

'I hear from her occasionally. Birthdays and Christmas. She's moved on from Spain. In Australia. Loving her life.'

'I'm sorry about that. Her upping and leaving like she did wasn't right.'

'We had Nan and Gramps here too, so Dad and I were always fine.'

'You were!' she says, with a firm nod. 'And you will be again. But I still don't know how she could have gone.'

And something hits me hard in the chest. A sharp pain that leaves a crushing feeling. We were fine, me and Dad, Nan and Gramps. But every now and again, I ask myself, *Why did she go? Was I not enough for her?* Sometimes I think that's what drives me now to be the best I can at my job. Showing I'm as good at what I do as I can be. Letting her know in occasional emails how well life is going for me.

'And then you'll be off on your holiday to the States.

All very exciting.' Myfanwy breaks into my thoughts but the pain in my chest remains.

'We'll be there soon,' says Matthew, pulling me close.

'I'll be off then,' says Myfanwy, and gives me the tiniest smile. 'I hope it all works out like you want it,' she says. 'Oh, and if I don't see you, happy Christmas. Hope it's everything you're wishing for.'

'And you, Myfanwy,' I say, reaching for my boots in the porch and slipping them on. I see Matthew look at them with horror, then back at Myfanwy.

'Yes, merry Christmas,' says Matthew, slipping into hospitality mode.

And suddenly Matthew being here doesn't feel quite right, as if there's something fake about the world he and I live in. Like a plastic Christmas tree, too bright for its surroundings. Standing here next to Matthew, I feel like a jigsaw piece in the wrong space. But I'm warmed by being home.

7

'Drive safely!' I wave as Matthew pulls away in his clean electric car and I can't help thinking he's rather too eager to get away – but I'm relieved that he's gone. Maybe it's just that I'm stressed about Dad. I want to focus on him and make sure he's okay before I leave. 'And remember to shut the gates!' I call after him. He gives me a thumbs-up.

I watch him go down the drive, slowly, trying to avoid the potholes that really need filling. Once he's out of sight, I step back into the kitchen, not wanting to let out any more of the heat, and close the door, with the dogs inside.

I grab the Land Rover keys from the Welsh dresser, pull on a scarf and Dad's coat, and head out across the yard. I climb into the Land Rover and try to start the engine. To say it needs a lot of encouragement is an understatement. It takes a while, and a few prayers to whoever might be listening, but finally it rattles and shudders into life.

'Yes!' I say, patting the steering wheel, like I would the dogs. 'Here we go.' I find first gear and release the handbrake. It's still raining, hard. The windscreen wipers are swishing back and forth without my having to turn them on. Like it's been raining for ever.

I set off down the uneven drive towards the front gate. Creak, swish, creak, swish go the wipers.

The Land Rover rocks and rolls along and I'm peering at the windscreen, squinting to see better through the rain. I grip the steering wheel – it feels like it's got a life of its own as I negotiate the neglected drive.

Swish, creak, swish, creak.

I'm hoping I'll be able to see a bit more clearly once I get onto the main road. I'm nearly at the gate. Right now, I can hardly see . . .

'Gah!'

I slam on the brakes. There's something or someone in front of me on the drive.

I pull on the handbrake and push open the stiff door with my shoulder, holding my other arm over my eyes.

A woman, almost camouflaged in a dark green wax jacket, dark brown boots and leather hat, is waving at me, and not in a welcoming way.

'Is everything okay?' I ask, concerned.

'No! It's not! There's a bloody big sheep and a horse loose in that field. They're chasing my dogs.'

'A sheep?'

I turn to look at the field beside Gramps's. I'd put Bertie and Harriet into their own field this morning. Now Bertie and his sidekick Harriet are cavorting around this one. I frown. 'They're not supposed to be there. Not in with the flock at this time of year! Not again!' And then I do a double-take and point. 'Are those your dogs?'

'Yes!' she replies angrily. 'And your animals are chasing them! You need to get them away! They could kill them!'

Suddenly my hackles are up. 'Shouldn't it be you getting your dogs back and leaving our stock alone? What are they doing running around this field in the first place?'

'It's a good walk for them!' she says indignantly. 'And on our doorstep!'

'On your doorstep? You live here?'

'Not exactly. Well, partially.'

I try not to roll my eyes. 'You have a second home here,' I say flatly.

'Thinking about it. I'm renting while I decide.' She pulls herself up to her full height. 'We keep the economy going here. If it wasn't for the likes of us . . .'

'Well, right now, you need to get your dogs back on the lead. This is private property.'

'But there's a footpath that runs along the edge of this field.'

I'm looking at the dogs and suddenly I can't bite my tongue. 'A footpath, yes. Not the right to let your dogs run amok on our land.'

'Your land?'

'My father's land. It's his farm. Our land.'

'Well, perhaps I should speak to your father. Get him to put better notices up. Fencing maybe. Where is he? He should be out here, keeping these animals under control.'

I sigh loudly. I'm feeling crosser by the moment. 'Call your dogs. I'm on my way to pick up my father from hospital.'

She looks as if she's about to say something but thinks better of it.

I'm watching the dogs and Bertie, kicking up his heels, with Harriet in hot pursuit. For a moment I want to laugh, but I do my best to suppress it. If Dad could see this, he'd laugh too.

'Cosmo! Hubert!' calls the woman, and raises a whistle to her lips, but Cosmo and Hubert just keep running in circles.

'Cosmo! Hubert!' Still nothing.

'Cos—'

'I don't think they're listening, do you?' I say, folding my arms.

The woman glares at me, then storms off in the

direction of the dogs. I take a deep breath and walk towards the chaos. The woman, in new designer outdoor wear, is shouting, 'Cosmo! Hubert!' at two excited black Labradors. 'That sheep is out of control! I could sue!'

Harriet is dipping and bucking but eventually I grab her forelock and pull her towards me. She swings her head back to the action, the woman trying to lasso her dogs with the leads. 'Very bad! Very bad!' She gasps.

I reach into Dad's coat pocket, for what I'm expecting to find there, and pull out the packet of Polo mints he always carries. 'You never know when they might come in handy,' he would tell me, when I was little. And he was right.

Harriet turns her head towards my outstretched hand and snaffles up the Polo, taking a feisty nip at my fingers.

'Ouch!'

I pull out another Polo and hold it in front of her. She starts to move in the right direction, back towards the gate that had clearly been left open. Frankly, with the state of the fence, they could probably have got out without needing the enticement of an open gate.

Bertie is chasing the woman, trying to butt her in the back of the shins, when he sees Harriet leaving, turns and hurries after her. Clearly, where Harriet goes, Bertie follows. And with a couple more Polos for encouragement, I have the two of them back in their field, the gate closed firmly behind me.

The same can't be said of the woman and her dogs. She is shouting at them, 'Lie down!' as they bounce around her. Eventually, she manages to grab one and flick a lead around its neck. And, in a stroke of what looks more like luck than judgement, she catches the other between her legs and clips on his lead. Then, with barely a backward glance, she lifts her chin and walks to the end of the field and the stile.

I watch her go, replaying her threats about suing for out-of-control animals. While I don't think she would and know that she has absolutely no right to, any kind of threat like that is a worry. I walk back to the Land Rover, which has stalled. I open the gate, lifting it on its hinges, and drive through, then close it carefully. It'll need fixing before I go, I think, and start making a mental list of things to be mended, including the gate and the listing fence on Bertie and Harriet's field. How long has it been like that? Has Bertie been able to get into the ewes' field and run free with them whenever he liked? It could create havoc around lambing if any of them have caught at the wrong time.

Just what I didn't need today. I pull my seatbelt around me, start the engine and put my foot on the accelerator, keen to get to the hospital and see Dad. I'm furious with the dog-walker for not respecting the footpath or our livestock. The Land Rover lurches down the final part of the drive, windscreen wipers working fast, and I'm about to swing out into the road, just as another car comes towards me at speed. The driver sees me, hits the brakes and slides off the road into the stone wall of the farm.

BANG! I hear, then the hissing of the airbags from the other car.

8

'Are you okay?' I jump out of the Land Rover and run towards the buckled car. 'I didn't see you. Sorry, I was a bit preoccupied.' I attempt to pull open the buckled door. 'A woman with her dogs loose!' I jabber, as I pull back the door and recognize the driver as Llew Griffiths.

'Oh, you're bleeding!' I say. Blood is oozing from just above his eyebrow. He must have hit the window when the car crashed into the wall. I dig into my pockets again for a tissue but instead I find a sock. Not very hygienic to put on the cut.

'I'm fine,' he says, clearing his throat. 'Left my phone in your kitchen when I took your number.'

I look at the front of the car. No wonder it was a loud bang. The wall has shifted and some of it has tumbled into the stream, which is flowing fast in the rain. 'Do you want an ambulance?' I pull out my phone, hoping for signal and holding it up as the rain pours down.

He waves a hand. 'No ambulance, thank you. I'll be okay.'

'Really?'

'No ambulance. Let's not make it more than it is.'

'I wasn't expecting someone to drive in. We don't get many visitors. Sorry.'

'You were going too fast,' he says. 'On the wrong side of the drive.'

'I – I was. Sorry. Like I say, I was in a rush.'

'I hit mud, I think. Wet road, slippery.'

I look down. There is a big skid in the mud on the road. 'You did.' I wince. 'Your car is pretty messed up.'

My heart is thudding, like horses' hoofs: I'm reminded of cantering across the fields when I was a child. Endless long summer holidays riding my pony Shadrach over Gramps's field, where Dad had made little jumps for me, and his collie would follow.

Llew Griffiths runs his hands through his hair and sees the blood from his forehead. 'I've got some tissues in the glove box,' he says. 'Could you help?' He points to the passenger side.

'Sure,' I say, and run round, but I can't get into the glove box due to the inflated airbag. 'Look, I'm going to the hospital to pick Dad up. Let me take you there. Just to check you're okay. I'd feel a lot happier.'

He attempts to move and winces. 'Maybe just a quick chat with a doctor,' he says, to my surprise. I'd thought he'd put up more of fight and I'd have to be firm about it.

'Okay, let's get you into the Land Rover.'

Again he tries to move and winces. The rain is rolling down my forehead, cheeks and face from my sodden hair.

He looks up at me and something inside me skips. It has to be the stress of the accident. 'I may need help,' he says.

'Sure,' I say, holding out a wet hand. He takes hold of it firmly and it feels very different from Matthew's soft hands. It's strong and powerful. And I have absolutely no idea why I'm thinking this when I'm partly to blame for his car coming off the road. He pulls on my hand and I lean back to help him to his feet. He hauls himself out stiffly, until he's upright, brushing at the gash on his head again.

Then he turns to the car, a mangled mess at the front, and the drop into the water, and I'm wondering if he's thinking the same as me. 'That could have been worse,' he says. 'Thank God for well-made walls.'

He was thinking the same as me.

He stares at the water tumbling over the rocks, where I used to paddle in the summer in the cold water running off the mountain. For a moment it looks as if he's somewhere else entirely.

Then he looks at the car. 'Don't worry. I'll get this sorted.'

'No rush,' I say. 'Let's get you checked over first.' I point him in the direction of the Land Rover, his shoulders stooped, accepting the sock to hold to the cut on his head.

By the time Dad is ready to leave and I've got him into the car, Llew Griffiths is coming out of A and E.

'Good to see you! Would you mind if I had a picture taken with you?' the doctor is asking, patting Llew on the shoulder.

Llew obliges politely and the selfie is taken, followed by a handshake.

'Good to meet you. And, again, I'm sorry for how things turned out.'

I frown. Clearly the doctor knows who Llew Griffiths is, even if I don't. All I know is that he's someone wanting to work with Dad on the farm. But there's clearly more to this.

'Just make sure you're not on your own this evening, and if you're concerned about anything, give us a call or get your wife to bring you back in.'

He nods to me. I wave a hand by explanation that I'm not his wife.

'Really, my wife won't be driving me anywhere,' Llew says, clearly half joking and maybe half not.

'Right,' I say, nodding to Dad in the Land Rover,

wearing a bobble hat I've brought for him, coat and scarf. 'Can I give you a lift somewhere?'

'I'd better get my stuff from the car and arrange to have it picked up. I'm sure they'll get it fixed as soon as possible,' he says. 'Or find a replacement.'

'Fine. Follow me.'

'Keep up the painkillers. But you should be right as rain after a good night's sleep,' says the doctor.

At the car Dad and Llew Griffiths greet each other. Dad is weak, but nods a hello, while looking at me. I can't work out what's going on. But maybe that's because Dad has been, and still is, really ill. *Could have been so much worse.* Llew's words come back to haunt me.

In the car, I realize the rain has eased. I turn the heater on but it circulates dog hair around the interior. It's like being inside the tube of a vacuum cleaner, so I turn it off again.

Dad is dozing and Llew is saying very little, probably shaken by his accident and what might have been.

As we approach the farm I slow right down. Dad wakes and sees the wreckage of the car. I pull up beside it. 'Do you need a hand?' I ask Llew.

'I'll just get my stuff together. Book into a hotel until I've sorted this.'

'You won't find much in town,' Dad murmurs. 'It's not what it was once.'

'Look, I feel bad for what happened, and it was partly my fault. You can stay here if you like. That's okay, isn't it, Dad?'

Dad nods cautiously, which is unlike him. I'm putting that down to the sepsis. 'Of course,' he says, and I'm sure he means it, even if he doesn't sound it. Dad would always welcome anyone who needed a hand.

'I don't want to impose.'

'Really, it's not an imposition. There's a spare room – I'll make up the bed – and the heating is back on, so it's warm. It's no bother.' I look sideways at Dad: he'll be embarrassed that I know the oil ran out. 'And once the two of you have had some rest you can tell me about your business plans to work together.' I glance between them. 'It's a chance for us to have a good catch-up. You can tell me everything that's going on, Dad.' I smile. 'Put my mind at rest before I have to go again.'

I see him look into the rear-view mirror at Llew.

'You're very kind but I'll be fine.' Llew pushes open the stiff back door, and as he does so, his legs nearly give way.

'Whoa,' I say, jumping out to help him. 'That's settled. You'll stay with us. The doctor says you shouldn't be on your own tonight and, by the sound of it, your wife isn't coming to collect you.'

He laughs as I hold his elbow, a big bear of a man, clearly having had the wind taken out of his sails.

'I feel like I've been hit by the entire front row of the All Blacks,' he says. He looks at me. 'No, I won't be ringing my wife, or ex-wife as she is. I don't think she or her new husband would appreciate that.'

'Ah,' I say, and give him a gentle nudge back into the Land Rover. 'Come on, let's get you two inside. Plenty of time to sort out the car and explain your plans.'

I open the gate, with difficulty, drive through and shut it again. That's one of the first jobs I have to do.

I check that all the sheep are in the right place and that the dog-walker isn't back with Cosmo and Hubert, then drive us up to the farmhouse, where the dogs are waiting to welcome Dad home.

'Gently,' I say to Ffion and Dewi, the pup, now that Dad has reminded me of his name.

'It's good to be home,' he says, sitting in the living room in front of the fire.

'It is,' I find myself saying. 'It really is.' I run upstairs and gather sheets and pillow cases for the spare room, which looks out over Gramps's field and the ewes. I'm not thinking about schedules, staffing rotas or suppliers. I'm just here, feeling happy, feeling home.

9

The next morning I'm up early. It's a dark Monday, but the farmhouse is warm. Matthew messages to say he got home safely yesterday. I can picture him in our apartment in the centre of Cardiff, turning on the coffee machine in the temperature-controlled room. Unlike here: your comfort depends on whether you're standing by the range or near the front door, where a draught slips around the frame if the curtain isn't drawn properly.

I feed the dogs and go outside, turning on my head torch, to check the ewes and load up their rack with hay. I'll take the old quad bike, I decide. I pick up a bucket of ewe nuts: I don't know if they've been scanned yet to see who's carrying multiple lambs and needs extra feed. I'm slipping back into the natural rhythm of farming life, away from planning wedding fairs and Christmas parties in January. Ffion jumps up behind me on the seat of the old quad, as if it's the most natural thing in the world for me to be here, driving it. I also find the tools I need to fix the gate and put them into the front basket. I can probably deal with the hinges, but may need a hand to re-hang it. I also consider making a sign that tells people to keep their dogs on leads and stick to the footpath. Respect our animals. I put a lot of energy into sorting out the hinges. It's heavy, hard, wet work, not something I've done in a long time.

Later, returning to the farmhouse I'm wet and I ache everywhere. I'd forgotten how cold and isolated you can feel when it's just you and the animals in the dark with only the light thrown from the head torch. Ffion and Dewi are now making for the warmth in front of the range, and Dolly, the Jack Russell, will be reluctant to share the space she hasn't moved from yet today.

As I ease off my wellingtons I see on the bench in the porch a tea-towel, with a loaf of bread wrapped up in it and a little jar beside it, with a label on it: 'sourdough starter'. I'm guessing Myfanwy's come over the fields and delivered it while I was at the gate. There's a tin, too, and I'm guessing it contains warm Welsh cakes. I lift the bread to my nose and can feel it revitalizing me. I push my boots under the bench and head into the kitchen.

The bread smells amazing as I slice, then toast it on the hotplate until it turns golden brown. I make tea in the big pot, spread butter on the toast and take it to Dad in bed. He's looking pale and weak. I put the tea and toast on the bedside table and sit on the bed beside him.

'Well, that's a treat,' he says, trying to lift himself up. I stand, step forward and slip my hand under his arm to help him, then plump up the pillows behind him. 'I must have overslept. Not like me. Need to get up and check the stock.'

I put a hand on his shoulder. 'It's fine, Dad. I've done them. How are you feeling?'

'I'll be great,' he says, in his usual no-fuss-needed way. 'Just a little blip. You should be on your way back to your office. You don't need to be here, looking after me. I can manage.' But his voice is thin, and I can hear the shake in it.

'Well, I'd like to see that for myself before I leave,' I say, patting his hand, then standing to pull back the curtains. 'Besides, I'm quite enjoying having you to myself for a few days and being home. I know you're not going to like this, but you do need to take it easy.'

He gives a *phhffff*. But I get the feeling he won't have much choice. His body won't let him pick up where he left off.

'Dad, there's something I want to talk to you about when you're feeling better.'

He nods and smiles at me, patting my hand on his. 'Me too, Jem-Jem.' His pet name for me when I was a child.

'It's good news,' I add.

'Mine too,' he says, with a tired smile.

'Okay, well, just rest. We'll talk later.' I lean in and give him a peck on his forehead.

In the kitchen, Llew is gazing at the range. 'No electric kettle, I take it?'

'There is, but we use the stove when the range is on,' I say. 'Let me.' I push up the lid of the hotplate and put the kettle on to boil.

'I don't want to be any trouble. I'll be out of your hair as soon as I have the car collected and a replacement sorted.'

'Hmm. Could take a while out here,' I say. 'It's fine. Besides, I'm keen to hear your and Dad's plans.'

He sits at the table, holding his iPad. His hair is on end, butterfly stitches on his forehead.

I make a pot of tea and put it on the table. 'Help yourself,' I say, pushing the milk jug and a mug towards him. He looks at me and I can't help but think how attractive he is, with his hair standing up in places.

He picks up the mug. 'That's kind. Thank you. You didn't have to.'

'No, but I wanted to. Like I say, it's the least I can do. And hospitality is my thing, so it's nothing.'

He pours the milk into his mug, then the tea. 'You work in hospitality?'

I nod. 'Area manager for the Catref Group, a hotel chain.'

'I know them.'

'They're doing well, expanding now.'

'Sounds good,' he says.

'I'm hoping to take up a new post in January. Just visiting Dad before the Christmas rush.'

'Ah, I see,' he says, sipping the tea.

For a moment we say nothing more. Something makes me want to sit and ask him to tell me his plans for working with Dad, knowing I'll feel better about leaving once I know Dad has help. But it can wait. I'm just glad, that's all.

'I have some more chores to do outside. Help yourself to toast and Welsh cakes. They're in the tin on the kitchen table.'

'Any chance of the Wi-Fi code?'

'Ah . . . No Wi-Fi, and I'm afraid the phone signal isn't great here. Dad's quite hard to get hold of, unless it's on the landline. Best place for signal is up at the feed shed or on Gramps's field on the bench there.'

'I know it. Thank you. I'll get on to my company. Have the car replaced.'

'Take your time,' I say, desperate to hear about his

and Dad's partnership but forcing myself to wait until they're both downstairs and awake.

I go into the little living room and give it a quick tidy. Puff up the cushions and empty the ashes from the fire into the bucket there, then lay another with scraps of paper and kindling. I stand up just as Dewi, the pup, comes in to jump at me, knocking over the little table with Dad's phone on it, next to his chair.

The pup bounces around in delight, making me laugh.

'Whoa!' I say, picking up the table, the phone and the letter under it and replacing them on the table. Then I walk back into the kitchen. 'I'm going out to check the fences now,' I tell Llew, 'but I could do with a hand re-hanging the gate, if you're feeling up to it. I can show you where we get signal in the feed shed.'

He looks up at me and I feel a little spark flicker inside me. 'Fresh air is exactly what I need,' he says. 'Especially after such delicious toast. That would be great. I'll get my coat.'

I find myself feeling quite pleased to have Dad's new worker here to help me, wishing I didn't find him so attractive. I must remember I'm only here for a few days. Then I'll be back at the hotel with Matthew . . . the man I'm planning to get engaged to and move to Seattle with! It'll be a long way from Hollybush Farm . . . I suddenly wish it wasn't, or that Matthew and I aren't miles apart, in distance and in how this place makes me feel. I'm falling in love with the farm all over again. I give Llew a sideways glance and meet his eyes. One thing I do know is that I'm not going to fall in love with this man. He's here to help Dad, and I'm grateful. The last thing I need is for him to look at me like that. He's just a helping hand on the gate and the farm. I need to remember that.

I pull on my pink wellingtons, to his laughter. 'What? I loved these boots!' I remonstrate, looking down at them.

'I can see why! Colourful!'

'Individual!' I say. 'A bit like this place. They make me happy!' I try not to feel that little connection between us when he smiles at me, and fail. But it feels nice. And he likes my boots. Unlike Matthew. In fact there's a lot about Llew Griffiths that's very different from Matthew.

10

'I need to get the gate back on its hinges, then fix some fence posts where I think Bertie and Harriet have been getting out,' I tell him, as we walk with the dogs bounding around our feet. The rain has stopped and the temperature seems to have dropped, creating a mist that's curling its way across Gramps's field. It's cold, but totally stunning. The wet grass, heavy with rainfall, is now looking whitewashed in the mist. It's crisp and sparkling, like a child's Christmas painting. The water butts will need checking tonight and I'll smash any ice in them.

We work our way down the drive towards the front gates. I look across the valley to the right and the tractor tyre marks leading to Myfanwy's farm.

'This is Gramps's field. It's the best on the farm. Best for grazing, access and views.' I'm gazing out over the white-tipped trees down to the road below. 'My grandparents were tenants here and my dad bought the farm. The chance came up to buy it and he used his and Mum's wedding fund as a deposit. She was furious! She'd thought he'd want to leave the place, not stay for ever.' I find myself telling Llew all the things I'd planned to tell Matthew when we got here and I was showing him around. 'Eventually they had a small wedding in town, and all the local farmers pitched in, but I don't think Mum ever forgave him.' It's strange how comfortable I feel with this complete stranger, but he's going to help Dad, and I like that very much. 'In fact, I know she didn't.' I give an ironic laugh. 'She left when I was still in primary school. I came home one day to be told by Dad she'd gone. It was what she needed to do. We had to understand that. And that we'd be fine.' I take a deep breath. 'Didn't even wait to tell me herself.'

'That's tough.'

I shrug.

'It's only now that I'm beginning to realize it,' I say. But it's true. I was only seven. 'But Dad was right. We were fine. I had the best growing up. I loved it here.'

'And you've never thought of moving back?'

'No,' I say, and a whole load of emotions stir inside me. 'No, I haven't. I have my job, my life. It's never been on the cards.'

We walk side by side down the stony driveway, the

grassy edges crunching under our feet. My pink wellingtons are cracking because they've sat too long in the porch.

'So, what about you? What brings you to Hollybush Farm?' I say, my lungs filling with fresh air. I can feel my cheeks turning pink. It's so different from my job, where I never see the light of day. I'm either in air-conditioned or centrally heated spaces, with a coffee in one hand and an iPad in the other. Right now, I'm just here, in the moment. A robin darts in front of us, the red of his breast vibrant against the white of the grasses and brambles in the mist. I feel as if I'm in a Christmas card, but I'm here, at home, and I wish I'd come back more, done more of this. It took Dad becoming ill to make me realize. I remember how I felt when I left, with Dad's encouragement, to see the world. I was homesick, but thought I was making him proud as I worked my way up the corporate ladder.

'Gramps said that if ever I felt homesick I should look up at the stars and know that he, Nan and Dad would be looking up at the same stars. To find the brightest one and know we would all be looking at it together.'

'That must have been comforting.'

'It was. To start with, I hated being away. And you?'

'Left school as soon as I could,' he says. 'I didn't like classrooms. I did my learning outside, on the rugby field. I moved on pretty quick.'

'Dad didn't want me to feel trapped here,' I say, as we walk. I see a listing fence post in Bertie and Harriet's field and walk towards it. I straighten it, and Llew steps forward to hold it.

'You sure?' I say.

'Yes. All good. Go for it! I'm used to feeling the fear!' He puts his shoulder to the stake as I swing the long-handled mallet several times to make sure it's firmly in and straight. Then I test it. Hopefully Bertie and Harriet are safely penned in now.

'So your dad wanted you to go? To leave here?'

I hit the stake once more with the mallet for good measure. 'Yup,' I say, out of puff. 'He never wanted to be anywhere else. But for Mum, it was like a prison sentence. She wanted out. And she found her way. He never wanted me to feel like that.'

We walk on.

'Here, I can help,' he says, as I take hold of another loose fence post.

'Are you sure?'

He gives a little shrug. 'Bit stiff still but this is helping,' he says. 'Just being out and about.'

'So, what about you? You weren't brought up on a farm, then?' I ask, as he holds the post and I hit it into the hard ground, making my arms ache. 'Better than any gym workout,' I say breathing out plumes of hot air as I let the mallet settle at my side. He gives the stake a shake and nods, satisfied.

'No, not farming. Like I say, rugby was my thing from a young age. I was spotted and signed. I went pretty far. Even got capped for the country a couple of times.'

'Ah, so that'll be where I've seen you, then. And the doctor at the hospital. Dad never misses a game on the telly. Loves his rugby. He'd go to the pub in the past, but I think he stays at home on his own now to watch it.'

We walk on some more and Dewi chases crisp, crystallizing leaves as the day gets even colder.

'And are you still playing? Or have you discovered farming is much more your thing?'

He shakes his head. 'No, not playing. I had an injury.'

'Oh, I'm sorry,' I say, the cold nipping at my cheeks.

'It was just bad luck. A fracture in my back.'

'On the field?'

'I fell from a ladder. We were getting ready for a party at home and my wife wanted bunting put up. I slipped and fell, broke my back and didn't play again.'

'Oh, no!'

'It's why I didn't argue when you suggested getting checked out yesterday at the hospital. Just to keep an eye on things.'

'And your wife? Did you need to call her?'

'Like I said at the hospital, we're not together any more.'

'Ah, yes . . .'

I stand at the top of Gramps's field and look out. 'It must have been hard, giving up something you love.'

He nods. 'It was. And the whole social-media thing got to me. Lots of people commenting on me, how I played. I just . . . lost confidence. Never went back to it. Just fell out of love with the game. And social media.'

'I'll get that gate back on.' I jerk a thumb at it, next to the car, which is crumpled against the wall. I can't help thinking again that either of us could have ended up in the river. I shudder. I'm suddenly very grateful to be here, on the farm, a place I love, with my dad. Work, with the hustle and bustle of the run-up to Christmas in the big hotel, seems very far away. I can breathe here, really breathe.

'I can help,' he says.

'Are you sure? I don't want you to hurt your back.'

'It's fine. Doctor wasn't worried. This is just lifting the gate onto its hinges.'

'Okay, if you're sure.'

Between us, we lift the gate and gently put it back on its hinges, and while we're there, we fix the listing farm sign so it hangs straight now.

I stand and stare at it, with the pride I know Dad feels for this place. I couldn't be happier that he is going to have someone working with him again, keeping the farm going.

'Thanks. I should probably head back and check on Dad,' I say, feeling I could stand here all day right now.

'Yes, of course. And thank you. Good to get out and get moving.'

'You're welcome. And don't feel you have to rush off. Get your car sorted.'

'Thank you. I will.' He looks at me and, for just a moment, there's that spark again, just a zip to and fro between us. But it's more than that. It was good to share this walk with someone. Just like I'd hoped to do with Matthew.

'I'll head to the feed shed. That one up there, is it?' He points to the top of the drive, above the yard.

I smile. 'Best service around here,' I say. 'Serves as a useful little office. And if you get cold, there's some sheepskin rugs you can sit on, or whatever. Help yourself to tea from the farmhouse if you want it.'

He waves his phone at me and heads towards it.

I stand and breathe it all in, just a little longer, enjoying the peace.

I stroke Ffion's head as she sits beside me looking out over the flock on the lower field, ever vigilant, always there. And I'm so glad she was here for Dad when he fell ill, and when I go back to work, she'll be his companion, with Llew Griffiths to help. I smile.

'It's all going to be okay, Ffi,' I say, hearing Dad's voice all those years ago, reassuring me. Because it is.

11

Back in the farmhouse I pull off my hat and coat and hang them by the back door. I slide off my boots and notice that the cracks are getting bigger. I find some tape in the drawer on the dresser and patch them up. That should last for now, I think. This time next week I'll be back in smart black court shoes and suits.

I walk to the range, almost as if it's pulling me towards its warmth. The kettle is still hot. I make Dad another cup of tea and put a Welsh cake on a plate, then take it upstairs to him in bed.

'I was just getting up,' he says, his legs out of bed. I put the tea on the chest of drawers and slide them back under the covers.

'Dad! You're not well. You've got to take it easy.'

'I can't stay here in bed all day, Jem love. It goes

81

against everything I know. I need to check on things. See the flock.'

'The flock is fine. I've fed them. The dogs are sorted too. And I've even been round checking some of the fence posts with Llew.'

'With Llew?'

'Yes. He's up in the feed shed, trying to get his car sorted. We fixed some of the fence posts to make sure Bertie and Harriet can't escape again, and put the gate back on its hinges. He even helped me straighten the farm sign,' I say happily. 'I think he's going to be a great addition around here, Dad.'

'And . . . how did—' He starts to cough.

'Take it easy, Dad. Honestly, everything is fine, I promise. I like him. He seems nice. Getting him on board to help here could be great. Bring some fresh ideas to the farm. Owen's good, but I can see why you might be open to listening to some new ideas.'

'But—' He coughs again. 'I need to explain . . .'

'Dad, plenty of time. I'm pleased – really. Now, drink your tea and stay in bed. At least for today.'

He leans back on the pillows, all the energy knocked out of him. I give his legs another little push back into the bed and pull the covers over him.

'Take it easy, Dad. I'm here to help.'

'But you need to get back. You have Christmas coming! And your holiday!'

'I know, I know. But work will cope. I've been planning this Christmas since January. Everything's in place, running like clockwork. It's what I do. I put the hard work in early on to make sure it all runs smoothly when the time comes. *Mise en place!* I say, smiling. 'Everything in its place. Just like they taught us in hospitality at college.'

'But I need to make a delivery. From the shed. Potatoes, from the allotment.'

'Dad, this is not the time to be worrying about your potatoes.'

He shakes his head. 'You don't understand. I have to deliver a bag to the café, in town.'

'Beti's?'

He coughs. 'Yes,' he says, sounding weaker. 'We have . . . an agreement.'

'What kind of agreement?'

'I take in potatoes to Mae, the waitress. She pays me cash in hand.'

'Ah.'

'She'll be waiting for them.'

'No worries. I can do that.'

'Every little helps, these days,' he says, and closes his eyes. I know he's exhausted: he's not arguing that he needs to get up.

I head out of the room, pull the door to and head downstairs into the warm, cosy kitchen. All of a sudden I get a wave of longing, of homesickness, or as we say in Wales, *hiraeth*. A sense of belonging. I wish I wasn't leaving and heading back to Christmas at the hotels. I wish I was here, having Christmas with Dad in the farmhouse kitchen, like we always did.

I decide to do some tidying up before Dad refuses to stay in bed any longer, gets up and tells me not to fuss, like I know he will. He'll want me to sit and tell him about the hotels and the plans made for Christmas. Now is my chance to get as much done as I can, while he's sleeping, occasionally waking and letting me know he's happy I'm here. And right here is where I need to be. I can't believe I've left it so long to come home. I shouldn't have listened when he kept telling me he was fine, that I should go and enjoy myself. But first I'll find the potatoes.

I go out to the shed, which is next to the vegetable plot. His pride and joy, and Gramps's before that. I pull open the door to the whitewashed stone shed and smile. I should have known Dad wouldn't be living on fresh air and mouldy bread. The smell is wonderful and earthy. In front of me there are sacks of potatoes, onions plaited up and hanging from the ceiling, next to strings of garlic, all home-grown. There are carrots too, and I'm thinking they might need using up, along with turnips and swedes. I grab a bag of potatoes, put it over my shoulder, then take some carrots and a swede.

I close the door behind me, walk to the Land Rover

and put the sack of potatoes into the back. Then I return to the warm kitchen. I begin by wiping out the cupboard. Not that there's much in there, but that's because Dad has been eating, as we always did, from the vegetable garden, and the eggs from the hens. We'd have bacon from the farm next door, when he and Myfanwy were speaking still, and ham. Ham, egg and chips is still one of my favourites and I wonder when I last ate it, my mouth watering. I wipe down the surfaces and wash the floor.

Then I fetch some logs in from outside to stack beside the living-room hearth to light the fire later. A lot has happened since Matthew and I sat here on the sofa and I had plans to show him around the farm, introduce him to Dad, and warn him about his corny jokes, his wicked sense of humour and strange collection of hats.

I find the vacuum-cleaner in the cupboard under the stairs, along with the box of Christmas decorations that hasn't seen the light of day this year . . . or for a while, I'd imagine. I can't think Dad's decorated the place when I haven't been able to get back for Christmas. My heart twists at the thought of him here alone, the memory of finding him so sick in the chair coming back to haunt me. I need to find a way to change this. Maybe invite him away with us, but I'm not sure how Matthew would feel about that, or if Dad would ever leave the farm. But he has help now in Llew so he could come and stay with us in Seattle. Start to take things a bit easier.

I plump up the worn but comfy cushions on the sofa, then turn on the vacuum-cleaner. Dewi leaps about with shock and excitement, barking.

'Sssh! Sssh!' I laugh. But he runs around the room, bouncing off the sofa and Dad's chair. I try to move the vacuum-cleaner but he barks and whizzes about some more, knocking over the side table next to Dad's chair in a cacophony of joyous barking and playfulness.

'Whoa!' I say, switching off the vacuum-cleaner. The barking stops.

I see Llew standing in the doorway, practically filling it. 'Oh, hi! I'm just trying to get things sorted here.' I stretch my arm for the upturned table.

He steps forward, crossing nearly the whole room in one stride. 'Can I help?' He reaches out towards the toppled table.

'No, it's fine. You're the one who needs to be careful,' I say, picking up the papers that were there, as Dewi leaps and bounds for them.

'Sit, good boy!' I say, then look down at the papers.

'My car's going to be towed away,' Llew is saying. 'They'll see if they can fix it. Might take a few days. They're struggling to get me a replacement at the moment.'

'Well, it's good that they're going to fix yours,' I say.

'I'll collect up my stuff and get out of your hair.'

And I feel a little disappointment. 'It was nice having you here,' I say, thinking that perhaps I'm being a little flirtatious too and I shouldn't be. I have a partner, Matthew. But I mean it. I enjoyed Llew's company today. But I shouldn't be giving any wrong signals and suddenly feel a little embarrassed. 'I didn't mean anything by that. It was just nice. Nice to have some company. The farm can be lonely at times. It's hard doing this on your own. Don't know how Dad keeps on with it. I've suggested he leave but I know he won't. Maybe I'll try to persuade him again, to come with me. Especially if you're going to be working together. Get him to come on a long holiday to stay with me – us,' I correct myself.

I look down at the papers in my hand, and see something I recognize. 'Oh, it's from you!' I look at the familiar name again. 'Llew Griffiths.'

He looks at me, saying nothing, just watching my face. I get a fizzing feeling in my stomach again. I glance down at the letter. Maybe I get to find out exactly what 'the plan' is, with him and Dad, and read until I reach the end.

I look at the logo at the top of the page, trying to take in what I've read. I look up at him. He still says nothing, and I reread it, the colour draining from my face.

'You . . .' My tongue feels as if it's got twisted in

my mouth. 'Is this you?' I look up at him to double-check. He isn't smiling. His face is harder now. We're not making friends, fixing fence posts and enjoying being outdoors.

'It is,' he says slowly, holding my stare steadily. 'Your dad and I have been in talks for some weeks now. I was hoping he'd discussed it with you.'

All of sudden I feel cold, very cold. The dogs slide into the kitchen onto the mat in front of the range as if they're feeling the temperature change in the room. I lift my chin. 'No. He hasn't. He did say he had something to discuss . . .'

'It's . . . a very good offer,' he says, with a little cough, slipping into business mode, as do I.

I say very slowly, as if I'm processing the offer, 'You want to buy Gramps's field?'

'Yes.' He nods.

'And,' I raise an eyebrow, 'put solar panels on it?'

'We work with companies who want to give something back, offset any carbon footprint by producing cleaner energy.'

For a moment I say nothing.

'It's a good offer,' he repeats.

'And, this cleaner energy, does it help the people around here? The ones struggling with fuel bills, who'll have to put up with the panels instead of livestock on the countryside. Will it make their lives better?'

'It . . . goes to the national grid,' he says.

'So it doesn't benefit the community at all?'

'No, but it will help your dad to stay here for longer.'

'By selling off parcels to you to ease the consciences of big business!' And I'm not sure where this fury is bubbling up from. Suddenly I feel like battle lines have been drawn. He's on one side and I'm on the other.

'Well, yes, the likes of you and your bosses. Flying around the world, sourcing products for price more than provenance!' he retorts. 'We're all here to try to make a living.'

Touché! I feel like I've been slapped.

The words sting. He's right. I'm as bad as the people wanting to buy up the land and put their solar panels on it. I turn away and look into the fire.

'I'll get my things. Let me know if you want to talk.'

I say nothing. Then, in disbelief, I turn back to him and say again, 'You want to buy Gramps's field.'

'Yes. Your dad, Edwin, was saying the farm was becoming too much for him. We've made an offer to buy the land.'

'And put solar panels on it.'

'That's right. Renewable energy.'

'But not for the town!'

'Er, no. The power doesn't supply the local area.'

'So you sell it elsewhere?'

'Yup,' he says, sipping the tea.

'And why?'

'Well, certain businesses want to help the planet. Much like the one you work for, I imagine.'

Suddenly I feel as if I've got a foot in each camp and am being torn.

'But that field is full of sheep. Fields should be covered by crops or livestock to support the local area!' I say, realizing where my priorities really lie and that I and the company I work for are part of the problem, part of what's happened to the town I left behind. 'We should be supporting local workers, keeping them in jobs.' Suddenly I'm getting worked up, thinking about Owen, Dad unable to pay his bills and the farm being turned into fields of solar panels that won't make energy cheaper for the local people. 'I'm not sure what Dad told you, or agreed to, but he won't be selling Gramps's field to you or anyone else right now. Not while I'm here to help on the farm.'

'Have a chat when he's feeling better. I can come back,' he says, clearly feeling the frosty atmosphere between us.

'Please don't bother. We're not selling!'

He lets out a long sigh. 'You have my number.' He points to the letter. 'Call me when your dad is feeling better.'

'Don't count on it,' I say, as he pulls on his coat and makes for the door. He looks as if he's going to say something else, but doesn't. Selling Gramps's field is not going to happen. Not while I'm here. And I'm going to have to stay to make sure it doesn't. I can't leave any time soon.

He strides upstairs and, head spinning, I grab Dad's keys to the Land Rover and pray it'll start but I have no idea where I'm going. Just somewhere to clear my head.

12

Solar panel installation. The words repeat in my head, like an earworm. *Like the big business you work for.* I turn on the radio but it just hisses and I switch it off again. I want Llew Griffiths to be gone by the time I get back. How could I have been so foolish, talking to him, even feeling there was some kind of connection, when I have a partner to go back to? What was I thinking? I let myself be taken in by that charmer. Or am I just cross that the work I do makes me part of the problem, buying cheaper and selling wider, to all the hotels?

I think about what the letter said. It offered Dad a sum of money, for Gramps's field, for solar panel installation, offsetting the carbon footprint of Llew's client, who is doing their bit to give back to the planet.

Could Dad really be thinking about selling Gramps's field? For solar panels?

I'm desperate to ask him about it, but I have to wait until he's less exhausted.

I stick the Land Rover key into the ignition. The engine turns over but doesn't start immediately. Finally it shudders into life. I push it into gear and drive, wanting to get away from the farm for a while. Clear my head. He wants to buy Gramps's field, cover it with solar panels. But the money would be good for Dad and he could get Owen back to work on the farm. But solar panels? There must be another way. So this was what Dad wanted to talk about.

I head down the drive, checking on the sheep again and that Bertie is still in his own field, where he should be. I negotiate the gate and drive over the river. Llew Griffiths's car is still there, its bonnet buckled. I swing around it. So that's what he was doing here: trying to get Dad to seal the deal. What if I hadn't been here? Would Dad have just signed without telling me? Sold off the field?

I drive away from town and over the mountain. Wild ponies are grazing on the common land, together as a family group, keeping close, as if showing there is safety in numbers. The stallion stands tall and proud, his long mane lifting in the wind, nostrils large as he lets out a loud neigh: he's here, with his family, and he's not going anywhere, protecting his patch. Around here they're a part of the landscape, along with the sheep. Unlike bloody solar panels!

I watch him as I drive past and I think he may be watching me too. They've always been here, the mountain ponies. And though many have tried to catch and tame them they have continued to thrive up here, in the hardest of conditions. And I can't help but think that that's how I feel. There are people like Llew Griffiths, wanting to change the landscape, the way we live, and someone has to fight for it to stay as it is, recreating the past to give us all a future. If there were fewer coffee bars and fast-food outlets, maybe people would pay a little more for quality produce, food reared well, not just to be cheap. The past is slipping away, given up to newly built roundabouts next to supermarkets, there for ease and convenience. Cheap produce is flown in from abroad. The way things are, farmers will disappear. There has to be a way we can all work together, reducing the carbon footprint and leaving the fields for flocks to graze on and crops to be grown. How could I ever have let myself become a part of this? I'm furious. Furious with Llew Griffiths, but furious with myself for helping to create a situation in which farms are struggling to survive while society has forgotten where food comes from and how to cook it.

I'm over the mountain now, continuing towards the coast and the sea, winding down my window with difficulty and breathing in the cold air, salty and fresh. I pull up and sit for a while to watch the waves by the shingle and sand shore, the seagulls and gannets diving, then start the Land Rover again and head back, away from the second homes and holiday cottages.

As I drive into our little town, up the high street, I know what I want. My stomach is rumbling and I see a parking space outside Beti's Café and swing into it, with the satisfaction that comes from finding the perfect spot – and that I haven't forgotten how to park the Land Rover.

I open the creaking door and jump out. As I walk round to the pavement, I remember going to Beti's after school or on a Saturday. The outside hasn't changed a bit. Literally. The same paintwork is peeling on the door and window frame. And the *i* on Beti's has been missing since I was last here. But if Beti's hasn't changed, lots around here has. There are closed-up shops all around it. What were once the butcher's, the baker's, the post office, at least two pubs, and a sweet shop on the square have all gone. I sigh. The holidaymakers are at the smarter town down the road, with its bistro bars and waterside restaurants. The younger people drift to the out-of-town places to get Wi-Fi or sit in their cars eating plastic burgers and drinking sweet milky coffee.

I open the back door of the Land Rover, pull out

the sack of potatoes and sling it over my shoulder, then head to the café and reach for the door. It opens and I practically fall into the place. I narrowly avoid running into someone coming out. I jump back, as if I've been electrocuted.

I clear my throat. 'Still here?' is all I can think of saying to Llew Griffiths, holding a coffee in one hand and his phone in the other.

'I am,' he says. 'Like I say, sorting out my car. And then I hope I'll be on my way.'

Suddenly I'm furious. Everything I've been thinking about on my drive tumbles out in one waspish statement. 'Looking for more hard-working farmers to prey on in the meantime!'

The man I'd thought so easy to be with as we walked across the farm was really there to butter me up to seal his deal with Dad.

His face darkens and he frowns. 'Look, I'm just offering a lifeline for farmers who are struggling.'

'But not for the people of the area to help them get cheaper fuel or keep their farms going so that we have food in this country.'

He shakes his head. 'I can see we're not going to agree on this.'

'We are not.' I glare at him.

'Have a chat with your dad and I'll be in touch when he's feeling better.'

'I'll save you the trouble. Don't bother.'

He sighs and takes a deep breath. 'And thank you for letting me stay last night. Thank you for making me feel . . . welcome.'

That wrongfoots me, but I manage to stop myself saying, 'Any time.'

Because, as nice as it was having him to stay, and as well as we got on, now that I know who he is, and what he's after from the farm, he's the last person I want to spend time with. I just wish it didn't make me feel so confused.

I go to sidestep him as he does the same, then back the other way, like we're doing some kind of formation dance, before we swerve around each other and I dive through the door, hoping for that feeling of familiarity.

Somehow I can't help turning to watch him walk away and wondering how he'll get around, or where he's staying while his car is being sorted. I shake myself. Not my business. I do not need to feel compelled to make sure everyone is well looked after. It's my job, not something I do with people trying to take over my family home.

My cheeks are flushed. I stand inside Beti's, and memories flood back. Saturdays in here with Owen, or after the sheep market, with Dad, when it still happened in the town. When he'd sold his lambs and been paid.

The café is practically empty. This used to be the

place to go in the town. Nowadays, it seems it has all but gone. Nothing about it has changed. The seventies Formica tables from when Beti revamped the place, the old piano that was Beti's mother's still in the corner. The little log-burner. It's a mix of cosy and kitsch.

'Hi, I'll be with you now,' says the server, younger than me, clearing the table that Llew Griffiths has obviously just vacated in the steamy window.

'Have a seat by the fire,' she says mildly. 'It's horrid out there. Oh, are they for me?'

'Erm, if you're Mae, then yes,' I say. 'I'm Jem, Edwin's daughter. He asked me to deliver them. He's not been well.'

She looks around as if checking we're not being watched. 'I'm Mae, yes,' she says, and smiles.

'And this is for Edwin,' she says, pulling out an envelope from the pocket of her apron. 'I hope he's okay. And tell him I said thank you and to get well soon.'

'I will,' I say, dropping the potatoes to the floor and putting the envelope into my pocket.

'Let me get you a cup of tea for your trouble,' she says. 'Have a seat.'

'Thanks.' I sit at the table she's just wiped, as she takes the potatoes behind the counter, and I pick up the menu from between the ketchup bottle and the condiments.

I look at the familiar wording on Beti's menu, which is worn around the edges, chewed and abused by children and adults alike over the years. It hasn't changed. A bit like the décor. It's a bizarre mix but we always came here. I'm still staring at the menu when Mae comes back to the table. 'What can I get you? Tea?' she asks softly, but she's looking rather fraught. Her phone rings and she pulls it out. She looks at it, sighs and pushes it back into her jeans pocket.

I have no idea what to order. I can see Mae is feeling a little flustered as the phone rings again. She gets it out once more, hangs up again and puts it away.

'All okay?' I find myself asking. 'I can wait if you need to take that. They seem quite insistent.'

She drops her head. 'Sorry, just school again.' She sighs. 'Wanting to know why I haven't paid for the school photographs.'

'Ah,' I say, and then, because I'm not sure what else to say, 'Expensive, children.' I try to smile.

She nods and I see her eyes fill with tears. Then she says, 'You got some?'

I shake my head as a wave of something, regret, longing, I'm not sure which, washes over me. I look down at the menu again. 'Think I'll just have tea.'

She sniffs and rubs her nose with the back of her hand. 'I don't blame you. The rubbish this place serves.' She takes away the grubby menu, making me laugh unexpectedly. She joins in. 'Sorry, I shouldn't say that. Just, y'know, one of those days.'

'I do know,' I say, and look around. 'It used to be great when Beti had it,' I say.

'Yeah, and when she died her son took over. It's all microwave burgers and plastic-wrapped pizzas now.'

'Shame. So how do you know my dad? How did you two get involved in potato trading?'

She chuckles. 'Actually, I think you and I used to be at school together. You were older than me.'

'Were we?'

She nods. 'You wouldn't remember me. You were one of the cool kids. You lived up the mountain on the farm . . . and weren't you with Owen?'

I laugh. 'I was, but I wasn't one of the cool kids.'

'Oh yes, you were. Living up the mountain. No streetlights up there, scary! And you didn't care what others thought or said. You did your own thing. Loved life on the farm where you lived. And then, of course, you and Owen were the steady couple.'

'Ah, yes! They were good times. But it's quiet on the farm now. Not like back then when Dad had help and I'd have friends back, camping in the summer and bonfires in the winter. I don't know how people do it now, long days on their own.'

'We all need a little company,' she says. 'Owen still comes in.'

'That's good.' I swallow. I feel bad about laying into

him at the pub, the fact he's out of work and with a small herd to sell or get through the winter.

'He was good to me in school,' Mae goes on. 'He probably doesn't remember, but he stepped in once, when some of the other kids were giving me a hard time, telling me I was poor and smelt, because I was wearing second-hand clothes. I was in tears and Owen saw them off, telling them they should be ashamed of themselves and that we all looked out for each other around here. I've never forgotten it.'

'Sounds like Owen. He's a good man,' I say, remembering his kindness, always. He was the one people turned to when they needed a hand.

'It was such a shame, what happened,' she says.

'What did happen?'

'Oh, it's . . . it's just a tough time out there,' she says, and then, 'Bloody moneygrabbers!' She pulls out her phone and shoves it back into her pocket. 'How am I supposed to choose between getting a new coat for my kid, because his last one was stolen, and stupid school photos? Sorry, I shouldn't be talking about this to you. You're a customer. I'll get your tea,' and then quietly, 'I could do you a jacket potato, if you like.'

I smile. 'That's just what I'd like! How did you know?'

'It's how your dad and I got talking. He came in for tea one day. He couldn't find anything on the menu he wanted and said what he fancied was a jacket potato. I said if he brought in the potatoes I'd make them. And the following day he did. He liked to come in for a bit of company. I take them home for the kids too. Way better than all the processed food in the supermarkets.'

'You're right,' I say, mouth already watering at the thought of a hot, crisp-skinned potato with a steaming, fluffy inside.

'Butter and cheese?'

'Perfect!' I beam.

'Don't tell anyone. Just for those who know,' she says, with a very lovely smile. 'I put a few on in the oven at home and bring them in with me, put them through the till as the daily special. Beti's son never asks. But people want something warming and home-cooked. And if it helps keep the place open and me hang on to my job,' she says, 'it's win-win.'

'That's a great idea,' I say, 'and Dad appreciates the money. Every bit counts at the moment.' I wonder again what happened to Owen and how he's coping without work.

The door opens, letting in a whoosh of cold air. 'Hi, Mae,' says the woman, shutting the door quickly.

'Hi, Evie . . . Usual?' Mae says, from behind the counter, which she can barely see over.

'Please. With tuna.'

'Ah, you know about the jacket potatoes too,' I say,

recognizing her name. She's the nurse from the GP practice who called the house, the one planning to visit Dad.

She strips off her long scarf and coat.

'Why not sit here, by the fire, keep the other tables clean?' I offer.

'If you don't mind.' Evie is wearing a cardigan over her blue nurse's uniform. 'Are you Jem? From Hollybush Farm?'

'I am. How did you know?'

'Your dad said you were out delivering potatoes and would have come here. I've just been up to see him. Hope it's okay, I let myself in.'

'Oh, yes, sorry.' I pull out my phone and see a missed call. 'I should have been there.'

'It's fine. A man was there. Llew Griffiths? He was sorting out something to do with his car at the end of the drive. He pointed me in the right direction. Me and your dad had a lovely chat while I gave him a health check. He's very proud of you. I stayed and made him a cuppa and took him a Welsh cake. They were delicious.'

I smile. 'His neighbour makes them. And amazing sourdough bread.'

The fact that Llew Griffiths is still hanging around doesn't surprise me. I hope the car gets picked up soon and he departs for good. He must have come here after leaving the farm. Maybe he's gone.

'Here we go,' says Mae, putting a jacket potato in front of me. The steam curls upwards and I breathe it in. I pick up my knife and fork. The grated cheese is already melting at the edges. I cut into the soft white flesh creating a yellow pool in the middle as the melting butter oozes into the well I've made. I load my fork with fluffy potato, creating strings of cheese from the plate to my lips. It's a reminder of the connection between field, farmer and fork. Simple, home-cooked food. I breathe in, then bite and let the buttery, salty, cheesy mash melt in my mouth. It's delicious, like a comforting hug. I eat slowly, enjoying every mouthful. When I've finished the potato and drunk the tea, I'm suddenly feeling so much better. There must be something I can do to help the farm. There's always hope, right?

'That was great,' I say to Mae.

Evie is finishing hers too. She pulls out a bag with knitting in it and starts to knit with great big wooden needles.

'Something special?' I ask.

'No, not really. I just like how it makes me feel. It takes my mind off things. When I need to be in the moment and not worry about what's been or what's to come.'

I nod. 'That sounds like a very good place to be. Well,' I say, as I stand and pull on my coat, 'I'll see you again soon.'

'I'll be up tomorrow to check on your dad. He's a great character. He was exhausted and still trying to tell me a joke. How many eggs does a French person eat for breakfast?' She grins.

'Oh, I know! One, because one egg is an *oeuf*!' I say, and we giggle at the silliness of it. 'That's one of his favourites. He must be on the mend!'

I push in my chair and make for the till, where I pay up and pop something in the tips box for Mae, hoping it will help and that she didn't notice me do it. I know how important those tips can be and the difference they can make to staff. Not just in the pocket but how they feel about themselves too.

I turn to leave and see Owen coming in through the glass door. Outside, his battered old truck is parked behind the Land Rover, his dog on the front seat looking out of the open window.

'Hi, Owen,' I say. 'Look, about when I came for you . . .'

He holds up a hand. 'Forget it. How's your dad?'

'Home. Tired. But home.'

'Good.'

There's a bark from the truck outside and we glance at his chestnut and white collie.

'What's her name?' I ask.

'Jess. She's from the same litter as your dad's Ffion. They're sisters.'

'Ah,' I say.

'Glad he's home and doing okay,' he says.

'He needs to take it easy. He still thinks he can take on the world, well, the farm, single-handed. He needs to understand he can't.'

'Usual, Owen?' Mae says, from behind the counter.

'Please!' he says. 'And can you put it on my tab? I'll be able to pay it off really soon.'

'Sure,' she says, and smiles kindly.

'Really, I'll pay it off soon.' He's frowning and I wonder if I should offer to pay, but, knowing Owen, that would only offend.

My phone rings. 'Oh, it's Matthew,' I say, but it stops. I'm keen to hear his voice.

'Good to see you, Jem,' says Owen.

'Give my best to Rhi and the girls,' I say, not knowing his children's names.

'Yeah,' he says, frowning again.

He takes the jacket potato in silver foil and leaves, climbing into his truck.

Evie and the waitress are looking at each other.

'Did I say something?' I ask.

'Owen . . . Rhi left him. About a year ago now,' Mae says quietly.

Evie nods. 'Before Christmas. Took the girls. Went off with someone else's husband,' she says.

Mae's face darkens. 'Just like mine did.'

'He's finding it hard,' says Evie.

'Aren't we all!' says Mae. 'While Rhi and her new

106

man are planning trips to Disneyland Paris in the new year, we're having to check the times at the food bank.' She peers at her phone.

'I didn't know. But it seems there's a lot been going on here I didn't know about,' I say, remembering Llew Griffiths and his attempts to buy Dad's land.

'You planning on staying around?' asks Evie.

I shake my head. 'Just until Dad is on the mend, and I know everything is as it should be at the farm.'

'It's tough out there at the moment.'

'But at least the house is warm again and he's happy there,' I reply. But for how much longer? I should do something I should have done ages ago. It's time I took a look at the farm accounts.

13

After confirming what I suspected, during a depressing couple of hours with the farm accounts, my stomach rumbles. I stand up, leaving paperwork strewn over the kitchen table. The day is darkening. I need to make something for Dad to eat. He can't live on Welsh cakes and toast. I did a quick spin by the new supermarket on the outskirts of town on my way back from Beti's. The car park was chock-a-block. No wonder there's no one left in town. I bought essentials, tea, coffee, toilet rolls, but couldn't wait to get out of there. I'm not even sure I have the makings of a meal. It was so busy, light, bright and artificial, that I suddenly craved the quiet of the farm, a place of calm and sanctuary.

I go to the back door, shoving on a hat and my splitting boots, pulling my jumper up around my ears, the dogs at my feet, and stride to the shed behind the farmhouse where the chest freezer lives. The vegetable plot, despite the cold and wet, looks as tidy as ever and ready for a new year after its winter rest.

I open the door and breathe in the earthy smell: bags of potatoes, carrots, leeks and strings of onions, boxes of apples wrapped in newspaper. I open the chest freezer and my suspicions are confirmed. There may not have been much in the cupboards in the kitchen, but there's plenty out here and in the freezer. No one seems to be buying hogget or mutton right now.

I take out a bag of chopped meat, grab some potatoes, onions, carrots and leeks and take them back to the warmth of the kitchen, where I put them all on the table. For a moment, I'm not sure where to start, but then I remember. I sit down and start to prepare the vegetables. If there's one thing that can make us feel better it's a home-cooked meal, I realize, thinking of the jacket potato I had earlier. So simple, but so tasty and pleasing.

The comfort I feel when the chopped onions hit the pan, sizzle, soften and begin to caramelize is overwhelming. I'm right back to when I was younger, when Nan would be in the kitchen making cawl or shepherd's pie. In later years, Dad would do the same; those were his two go-to meals, ready and warm on the range for when we got in from the yard at whatever time of day or night it might have been. The cawl or shepherd's pie would have been in the bottom oven, staying warm. Sometimes there would be a weekend curry, with rice, and on special occasions, a roast.

I put the radio on. The kitchen is warm and I pour a glass of red wine from the bottle I brought, hoping it will give me some ideas to help the farm. I can't let Llew Griffiths's idea be the only offer on the table. There has to be another way.

With the cawl in the oven, I put on my coat, add a hat and the head torch and walk up to the feed shed with the dogs, where I settle into the corner by the window, on the straw bales, covered with sheepskins, and ring Matthew.

'Hey,' he says.

Suddenly I have an overwhelming urge to tell him everything I feel about the farm. How I'm scared for its future. For Dad's future. And if he can't make the farm pay for itself . . . What are other farmers doing? Where will our food come from?

'Everything okay?' he asks. And I falter, not knowing where to start.

'Yes, fine . . . Well, not really, no.'

There's a ping on his phone and I can hear him checking the message. 'Ah, that's HR, confirming our flights for the new year.' I can hear the smile in his voice. 'So, your dad's home. On the mend? You on your way back?'

I pause, again not knowing where to start. 'Not yet,' I reply. 'Just need a little longer. Dad's not on his feet yet and I need to see off some chancer who's trying to buy some of Dad's land to put solar panels on. But I won't be long. Is everything okay there? Managing without me?'

'Yes. All under control. You're so organized, every-thing's running fine. You make things look easy!' He laughs.

'That's because a lot of work went into it.' I'm feel-ing a bit scratchy. The Christmas schedules, bookings and events aren't just thrown together.

Matthew senses the irritation in my voice. 'I was just giving you a compliment.'

'Sorry.' I sigh. 'I'm just wound up by this guy trying to buy a piece of the farm without my knowing about it. I didn't mean to take it out on you.'

'It's fine. You've got a lot on your plate. But solar panels? That sounds good,' he says. 'Could be the answer.'

And now I'm really irritated. 'It's not, Matthew,' I say. 'For starters it would look terrible.'

'Yes, but if it brings in money for your dad, it could be more profitable than sheep and it is helping to save the environment.'

The comment hits me like a flick in the face with

a wet tea-towel. 'But this is a sheep farm. Always has been.'

'But, Jem, people have to change, adapt. Like you in work. You sort things when they happen, go with the flow to make sure things get done.'

'Well . . .' I try to gather my thoughts '. . . the super-markets could pay farmers what the product is worth. They're selling the lamb for less than it costs to prod-uce it sometimes.'

'Which is why,' he says slowly, as if he needs to spell it out for me, 'many people are moving to plant-based diets.'

I'm exasperated now.

'And solar power has got to be good for the planet,' he carries on.

'Not for the people round here, though,' I say, thinking about Mae in the café and Owen. 'It's not helping the people who actually live here.'

'But you don't live there,' he says.

'No, I don't.' And then a voice in my head says, loud and clear, surprising me, *But I wish I still did! I wish I'd never left!* I wonder how my mother and I could have brought ourselves to do it.

There's a pause.

'It's not really your problem as long as your dad has some money in his pocket.'

I don't say anything. Right now, that couldn't feel further from the truth. I'm thinking about Evie, the nurse, knitting to help herself relax after a stressful morning at work. 'It just keeps me in the here and now. It centres me.'

But wool is expensive. And Mae is using a food bank to feed her children. And Owen hasn't enough work to support himself or his family. It shouldn't be like this, I think. 'There has to be a different way.'

'See, you can't help yourself, trying to find answers,' he says. 'It's what you do. You solve problems. You're getting too close to it all. You'll be back here soon, once your dad is sorted. Maybe ask the neighbour to drop in. Then we can start getting ready for the big trip. I really want to enjoy every minute of this with you,' he says, finally making me smile and, for a moment, whisking me away from the worries that seem to have settled in my mind. 'We'll be meeting the owners of the hotel and deciding if we want to make it our new home.'

My timer goes off on my phone. 'I have to go. I'm cooking,' I say, standing up from my cosy corner by the window in the shed on the straw bales.

'Cooking?' He sounds surprised. 'You never cook.'

'I can though. It's what happens when you don't work in hospitality and have all your meals cooked by the hotel kitchen.' I add a little lightness to my voice, but he's right: when did we last shop or cook a meal together, instead of relying on the kitchen staff or smashed avocados on toast?

'Well' – I hear the smile in his voice – 'I look forward to tasting it when you're back.'

'My new-year resolution is to cook more! I'd forgotten how much I enjoy it.' I'm thinking about Evie again: knitting centres her, and I felt the same as I stirred the carrots and onions and browned the meat.

'In Seattle!' he says. 'Sounds good to me!'

'Goodbye, Matthew,' I say, and something inside me shifts. Like I'm at a crossroads and Matthew is there, his bags packed ready for the Seattle adventure, and I'm having to choose a path, but nothing is pointing me towards Seattle.

'Come home soon,' he says, and the voice inside me says, *But I already am.*

I press the red button, hang up and hold the phone to my chin, thinking about what he's just said. Maybe I am too close to it all. Maybe the answer is to sell Gramps's field for solar panels. What's the alternative? Selling the farm altogether?

I look out of the feed shed, towards the lights of the town. The temperature has dropped again. I take a picture of the stars as they start to pop out one by one over Gramps's field and post it on my Instagram account. #ThinkingofGramps #Home #Onthefarm.

Back in the farmhouse, I take Dad a bowl of cawl on a tray, prop him up on his pillows and lay it on his lap. He smiles a watery smile. '*Diolch, cariad*,' he says, his shaking hand holding the spoon.

'Here, let me help,' I say, taking his hand and guiding it to his mouth. He slurps. 'Just like you used to make?'

'Just like it! In the good old days.'

'Yes.' The word catches in my throat.

His eyes fill with tears. He leans back against his pillows and I know he's exhausted. 'It's gone, though. Those days . . .'

My eyes fill too. 'Not yet they haven't, Dad, not yet.'

'This place, it's not a family home any more. It's time to take what's on offer.'

I clear my throat and raise the spoon with more cawl. 'We still have plenty more cawl.' I smile at him. 'And hope.' But, in my heart of hearts, I know he's right . . . I can't for the life of me think of another solution.

Early the following morning, I put on my coat and wellies. The wind is flinging the rain into my face as soon as I step outside the front door, as if it's punishing me for staying away so long. I spend the next couple of hours feeding the ewes with hay and ewe nuts, and breaking up the ice that's formed overnight in the water butts.

With the ewes content, Bertie and Harriet fed, I go back to the feed shed and sit on a straw bale, Ffion and Dewi at my feet. I'm cold, wet and thoroughly miserable and, if I'm honest, alone. My hands are freezing from the water in the butts as I made sure they were running free. I pull off my gloves. My hands are red with cold. This is hard work and for what? For the fields to be turned over to solar panels.

I sit there, listening to the rain against the window. More like sleet, now the weather's turned colder. The feed shed has always been my place of safety. When my mother left, this was where I'd come, angry she'd hurt my dad so much. Sad to see him sad. But I realize now how he felt. Not good enough. And maybe that's how I feel. I've spent all this time working my way up the career ladder to feel good enough. Good enough for who? Or for what? For me?

I look at the metal stalls, ready for lambing. Something we always looked forward to, coming out of winter and into the brighter, lighter days of spring. I look at my phone, wanting to share how I'm feeling. But with whom? Clearly not Matthew, who doesn't get it. I want to share how sad and frustrated I feel that all this work has been for nothing. Two generations that have farmed the land, cared for the livestock, produced the best they could, for what? I want to say that I can't see any hope of people wanting to take on this job. The older farmers are getting out of farming and I don't blame the younger ones for looking to work elsewhere. There are jobs in the local supermarket that pay more.

But no one seems to know where their food has come from! It's not grown in the supermarkets. And that means animals have to be cared for. I look out at our sheep grazing on the fresh pasture I've just moved them to, with Ffion's help – Dewi's over-enthusiasm made the job take longer than it should have done. I love Ffion's patience with him and the ewes, doing what she has always done, working gently but firmly to move them to fresher pasture and give the fields a rest. It amazes me how she understands what needs doing, how the grass needs time to recover to make a better habitat for them, Nature working to give us what we need. I want to tell someone how fantastic it is out here, but also how blooming hard.

So who do I want to call? If not Matthew, who?

I put some music on but somehow the mix I've selected just seems to bring me further down.

What if we were to sell the farm? If Dad were to come with us to Seattle? But who would take this on? Why would anyone want to? It doesn't make money. It doesn't make sense . . .

And yet, leaving it, the ewes that have grazed on this land, feels like erasing the past.

Ffion settles down at my feet and Dewi chases wind-blown straw around the barn. I put my phone beside me. I look out of the window. I love this place.

The familiar view. I always have. I take a deep breath. I love the smell of the lambing shed, yet the feeling of isolation is almost overwhelming. I'm so used to having a phone in hand, pinging and vibrating when messages come in: WhatsApp, Facebook, Instagram, email. But right now, I feel as if I've fallen off the edge of the world. Would anyone even notice if I had? Matthew maybe. I'm missing him . . . At least, I think I am. Or maybe I'm missing the little messages throughout the day. The plans for drinks or dinner. There are no plans here. Just waiting. Waiting for Dad to get better. Waiting for the rain to subside. Waiting for the days to get longer and lighter. But then what? What are we waiting for? Waiting until something worse happens? Or someone buys all of the land for solar panels? Waiting to live again.

Phffff . . .

I pick up my phone and check for messages. Nothing. HR has clearly told everyone I'm not available and someone else is dealing with everything at work. I scroll through social media, see everyone living their best lives. I have no idea what will happen here. My muscles hurt. Everything hurts. And for what? For Dad still to be trying to keep the farm going on his own because he can't afford help. What's it all for? Tears spring to my eyes. I brush them away. Ffion looks up and snuggles closer to my legs, which I really appreciate. If only other people could see how beautiful it is here. That this is where their food comes from, not plastic packets in the supermarkets or on a moped, delivered by a struggling student.

I hear the ewes call in the rain, keeping in touch with each other, making sure they're all safe. I can see them huddling under one of the big oak trees, settled into their new field for the next few days. I lift my phone to take a picture.

My fingers are clumsy and I end up taking a picture of myself. I look at it. I hardly recognize the face in the photo.

I'm cold and wet. Worry is etched on my face, as I wonder what's going to happen to this place and to Dad when the inevitable occurs. If not Llew Griffiths then some other agent will be looking to buy land and plant trees or more solar panels. What will the future look like when farms like this are gone and we wonder where the green fields went? Who would want to carry on doing this thankless job? I look out again at the flock. A flock that has continued since my grandfather's day, cared for and part of the family.

I look down at the phone and lift it again. I don't know who, but I have to tell someone how I'm feeling about this. It can't all be for nothing. I have no idea if anyone out there will understand, but I turn the camera to take in the fields over my shoulder. This time, I press the live button on my Instagram account, deliberately.

'Three, two, one . . . you're live,' says the screen, and I'm like a rabbit caught in bright headlights. What am I doing? Who am I trying to tell, and what am I trying to tell them? That I'm lonely, scared for the future, worried for the farm and the flock?

I feel a nudge on my leg as Ffion leans into me again. I look down at her and she barks. A single, supportive woof.

'Um, yeah, hello.' I stare at my face. 'I'm Jem and I'm working on my family farm in west Wales.' I take a deep breath. 'I'm cold, tired and I've never felt lonelier. I just wanted to share that with someone. But I also know I don't want to give up on this farm. I don't want to sell our land so that solar panels can be installed here. I don't want to eat meat that's been flown halfway around the world or generated in a laboratory. Any food for that matter. Yesterday I ate a jacket potato and, for the first time in ages, it was real food. Comfort food. A basic jacket potato, with butter and cheese. It wasn't just me. There were a few of us. All enjoying something as simple as a jacket potato and the company of others. It's a lonely life being a farmer. It's hard work. But when I got home from that lunch, I pulled out the ingredients and made cawl for me and my dad. He's been ill. Cut himself and got sepsis. So, I've taken on the farm, just for a bit. Until . . .' I stop. No need to tell anyone it's until we decide what to do with it. I see an image of

Dad moving to Seattle with me. A confused, blurry image that doesn't sit right. Eating a pizza from a box arriving by Deliveroo. 'I made cawl. It made me feel better. And him . . .' I stop. I don't know why I'm doing this.

'Anyway, I just wanted to tell someone how it feels out here. People are buying cheaper meat . . . processed foods. Try a jacket potato. Or cawl.' That makes me smile. 'It's really easy. And if I can make it, you can.' That's why I'm saying this: because someone may hear it. It may make this job worthwhile to those working in the rain, the mud, feeling underpaid and undervalued. That is exactly how I'm feeling, how Dad must have felt for years. I'm angry about it. Someone has to hear this and it may as well be the internet. But a real person may hear my frustration.

'Try to remember how it feels to eat something that makes you feel good. And then remember who's making it happen. Remember the farmers, because without them there's no food, no jacket potatoes, no cawl, no shepherd's pie . . .' I may be wandering off the point now. 'Just don't forget where your food comes from. Don't forget your roots.'

I stare at the screen and try to see the off button, put on my reading glasses and screw up my eyes to see out of the rain-splattered lenses, steaming up with condensation. Finally, I tap it. Everything has gone quiet and I'm here again on my own. No idea why I did that. I doubt anyone will hear it. I lean back on the sheepskins draped over the bales. I feel better for saying it. It feels cosier here now. I take a deep breath and message Matthew: *I'm not going to let Dad sell the land, not if I can help it. I want to find another way!* I press send, then try to lighten the mood by adding #onceafarmersdaughteralwaysafarmersdaughter. And a laughing smiley face.

He messages back with half a dozen question marks, as if suggesting I'm mad.

I wonder how to reply, then watch the dancing bubbles on the screen telling me he's typing.

You need to be back here soon. They want you back. They need you! They're talking about bringing in a replacement to cover Christmas. And then there's Seattle.

Would they actually notice if it wasn't me? With all the systems I've put in place to make the hotels work seamlessly to a routine, budget, schedule and brand. To a script even! Telling the receptionists what to say, the waiters and housekeeping staff. I've made us all faceless. Would anyone notice if I wasn't in charge as long as the systems work? It's like the menus: all the same, the same suppliers. When did we forget about the people behind the food, the faces and families that bring the Christmas feast to the table, from the farm to the fork? When did I?

14

It's Friday. Dad is insistent on getting up and dressed and coming downstairs. Even if he does fall asleep in his armchair once he's down.

I check and feed the ewes, then clean the henhouse, and let the birds out to peck around the yard. I check for more wobbly fence posts that need securing. After I've done that, it's nearly lunchtime. I decide to go into town, bring something back for Dad. It's the end of the week, I've made it, and I feel the need to celebrate my little successes.

I shove my phone into Dad's old coat pocket. The dogs settle in front of the fire at his feet where he's dozing in the armchair and I pick up the Land Rover keys. One of Mae's jacket potatoes could be just what I need right now. That and a bit of company.

*

Evie the nurse is already in Beti's, her knitting on her knee. She and Mae are looking at Mae's phone. They turn and smile at me when they hear me come in. The warmth from the fire hits me and it feels good to see some familiar faces.

'Well, if it isn't our local celebrity!' Mae says, looking up from her phone.

'What?' I laugh. 'What are you talking about?'

'You!' says Evie.

Mae waggles her phone in its case. 'Your post!'

I'm confused. 'My post?'

'It's sharing all over the socials! My son just sent it to me from his phone,' she says.

'Oh, my post?' They're not talking about what the postman brings. Life has moved on since I left school.

'And one of the other nurses saw it and sent it to me, asking if I knew you.' Evie grins. 'I said I did. I hope that was okay.'

I sit down next to Evie, haul off my coat and look at Mae's phone. I frown. Then I pull out my phone. The screen is spattered with mud and there's a chip in the corner from when I was driving the quad bike and it fell out of my pocket. I know that social media is part of business these days, but I'm still finding it hard to keep up. With working on the farm all day, I've barely had time to log in, let alone do any scrolling. I look at the insights. There must be some mistake, or I'm not reading things properly. I point. 'All those people have liked it?'

'Yup!' says Evie, stopping mid-stitch to look at me and smile.

'And commented. Telling you to keep going. Keep your chin up. Saying thank you to you and other farmers.' Mae's fingernails click on the screen and she shows me the answers way quicker than I could find them. 'And look at the followers you're clocking up!'

Evie's knitting again. 'Looks like you'll have to keep posting now,' she says.

'You're like a cheerleader for the young farmers out there,' Mae says.

'Women farmers too!' says Evie. 'Loads of them! You said what they've all wanted to say! They're sharing it like mad!'

I stare at the screen, seeing a different me. No makeup, sodden, anxious. Where did the other me go? The one who arrived full of happiness to see her dad and her home, to tell him she's moving to Seattle. Now I'm just worn out and worried.

The door of the café opens and two schoolgirls, skirts short, blazers practically touching the hems, come in. One is staring at the screen of her phone. 'Hey, look, that woman shepherd. It's someone from round here!' she says, showing it to her friend, who turns down the corners of her mouth.

'No one knows where here even is!' she says.

125

'They do now,' say two more girls coming in behind them, also with skirts so short their bits must be freezing.

Where did the time go? What have I done with it? Well, apart from the obvious – went travelling, got a job, settled down with the wrong man . . . I've blinked and it's gone. And now . . . Now it may all go, if we sell off Gramps's field. What will be next? The rest of the farm. And the house will become a second home for people wanting to get out of the city. I'm sure Llew Griffiths will have contacts for that too. And no one will know where this place is and what a thriving community there used to be.

The girls are at the counter as Mae slips behind it to microwave pizzas and warm up rubbery burgers. I slide down in my chair, hoping they won't recognize me. I'm hardly seen on the screen, just the edge of my face. I listen to them banter.

'I think it's sad. I wouldn't do it!' says the one who ordered the burger.

'It's a brutal job.'

'And lonely.'

'Can't wait to get to uni,' says the first. 'Away from this place.'

'I think it's cool,' says another. 'But doubt there'll be any jobs in farming by the time I leave.'

'Nothing that pays you enough to live off anyway,' says another.

'New Zealand! That's the place to go for farming.'

'Or Australia!'

'Christmas on the beach!'

'Got to be better than here!'

I slide down further. I listen to the clack of Evie's knitting needles, feeling sad for the place this once was. These young people don't want to stay here. They don't have dreams that include this place. I didn't. I was so keen to prove I could make something of myself. So keen to do as Dad suggested and move away, like Mum did, to make him proud. But do I have dreams for this place now? I know I don't want our fields to become a solar farm. I know I don't want Dad to sell up. But what do I want? If I want to save the farm, where does that leave me and Matthew? Would he ever join me here? I know the answer to that. Matthew and my bosses are expecting me in Seattle in the new year. I have to work out a plan between now and then to save the farm and leave it in safe hands.

The door of the café opens, letting in a cold blast and the young, brave-against-the-cold girls, no coats, short skirts, nose piercings and colourful hair, leave, talking of life on the other side of the world where everything, apparently, is much better than it is here, from wages to jobs and weekend beach parties. They've seen it on the internet. Suddenly I feel very old, as if the world has passed me by. I've seen it all from the inside of hotel reception areas and guest suites, and in helping to create an idea of paradise I'd forgotten what I'd left behind. Maybe paradise was once here too.

The door opens and my past walks into the café. 'Hi.' Owen raises a hand and smiles. 'Hi,' he says to Mae. 'Can I take a jacket spud? I'll settle my account soon. Going to pick up some money for grass-cutting I'm still owed from the end of the summer. Some of the second-home owners are here and I'll be back with cash.'

'No worries. Oh, actually' – she grimaces – 'the boss is coming down tomorrow to check things over. Would be great if you could pay me before then.'

I see him dip his head.

'Really. I'm owed some money. I'll get it to you,' he promises. 'Thank you for letting me owe it.'

Mae's face creases. 'I hate to ask. I know how hard things are right now,' she says.

'For all of us,' he says. 'I know things are for you too. Can't be easy, this close to Christmas.'

She shrugs . . . her armour against the world. 'It's okay. I'll get by.'

'If there's anything I can do to help, you know where I am.' He's always there to help others.

'Thank you,' she says. 'I know. We seem to be a small group still looking out for each other around here.' She hands him the jacket potato wrapped in foil.

He thanks her again and goes to leave, then turns back. 'I'll see you in the morning, with the money I owe. I promise.'

'I know you will. No worries.'

Then he turns to me and stops. 'Great post on Instagram. Bloody brilliant!' It's a smile that looks like it hasn't seen the light of day recently.

'I just wanted to get some things off my chest. Maybe should have come here instead!' I try to hide my embarrassment behind the mug of tea Mae has put in front of me. 'Not sure what I was thinking of, to be honest.'

'Well, you certainly said what a lot of us are thinking,' he says. 'Well done.'

I hear a single bark from outside.

'Jess is waiting for me!' he says. His brown and white collie is in the front of his battered truck and I wonder if the food he's carrying is for himself or for her.

'Just . . . Good for you, Jem.' He puts a hand out and squeezes my shoulder. 'Someone needs to be saying it. You always were the one to take the lead and others followed.'

I laugh. 'I don't know about that.'

'Well, you left, and most of the town followed. Not many of us stayed. You were the one with the right idea. You always were independent-minded.' He adds, 'They were good times, Jem.'

129

Suddenly, I have no idea why, I feel a deep sense of betrayal: I let down the town. The farm and the town. The place where I had such a wonderful growing-up: I left and gave nothing back. Like Mum. Just ran away.

Owen nods shyly to Evie, then to me and raises a hand in farewell. 'See you around, if you're still here?' he says, and although I don't think he meant anything by it, it hurts.

My phone rings. It's Matthew.

'Hi!' I say.

He doesn't bother with pleasantries. 'What's all this about you on social media? I'm getting loads of messages.'

'Oh, that . . .' I try to laugh it off. 'It was just a bit of . . .' I can't say it was fun. 'Maybe I should have kept it to myself.'

'Well, it's not going to do us any favours if the bosses see it,' he snaps. I'm feeling told off. He's right. It's not 'on brand' for the hotel chain.

'You can barely see it's me in it.'

'Hardly recognizable, I agree, but it is from your account.'

'Yes, I know. I'll take it down.'

'Best you do,' he says, letting out a long sigh.

I feel as if a small flame thrower has ignited in the pit of my stomach. I want to tell him this is important to me and should be to him. Instead I stop myself and think of another way to get him to support this part of my life. 'Matthew, how do you feel about spending Christmas here at the farm?'

He laughs and I don't. There's an awkward pause.

'You're not serious,' he says, suddenly very serious.

'It could be fun!' I say, frowning at his response.

He takes a beat, then speaks slowly and clearly. 'We have Christmas plans. We work and then we leave for Seattle. It's all booked.'

'I know, I know.' I realize it's a big ask. It's almost as if I'm testing things . . . testing 'us'. 'And it'll be lovely. I'm just wondering . . . if we could postpone it.'

'Postpone the Seattle trip?' he says, as if he's misheard me. 'But we're meeting with the hotel owners.'

'Yes, but I'd like to stay here with Dad. What if we just said we're taking Christmas off? Going home!' My laugh sounds slightly hysterical. Any previous year I'd've been the first to say, 'The thought of it! Taking Christmas off when you work in hospitality? Ridiculous!' But that's exactly what I want to do.

'Are you okay, Jem?' he says, a little more quietly. 'Do you have a temperature? Can you get the nurse to check you over?'

I watch through the window as Owen gives the ham from his jacket potato to his dog. She swallows it as he drives away.

'It's just good catching up with people here. And then there's Dad.'

'I know he's your dad, but he's telling you to go and live your life. He'd want you to go to Seattle.'

'You're right. I'm not sure what I was thinking. I'll work it out. I'll be back.' I'm trying to snap out of the desire to stay and get back into work mode.

'This place is a dive. Wish school was closer to the outlet centre. At least we could get Greggs!' says a girl, arriving with friends in the café.

'Apparently she's from around here, but moved away. The one in the video,' says another, studying her phone. 'You can tell by the fields.'

'Okay, okay,' I say to Matthew. 'Look, I have to go. I need to get back to see Dad. I'll take down the post, don't worry.' I hang up, my finger hovering over the post's delete button.

'Looks like you're famous now!' says Mae, nudging me, listening to the girls' conversation. I look at them, then at Mae and Evie, and down at my phone.

'Looks like I have to take down the post. My bosses really won't approve.'

Evie smiles. 'Or your partner, for that matter,' she says, clearly having heard everything.

'I think she's great!'

Evie looks up at the girls, talking among themselves.

'I'm sharing it to my followers!'

Evie leans into me, shoulder to shoulder, whispering, 'Looks like social media isn't all bad!'

I decide to steer the conversation in a different direction and distract myself from the praise being uttered at the counter for the 'Social Shepherdess', as they're calling me, or the woman they've shared on social media who doesn't feel like me at all. It's a bit surreal.

'What's next? When you've finished that?' I ask her quickly. 'What keeps you knitting?'

'Not sure. Mad, with the price of wool. It's more expensive to make things than buy them.'

I remember what Dad was paid for the fleeces. 'Madness indeed.'

'But I can't stop,' she carries on. 'I love it. I like who I am when I'm doing it. Helps me to make sense when the world doesn't.'

'Maybe that's where I've been going wrong. Hiding in the process instead of letting myself be part of it,' I say. I keep my head down and eat the hot jacket potato, this time with beans, thankful no one has recognized me.

Evie is packing away her knitting. 'Better get back to work.'

I walk up to the counter and hand Mae my card to pay for my tea and the potato. 'And I'll pay Owen's tab, please,' I say quietly.

Mae looks at me. 'Are you sure?'

I nod. 'Don't tell him, though. Just thought it might help.'

She rings it through. 'It will, him and me too, when Beti's son gets here. Oh, and no jacket potatoes tomorrow. Back to burgers and pizzas from the microwave with the boss in town.'

'Got it.'

'How are things at the school?' I ask.

She sighs. 'Oh, same. Money for this and that. School trips, and PE kit I don't have money to replace. But at least I have this job. Thank goodness.'

'See you tomorrow, Mae,' I say, enjoying the sense of familiarity coming here has brought me.

Evie and I leave together. 'See you tomorrow?' she says, and I nod. It's good to get out.

'Definitely,' I say.

The one thing I can do is support this place while I'm here. Now all I have to do is work out how much longer I can stay. With Matthew turning down my idea of Christmas at the farmhouse, I suppose I should start making plans to go back.

15

At the farmhouse, Dad is keen to hear about my trip into town. He's sitting in his armchair by the fire, chortling at the idea of the illicit jacket potatoes, one of which I've brought back for him.

'It's delicious!' he says, tucking into beans and cheese. 'We used to have them on Bonfire Night, remember?'

'I do. A bonfire, with jacket potatoes in the embers. No fireworks because they'd scare the sheep. But the bonfire was great fun! You could make more of these for yourself,' I say. *Once I've gone.*

'Yes, I will,' he says.

After he's eaten, and I've made him a cup of tea, I see there's a fresh tin of Welsh cakes on the side.

'Has anyone been while I was out?' I call from the kitchen.

'Blooming woman from next door! Expect she thinks I need looking after. Will probably make an offer for Bertie if she finds out I'm strapped for cash. Tried to leave the tin without knocking, so I wouldn't know it was here.'

'Or maybe she was just being nice,' I call, putting two Welsh cakes on a plate and taking them to him. 'I'm going up to the feed shed. Need to sort out some emails,' I say, and kiss his forehead.

'It's good to have you here, Jem,' he says quietly, and I'm stopped in my tracks. Usually he'd be telling me I should get back to work. The words sit with me as I put on my coat. Ffion stays at Dad's feet with Dolly, but Dewi is keen for another walk so I open the door and let him out with me.

I take huge deep breaths as I walk up to the shed, fresh air filling my lungs, the wind nipping my cheeks. We go in and Dewi sits beside me. I reach down and stroke his soft head. 'It's not a bad place to be, is it?' I say to him.

Suddenly the spreadsheets, the delivery timetables of suppliers for the Christmas rush, the staffing schedules and laundry pick-ups seem so distant, so manufactured. My hotel base could be anywhere, at any time of year, with baubles, Christmas music and a festive menu created for its profit more than the pleasure it will bring. Again, I'm thinking about Christmas here, at the family table.

I pull out my phone. Matthew is right. If my bosses see this post, it could ruin everything for me . . . and for him.

I look at the post. My finger hovers over the delete button but doesn't press it. If no one speaks up, who will know what's going on? I remember the school-girls planning life on the other side of the world, where pay is better and the lifestyle is good. I think about the super-farms flooding the supermarkets with cheap meat and the farmland soon to be cov-ered with solar panels instead of livestock or crops. Where will this cheaper way of living end? I tap my phone in the palm of my hand. I've come a long way in my career, almost to the top of the mountain. The wrong mountain. I should have stayed, fought for what I believed in, where I was happy. I wipe away tears that are now falling fast down my face. I went because Dad didn't want me to feel trapped, like Mum. I went to make him proud. And to make her notice me, see that I was good enough, and the suc-cess I'd become, the girl she'd left behind. But is that enough reason to stay away? Or is it time to think about what and who I want to be, where I want to be?

Dewi barks in delight, seeing a squirrel dart out, then up a tree.

So, who is the Jem sitting here now? Certainly not the one who arrived with plans to go back to oversee the running of several hotels at Christmas.

I've done the job so flawlessly that they're offering to expand for me to do it all over again. Not that Jem. I'm the Jem who loves this place. Loves the farm, knowing where her food comes from, the care and love that go into it. Not the one who's forgotten it all for the sake of balance sheets. That Jem is part of the problem, part of a big business trying to offset its carbon footprint, flying to the States, encouraging more travel for pleasure.

The tears are still flowing freely down my cheeks.

Yesterday I felt sad for the farmers working hard and not being rewarded. Sad that no new young farmers will come into the industry. Today, I'm frustrated and angry: frustrated that I have been part of the process in which food on a plate is now about how it's presented and priced, forgetting the farmers. And I'm a farmer's daughter. Today, I must start to help put that right. No matter what Matthew says. I'm not the same Jem who arrived here. But I'm starting to remember the Jem I used to be.

I press 'live'.

'So, as you can see, it's a misty one here on the mountain today. The sheep are all fine. I've been out and counted them. Bertie the ram is firmly in his field with Harriet, the pony, his companion. Feeding them this morning was no mean feat . . .' I laugh. 'Anyway, that's me, saying hello to anyone out there who needs to hear it. Give me a wave or a comment.

You're not alone!' I say, the camera facing away from me to shoot the hill, the rolling fields below and Dewi chasing the squirrel. 'It may be cold and lonely out here, but at least you lot know why I'm doing this.' I smile and sign off.

I switch off the live stream, then watch as the likes and hearts travel up my screen.

It wasn't the same as yesterday's post. Today I just wanted to share a bit of life out here as a sheep farmer. But I can also feel the fire in my stomach that's strengthening every day.

I go back into the farmhouse, dogs at my feet, and check in on Dad. 'What are you doing?'

'Standing up!' he says, staggering to his feet. 'I can't just sit around here all day. And you need to be getting back to work and that man of yours. You have a new-year trip to go on.'

He tries to straighten. 'See, good as new.' He smiles and all the colour drains from his face. His legs buckle and I lurch forward, catching him under his arms.

'I'm not going anywhere just yet, Dad. I'm here for as long as you need me. I mean it. Work will cope without me. I made it so it would. The new-year trip can wait. I'll let them know. Right now, I want to be here.'

He looks at me from where I've lowered him into his armchair. 'We have to talk,' he says, his hand shaking and resting on mine.

I swallow. 'It's okay, Dad. I know.'

His tired eyes rest on me. 'This place. It's not working any more. The flock.'

'We can make it work, Dad. I'll think of something.'

He shakes his head. 'People won't pay. The supermarkets won't pay. There isn't a living to be made any more.'

'So we just cover the farm with solar panels?'

'Ah, you know about that too.' He pats my hand. 'It's the only option. Or sell the whole place.'

I think about Llew Griffiths and feel really angry with him.

Dad seems to know exactly what I'm thinking. 'It's not his fault, love. He's just making it possible. We all need to earn a living.'

I wonder what will happen to the flock if he decides to sell. 'You could come back with me, Dad. You know that.'

He nods. 'But it's not for me. Your mum, she was one for moving to sunny climes. This place has always felt like home. The solar panels will make it possible for me to stay. And you need to be thinking about getting back to work. I won't let you stay here for me, no matter how much I love having you home. I'm always so proud to tell people what you're doing.'

He's saying I should go. How can I tell him it's the last thing I want to do? What if I want to stay? I just have to find a way.

16

It's been a week of working on the farm, posting occasional live feeds of the fields and the animals, and popping into Beti's for my lunchtime jacket potato. Back at work everything will be ramping up now it's 1 December. Everything will be feeling festive. Here, it hardly feels like Christmas is only just under a month away.

'Did you see the video this morning?' I hear one of the schoolgirls I recognize from the café call to her friends, as I park the Land Rover, which has limped its way to the town this lunchtime. I pull on the handbrake and put it into first gear just in case.

'Yes, she's great!'

'Does anyone know who she is yet?'

I find myself smiling in the front seat.

'Really went to town on the supermarkets and

hotels this morning. Telling people why they should shop local!'

'People are calling her the Stand Up to Big Business Shepherdess!'

'I'd love to meet her!'

I smile again, watching the girls ambling towards the café.

'Perhaps Beti's should start listening to her and get local stuff instead of the disgusting burgers and pizzas we have to buy there,' says another.

'Speak for yourself. I'm not changing the way I eat,' says the girl I recognized. 'Farming is for losers. Who wants to spend their day in the rain with animals? Doesn't matter where food comes from. As long as it's cheap, my family's happy. We can't afford all that high-welfare stuff. My mum's got seven of us to feed.'

And my happy bubble pops. I don't know how this will ever change now.

The sun is trying to come out. It's wintry and there's very little Christmas cheer about the high street. But at least a crowd is waiting to get into Beti's, which is great. I must bring Dad tomorrow, I think. This will be good for him. He'd love a visit to the café, see some people. I'm pleased with the idea: things are getting better; he's on the mend.

I pull up the hood on my coat and look at the front of the café. Clearly burgers and pizza are in demand today, I think sadly. Or maybe word's got out about

Mae's jacket potatoes and they're queuing to order them. Maybe Beti's son let her put them on the menu after his visit.

I stand back and watch, wondering if it's going to be a long wait for a cup of tea. I could just go home. But this place has become part of my daily routine. A connection to people that helps when I've been outside in the cold and wet all morning. Contact with others has been my daily treat. I'm wondering if things are moving but the crowd isn't getting any smaller. In fact, as I look closer, the group of people around the door seems to be growing as passers-by stop and stare. An argument is going on outside the front door. I'm hoping it isn't about Beti's son having found out about Mae's jacket potatoes and she's in trouble. It's not like she wasn't charging people for them and putting the money through the till as the daily special. He should be grateful for her ingenuity. She's been keeping this place going. Or perhaps she's been giving too many people leeway and running tabs for them. Maybe Owen wasn't the only one with an account to settle. I should check that Mae's okay.

Owen's truck pulls up in front of the Land Rover. 'What's going on?' he says, as he gets out and stands beside me. Now I can see Mae with a man in a suit.

'Not sure, but looks like trouble,' I say, and walk towards her, not bothering to lock the Land Rover.

Owen's beside me and we quicken our pace towards Mae and the gathered crowd, where a heated debate is going on.

'No! No!' Mae is saying firmly. 'You can't do this!'

I look on from behind the interested schoolgirls and Owen, who seems to want to help but is apparently unsure of what to do.

'Mae? What's going on?' I call.

'What's happening?' Evie appears beside me, her knitting bag on her shoulder. 'Is anyone hurt?'

'I don't think so,' I tell her.

Mae spots us. 'They're shutting the café down!' she calls. 'From today!' She points to a sign Sellotaped to the front door, beside the closed sign in front of the drawn-down blinds.

'What?' We nudge our way through the crowd.

'That's why Beti's son came yesterday. He told me he'd lock up – he didn't tell me he was closing down.'

'Sorry, excuse me,' I say, pushing my way through.

'I'm sorry. It's just how it is. The café has been sold,' says a young man in a suit and a smart woollen coat, the sort you wear for best or funerals. The sort Matthew wears whenever we go out.

'It's been sold. By Beti's son!' Mae shouts to me, clearly furious.

The young man in the suit and big woollen coat pulls up his collar, uncomfortable with all the attention on him.

'By the previous owner's son, that's right,' he says steadily.

'But I'm owed wages!' Mae shouts.

'I'm sorry, you'll have to speak to him,' the young man says.

'I need that money! I have a coat to buy, a school trip . . . and what about Christmas?'

I can't stand by and do nothing. I step forward. 'Hang on, you can't just shut it down with no notice.'

He turns to me, shoulders up against the cold. His eyes narrow: he's clearly seeing me as another complication in his day. 'I'm sorry, I'm just doing what I was sent here to do. Everyone who works here is on zero-hours contracts.'

'Because we need the work!' Mae shouts. 'I have to make a living!'

For a moment, he's like a rabbit caught in the headlights. He gives a little cough and pulls himself up taller.

'And it's nearly Christmas!' someone calls from the group.

'Yeah!' shouts another.

'Boo!'

'Shame on you!' yells a voice from the back of the crowd. It's Myfanwy, who's come out of the hairdresser in her foils, with a towel wrapped around her shoulders, to see what all the fuss is about.

Twm Bach joins her and steps towards Mae, the

group standing aside to let him through. The chatty group goes quiet. Twm looks at the café window, and then at Mae, shivering in her worn, thin coat. 'So, it's not opening today, then,' he says.

'Not today,' says Mae. 'Sorry, Twm.' She glares at the man in front of her. 'There are new owners. They want to redecorate. Put their stamp on the place.'

Twm shakes his head and turns to walk away. I watch him go up the high street, past the closed shops and To Let signs, the scaffolding with the promise of work to be done that never happens, and I wonder where he'll eat that day.

'That's the only café, unless you go to the out-of-town place!' shouts the young hairdresser, with blue and pink stripes in her hair.

The young man turns to us and holds up his hands. 'I'm sorry. There's nothing I can do.'

Someone else is standing next to me. It's Llew Griffiths. My hackles rise. 'I suppose you think it's the right thing!'

'No,' I hear him say. His voice makes my nerve endings stand to attention. 'We all need to eat. They could have given notice,' he says, and I soften just a bit.

'Yes, it's not fair. Zero hours or not, you should have given notice! It's no way to treat people,' I call, and move closer to the door, where I can now read the 'Closed with Immediate Effect' notice more clearly.

I stand beside Mae.

'So, you've been sent by the company, have you?' I say, feeling as if I'm looking at myself in the mirror. Sent in to close down the old place and make it the same as all the others they've bought. I've been ironing out any individuality from hotels. It's why they want me to go to the States. I'll make another for the chain, where the reputation matters but the source of the restaurant's food doesn't. I'm suddenly angry that I've been a part of this. Destroying lives, businesses and communities so that I could work my way up the hospitality ladder. For what? 'Going to be another Starbucks or Costa, is it?'

'Actually, I like Starbucks,' says one of the schoolgirls.

'And me,' says another.

'Brilliant!' says a third.

I frown. 'Not brilliant!' I say, then turn back to the man, a younger version of me. 'The older generation won't come to Starbucks or Costa. Not least because it's too expensive! And it's faceless!' I'm on a roll, with nothing to lose. 'Mae and her jacket potatoes are holding this community together right now, what's left of it. Not least my father, who earns a small amount of money from growing the potatoes. Enough to help him keep going with the veg he also produces.'

He frowns. 'Her what?'

Mae gives me a look.

'Nothing,' I say quickly, but suddenly I love Mae

and her rebellious streak. The man goes to step around her: she's standing in front of the door.

'Wait!' Mae doesn't move, but puts an arm across the door. 'What am I supposed to do? How will I afford Christmas for my kids now?'

'Please, I'm sorry. I'm just doing my job. Move out of the way of the door. I need to get to it to lock up. Let's not make this any more of a fuss than it needs to be.' He stretches out a hand in front of me.

Suddenly Mae explodes. 'There needs to be a fuss!' she shouts, and shoots a look at me. I glance at Evie. I have a feeling that things are about to escalate and I'm here for Mae, as are Evie and Owen.

'You're not shutting down the café! We need it! I need it! These people need it!' shouts Mae. She lunges forward and grabs the keys from the man's hand.

'Hey!' he yells.

Mae tosses them to Evie. The young man turns towards her, completely at a loss, and puts out his hand. 'Come on now,' he says, as if he's in charge of herding a pack of cats and has no idea where to start. 'Let's not make this into a bigger drama than it needs to be.' He sounds like he's trying to stay in charge but there's a wobble in his voice.

Mae dodges round him and opens the café door. The young man walks towards Evie. The schoolgirls cheer.

'To me, to me!' they shout, as they would in a school netball team.

Evie tosses the keys to me and runs forward towards the door. The man makes a strange lunge while I run the other way around him to dart in through the open door. It's just ajar with Mae behind it. I squeeze through and thrust the keys into her hands. She grapples with them, and he goes to pull the door handle. She drops the keys with a clatter. The young man looks down as does Mae.

'Quick!' Evie and I squeal.

She scoops them up from the floor and I feel like one of the girls outside. I was never really in trouble, but I do remember the thrill of risk-taking, riding the horses with no bridles around the field, hoping not to be the first to fall, being young and alive and willing to take risks. Not a management professional about to embark on her fortieth year on the planet. Somehow, it feels thrilling and exhilarating as the keys tumble into her hands just as the new owner's representative is pulling open the door. Suddenly it slams shut and I hear a familiar voice say, 'Sorry. Didn't mean to do that. Thought I was helping, that the door opened the other way.'

I look at Llew Griffiths in complete surprise. We hold each other's gaze just for a moment, while I hear the clunk of the lock as Mae secures the door from the inside. The thrill I feel as I stare at Llew Griffiths leaves me a little breathless.

'Bolts,' Mae commands, and I'm catapulted out of

149

the bubble from which I'm staring at a man I find attractive but want nothing to do with. Or do I?

I reach for the top bolt. Evie bobs down and pulls across the bottom one.

We straighten. The door is bolted and locked, with us inside.

'You're not closing this building today!' shouts Mae, at the shocked young man.

Llew puts a hand on his shoulder and pats it. 'Sorry, mate. Like I say, I thought I was helping there.'

'Thanks anyway,' he says, baffled and beaten. For a moment, I feel sorry for him. Like the rest of us, he's just trying to make a living. He produces his phone. 'Looks like I'm going to have to tell the office what's going on,' he says to Llew, then, into the phone, 'Hi, it's Josh. Can you put me through to Acquisitions?' He waits. 'Hi, yeah, about the new place, Beti's Café. We've got a problem. We're going to have to come back another day.'

Llew is walking away, but turns suddenly and looks back at me. I feel myself shiver as he gives the slightest nod and a smile tugs at the corners of his mouth. I want to thank him, but don't, before he walks away. Did he do that on purpose or was it a genuine mistake?

Josh, the management man, walks back to his car, which opens up with a blink-blink of lights. He slides into the driver's seat, starts the engine and drives off.

The crowd outside starts to chatter, laugh and move off in different directions. A strange quiet falls over the place but I swear I can hear the adrenaline thundering around my veins as I watch Llew Griffiths go. My world has turned upside down since he arrived in it and I'm not sure if I like or hate it.

Mae, Evie and I turn to each other and say at the same time: 'Now what?'

17

'Well, we'll just camp out here until they agree to keep it open,' says Mae.

Evie and I stare at quiet, shy Mae, who has most definitely come out of her shell.

She looks at us. 'I had to do something! These people don't realize how their decisions affect us. We're trying to get by, day by day. Feed our kids and families. Coming to work when we should be in bed because we're ill but we can't afford to take time off. Trying to encourage our kids to have dreams when we lost ours a long time ago.'

We stare at her and nod.

'I need to phone the rugby club,' Mae says. 'Get someone to have the boys.'

'I can pick up the kids, if you like,' says Evie. 'If you let them know.'

'Can you take them to my mum's?'

'Of course. I'm licensed to drive passengers around.'

'Mum doesn't really go out, but the kids will be safe at hers.'

I look at the time, feeling I'm deserting Mae and Evie but I need to check on Dad.

'You go,' Mae says. 'I'll be here.' She's in the kitchen, opening cupboards and closing them.

'I'll be back. I promise. We won't leave you to do this on your own. Enough is enough!' I hear myself say, and suddenly feel more like me than I have in a long time.

'*Phffff . . .*' Mae says. 'Nothing to eat!' She shuts the cupboards. 'They must have cancelled today's delivery and I didn't do jacket potatoes, in case Beti's son was still hanging around.'

'Looks like he's taken the money and run,' I say, glancing around the empty café. 'I'll sort something when I'm out. Bring something back for you to eat. And more potatoes.'

'If your mum needs a break,' says Evie, 'the children can stay with me. I have the room.'

'No children of your own?' I ask. She shakes her head and, for a moment, I think she won't say any more, until she does.

'My husband . . . died suddenly. We didn't know, until it was too late. He didn't say he was feeling unwell.'

At first neither of us says anything . . . and it all falls into place, the knitting, the being in the here and now. 'I'm sorry,' I say.

'Yes, and me,' adds Mae.

Evie gives a sniffly laugh. 'I never know what to say when people say that. It wasn't their fault.'

'What should we say?' asks Mae.

'I'm not sure. But saying anything is better than being embarrassed and crossing the road. Some people are just too scared to do or say anything.'

'Actions count,' I say, and then to Mae, 'Is this really what you want to do? Stage a sit-in? You don't have to go through with it. We could just say it was a moment of madness.'

'I don't want to, no.' Mae takes a deep breath. 'But it's all I can think to do at the moment. And I have to. My kids need me to have this job. I'm fed up of being hung out to dry.'

'Then I'm here to help,' I say.

'Me too,' says Evie.

'And me.' We turn to the kitchen and Owen is standing there. 'I don't know who paid my bill yesterday but I owe them one. I can help.'

We smile at him, then frown.

'How did you get in?' I ask.

He points over his shoulder. 'Back door.'

Mae grabs the keys. 'Quick, lock it!' she says. 'And put a chair in front of it, just in case.'

'Right. Let's work out a rota so someone's always here,' I say. 'But we don't all have to be here at the same time.' We sit at a table and I grab my iPad from my bag.

We're plunged into darkness as the lights go out.

'Looks like they've pulled the plug on us already,' says Mae.

The one person I have to explain things to is Matthew. I just hope he understands that this is something I need to do. If I mean anything to him, he will.

18

That evening we eat the cawl I made at home and brought back with me, and drink a flask of tea.

'Are you sure you'll be okay here tonight?' I ask.

'I'll be fine,' says Mae. 'The children are at Mum's. And it's my ex Rob's turn to have them tomorrow.'

I hate to leave her here, but I have to get back to Dad. It's important to me to stand up against what's happening to the hospitality and farming industries, but Dad has to be my priority.

'Of course I'll be fine!' she says, far braver than I'm expecting. 'It'll be like a holiday.'

'And hopefully tomorrow they'll rethink and reopen, not leave the town with another empty shell on the high street,' I say.

'I'll stay,' says Owen. 'If you'd like me to. I'd need to bring Jess in. But I just feel some of this is down to me. If I hadn't had a tab running, leaving the till short, the figures might have looked different. Beti's son might have been persuaded to keep it going if people like me didn't owe the place money. I should have been firmer with the people who owed me and been able to pay my way, instead of passing on the debt to others to deal with.'

'It's not down to you, Owen,' says Mae, reassuringly.

'I should have found a way to earn more money. Maybe then I wouldn't have messed things up with my wife and she wouldn't have walked out on me,' he says. 'Maybe if I'd fought a little harder for what was important to me.'

'Oh, Owen, you can't think like that,' I say.

'But I do. If I'd been able to give her a better life, look after them all properly, she wouldn't have looked elsewhere. Same as this place – if people had supported it more, put more money in the till, we wouldn't have lost it.'

'Owen, none of this mess is your fault.'

'Maybe not, but Beti's has been a lifeline when I've needed it. Maybe if I'd asked you not to leave, Jem, we'd be running our own farm by now, with children and even grandchildren on the way.' He laughs and so do I.

'Or up to our eyes in debt, divorced and miserable.' We laugh again.

'We can't predict the future. Life has a way of throwing curve balls at us,' says Evie.

'We just have to learn to roll with them,' I say, realizing I'm dodging the curve ball in my life. I don't want to go back to my job. I don't want the promotion. I'm not even sure I want to be with Matthew.

'I can stay here with you, Mae, rather than leaving you on your own,' says Owen.

'Well, if that's okay,' she says, glancing between me and Owen.

'More than okay,' I say. 'Really, Owen and I were a long time ago.'

'We were. But we'll always be friends.'

'I'm glad you're here, Owen,' I say, 'and happy to have you back in my life as a friend.'

'Me too,' says Owen. 'Really, I just want to help. Give something back Mae, for all the help you've given me, letting me have lunches when I needed them.' A glimmer of the old Owen. 'Hopefully you won't find me as boring as my ex did.'

'Actually,' she beams, 'that would be lovely. And thank you for being here as my friend. Jess, too.'

I hug them, as does Evie, and then we slip out of the door into the darkening afternoon.

I toss my phone and my bag onto the Land Rover's passenger seat. Thankfully, the engine starts and I drive back to the farm, trying not to imagine what my current employers would say if they knew I'd just been helping to stage a sit-in at the local café. But the idea just makes me smile. Much more than any of my day-to-day work ever did.

My phone rings and I can see it's Matthew. I should answer. Tell him I'm having doubts about the new job. Instead, I let it ring out. Now, I have no idea what to say.

19

The following morning, after a freezing start with the ewes, I run into the farmhouse kitchen. Dad is in his armchair, with a blanket over his legs. 'I'm going to the café, Dad.'

'For the sit-in?' His eyes dance with excitement.

'Yes. I'm going to take some more cawl and some of Myfanwy's Welsh cakes. I've made sourdough too. I don't think it's come out too badly – hers is better, of course.'

'I can come!' he says, pushing the blanket off his legs.

'Evie wouldn't approve of that.' I adjust the blanket. 'You still need to rest.'

'But I've been sitting here for bloomin' ages! It's been nearly two weeks! How do people do it? Just sit and watch TV all day?'

'It's not for much longer,' I say, without knowing how much longer, but I do know I must keep him safe and well. He's all I have, apart from Matthew and work. And suddenly I'm thinking about a different life, a million miles away from this one. A life I used to live. I'm not sure I want to go back to it.

I put the key into the Land Rover and it seems to take even longer than usual to start. 'Come on, come on!' I cajole the vehicle.

I have the pot of cawl on the front seat, with the seatbelt around it.

The engine growls but doesn't ignite.

'Woof!' Ffion barks.

Dad is standing outside, dressed and wearing a pink hat he's clearly just picked off the hooks. It could be an old one of mine or even Nan's, with a bow at the front. He's wearing a big coat, which he used to fill but which now hangs from his shoulders.

I push open the Land Rover's stiff door. 'Dad? What are you doing out here?' I call over the wind and the rain that is freckling my face.

I jump out and run across the yard to him, coat flapping.

'Coming with you,' he says matter-of-factly. 'I told you. I can't just sit around any more. It's not good for me or my mental health. I saw it on one of those morning TV programmes. You have to keep physically and mentally active. I'm going mad with boredom just sitting in the farmhouse. I could do with a bowl of cawl and some company.'

'You can't! The café isn't open. Remember, I told you!'

'I know. I may have had sepsis, but I'm not going doo-lally. You've taken over the café. And if there's a sit-in going on, the one thing I can do is sit.' He gives a wonky but familiar smile.

'Dad, you're—'

'Ill? Or sick? Sick of worrying about what I'm going to do with this place? Sick of thinking about solar bloody panels? Or how I'm going to pay for the next oil delivery and feed bill?'

I drop my head.

'I'm not stupid, Jem, I really am out of options. I don't know how to make the farm pay any more.'

'Does that mean we're going to have to sell Gramps's field?'

'I can't see any other option. I may be a bit creaky in the joints, but my mind is still going. Still whirring. It'll be good to take it elsewhere for a little while. Be good to see some people. Conjure up a bit of mischief!'

I can't help but smile: the Dad I know and love is back. 'Come on, then. But you have to promise to sit and not do anything taxing. Apart from carry the cawl on your lap.'

'Promise!' He grins.

I take his arm and steady him to the Land Rover, open the passenger door and help him in, then lay a blanket over his legs. He tells me to stop fussing but lets me do it anyway.

I pull the seatbelt over him and place the pot of cawl on his lap. It's warm – it'll be like a hot-water bottle.

'Right, come on, old girl.' I pat the Land Rover's steering wheel, take a deep breath and turn the key again. I press the accelerator and she roars into life.

'Stay there, Ffion! Guard the house – especially against solar-panel salesmen,' I instruct the dog, standing in the covered porch. She lies down with Dewi next to her, not minding the wind or rain. She has a job to do.

As I manoeuvre the Land Rover out of the drive, the rain eases and, on the horizon, the other side of the valley, the sun makes an appearance, reminding me of the beautiful days I spent here on the farm growing up. When I imagine it covered with solar panels, my teeth grind, like the gears of the Land Rover.

We bump down the drive to the gates. I get out to open them, drive through, then shut them firmly to keep Bertie and Harriet where they're supposed to be.

'Um, talking of Bertie. He got out.'

'Did he?'

'That annoying woman in the cottage told me he'd

attacked her before. But I'm guessing he's been getting out and in with the ewes.'

'I'm afraid so.'

'Some of them could have been pregnant before they were meant to be.'

Dad goes silent.

'Don't worry,' I comfort him, as he owns up to one of the balls he's dropped lately. 'I've mended the fence.'

'Thank you. I've been meaning to do it. But with so much else to manage, and it being just me . . .'

'I can stay on, Dad,' I say.

He shakes his head, and the pink hat wobbles. 'No, Jem, I can't let you. You have a job to get back to and a trip you're going to tell me about. You don't want to be here looking after me. I'll be fine.'

'That's what you always say,' I remind him crossly. 'And, clearly, it's not fine! Besides, it's not just a trip, Dad. It's not a holiday. They want me to move out there. Take over a new hotel. Extend the brand. Me and Matthew. I know you wanted me to spread my wings, see the world, Dad, and that's what this is. But I don't want to leave. I'm not Mum. And I don't need to prove anything to anyone, especially not to Mum.'

I notice Llew Griffiths's car has gone and wonder if he has too.

'Okay, so maybe fine's pushing it a bit. But I'm getting by, Jem. I can't let you stay for me.'

'Getting by, but only just, with money from the potatoes you're selling to the café.'

'I know, I know,' he says, brushing me off, and peering out of the window as we pass the flock. This place, the sheep, the way of life, makes him happy. And if people like Dad aren't producing food to put on our tables, who is? Super-farmers from the States or elsewhere, and the last thing on their minds is the welfare of the animals. I get cross all over again.

I put the windscreen wipers on as the rain returns.

'It's just it's not easy for one. I don't have the same energy to do it just for me. But I'll do better when you go, I promise,' he says, not catching my eye.

We drive in silence for a while, looking at the hedges still heavy with berries.

'Going to be a cold one,' I say. 'Isn't that what you always said if the hedges were full of berries?'

'Or maybe just a tough one,' says Dad, thoughtfully. 'But Mother Nature seems to find ways of providing.'

If only she would for Dad and the farm.

I pull up outside the café. The blinds are drawn. For a moment I think about the new job in Seattle. I *should* be thinking about it. I know Dad thinks I should take it. But I can't stop thinking about this place, the big companies taking over the independents, the farmers who can't feed their families. I get out of the Land Rover and pull my coat around me.

I knock on the café door. There's no reply. 'Mae, it's Jem.'

The blind is pulled back, just a bit. There she is, the shy girl from school, who wouldn't say boo to a goose but has taken on her bosses. She waves and beckons me in. She opens the door a little way.

'Are you okay? Cold?' I ask.

'I'm fine. The fire's in.' She points to the wood-burner.

'Anyone been here?' I ask

She shakes her head. 'It's just me. Owen's gone to check on his heifers. He'll be back soon.'

'I brought you some cawl. Thought we could take some to Twm Bach as well for lunch.'

'Good idea! I'm starving – I've eaten all the ice-cream wafers and the cheese and onion crisps.'

'I've got Dad in the Land Rover. Can he come in too?'

'Of course!'

She holds the door while I run back to get Dad and the bowl of cawl. 'Looks like I came at the right time,' says a voice from beside Dad.

'Owen!' I smile, as does Dad.

'Good to see you, lad. You doing okay? I'm still feeling so bad about having to lay you off.'

'We've all got to take care of ourselves now, Edwin. You included. And you know if you need anything you can always ask.'

'I was just embarrassed, having had to—'

'No need. We're old friends. We go way back. You just ask.'

'*Diolch*, son. Thank you,' says Dad, a little choked.

Tears spring to my eyes and, just for a moment, I wonder how it would have been, if Owen and I . . . What would life have been like? Would we have made the farm work?

'Come on, let's get you in,' he says, leading Dad to the café door, and I watch them go in.

Mae is beckoning. 'Come on, quick!'

I hurry after them and she locks the door behind me, then pushes the sideboard over it.

'Here, let me!' says Owen, helping her. 'But hang on. I've got something in the truck.'

'Dad, you sit here.' I point to one of Beti's armchairs by the fire. 'Mae, this is my dad. Mae and I were at school together Dad, but we didn't really know each other then.'

'She was one of the older, cooler kids,' Mae says.

'Who's the cool one now?' I giggle.

'Pleased to meet you. And well done on what you're doing. We all need to find a way to be heard right now.' He does as he's told and sits in one of Beti's chairs by the fire.

I put the cawl on the table. 'Now what?' I answer myself. 'Well, first off, I wish we could have a cuppa. I should have brought flasks.'

There's a knock at the door. Owen is there carrying

something big. We push back the sideboard. 'A generator. Thought you could use this for leccy! Get some spuds on the go, that sort of thing. And make tea.'

'Brilliant!' says Mae.

And we do.

There's another knock. Mae looks out and so do I.

'It's Myfanwy!'

Mae shoves back the sideboard.

'I've brought bara brith – I heard what you were doing. Well done!' Myfanwy says, with a grin.

'Come in,' says Mae. 'Have a cup of tea.'

Myfanwy slides through the door and joins Dad by the fire. They nod at each other, stiffly at first.

'Best bit of excitement around here in ages,' he says, and she can't help smiling back, despite their past hostilities.

'We need to work out a plan for how to get the bosses to meet our demands,' I say. 'If this place goes, who's next? Maybe Hollybush Farm.'

'Well, we should let everyone know what you're doing,' says Myfanwy.

'No point in us being here if no one knows about it,' says Dad. 'Open the blinds. Let people know we're staging a sit-in.'

'He's right,' says Owen. 'No point in putting on a protest that no one knows about.'

We step forward and open the blinds.

A group of schoolkids goes past and gives us a little cheer.

We wave.

'I'll take some cawl to Twm Bach,' I say.

'I'll go,' says Owen. 'You work out how to let people know you're here, and why. You're more use here.'

'Thanks, Owen,' I say, as he takes the bowl, with a chunk of bread and butter, and makes for the back door, where there's a knock.

'It's me, Evie.'

I open the door a crack. 'Are you on your own?'

'Yes! Of course!'

'What's the password?' Dad chortles.

'Twenty-four days until Christmas,' she replies, and slips inside.

'Excellent,' I hear Dad say.

'Still the joker, Edwin,' I hear Myfanwy say, but there's a definite softening to her tone.

It makes me smile. I'd like Dad to find happiness, like I've done. Something in me jolts: the happiness isn't where it should be. It's being here. I need to speak to Matthew. I need to tell him how I'm feeling, what's going on. I can't put this off much longer. I need to listen to my heart.

Evie has taken off her coat. 'I've just come from your farm. I was looking for the patient. And here you are!' she says, smiling at Dad.

'Found me!' He grins naughtily. 'Guilty as charged!'

'Well, I had a good idea where you might be. I spent a few lovely minutes with your sheepdog and the pup.'

'Not such a good guard dog, then.' He chuckles, shoulders shaking.

'Okay if I do your blood pressure?'

'Work away,' he says. 'But I'm having another of Myfanwy's Welsh cakes. You'd better try one, just to make sure she hasn't come here to poison me. She's had it in for me for years.'

'I'd have done it a long time ago if I'd known it was as easy as plying him with Welsh cakes and bara brith!' She laughs and the friction between them seems to disappear, all those years of not speaking wiped away over a tin of Welsh cakes. 'How about a cup of tea to go with it?' says Myfanwy to Evie, standing and picking up the kettle. 'You couldn't do my blood pressure too, while we're here? I've been meaning to go for a check-up, but what with trying to keep on top of things at the farm and trying to get an appointment at the surgery, I've been putting it off.'

'Of course,' says Evie.

'Smashing,' says Dad, and I can see the old Dad coming back to life right in front of me.

'It's amazing what a cup of tea and some company can do,' says Evie, with a little wink.

'And the Welsh cakes. Don't forget Myfanwy's

Welsh cakes!' Dad laughs. 'Can't believe how good they are. I'd have given her Bertie years ago if I'd known she made Welsh cakes like these.'

'Well, I've no one to make them for now the kids have gone,' she says. 'It's nice to have people to cook for again.'

'Oh, and your mum messaged me, Mae,' says Evie. 'She said she'd baked some jacket potatoes in case you got hungry. I picked them up. The boys send kisses and said you're Superwoman.' She's holding a tray of foil-wrapped potatoes.

'Those could feed an army!' I laugh. 'At least we won't starve. And I've brought cawl.'

People pass the window and wave as we drink tea. But, really, I'm not sure what good we're doing here.

We watch as Owen appears and makes his way round to the back. Evie opens the door to him.

'Twm Bach says the cawl was fantastic!' He's brought back the empty bowl. 'And he can't wait to see what you're going to put on your social-media feed next.'

'What's this?' Dad asks.

'Old boy Twm said that?' I ask.

'He's been following you.'

I look at Evie, then at Dad.

'What's this about social feeding?' asks Dad.

'Social media, Dad. I've been putting up some posts about farm life with the sheep. Saying how

171

cross it makes me that it's a hard, lonely job and barely makes a living.'

He scoffs. 'You can say that again.'

'Anyway, people like seeing the farm and I feel less alone when I'm out there.'

He raises his eyebrows. 'And it's going well?'

'It is. You don't mind, do you?'

He beams. 'Of course not, especially if it gets the word out.'

'They call her the Social Shepherdess!' Mae joins in.

'And other cool names too. Got loads of followers, she has,' says Evie.

'Well, that's good! Best get socializing now, then!' says Dad.

'What?'

'Well, as I said before, what's the point of doing this sit-in if no one knows about it?'

'He's right. The way to get the new owners to hear us is to make a noise,' Mae says.

I said to Matthew I wouldn't do any more. But somehow I can't stop myself. After all, this is the way to be heard now. 'Well, social media is a way to get the word out there. Look at the response I've had to my last couple of posts.'

'Tell 'em what's going on, there's a good girl,' says Dad.

I take a deep breath, hold up my phone and press 'live'. 'It's not just the farmers who are finding it hard, but hospitality businesses. Pubs and restaurants are shutting, it's just over three weeks until Christmas and there's no Christmas spirit for these workers! The only bank they'll be visiting is the food bank! Where have we got to when we can't produce the food to feed our families any more? This café needs to stay open, for its workers and the community, who come here to see people and get a hot meal. We need to support our farmers and those working in hospitality. Oh, and if you're in the area, and you're looking for hot jacket potatoes, come to the café, let us know the password – how many days until Christmas – and you'll be served!'

I stare into the screen, hit 'send' and lower the phone.

'Well done, girl!' says Dad, proud as Punch with a tear in his eye, and the others burst into applause.

My phone rings. It's head office.

20

As soon as I hang up, the phone rings again. Matthew's name flashes up. Instead of filling me with joy and even excitement, I'm feeling dread. I take a deep breath and press the green button. 'Hi!' I say, as cheerily as I can.

'Where are you?' he demands.

'I'm . . .' I take a moment. No 'hello' or 'how are you?' I realize that calls from Matthew have become an irritation rather than a pleasure, and I dread them more and more. I take another deep breath. 'I'm in town,' I say. 'Why?'

'I'm here!' he says, not hiding the annoyance in his voice like I tried to.

'Here?' I repeat.

'Yes, here. At your dad's farm.'

'At the farm?' I smile. 'Really?'

I soften. He's had a rethink. He's going to join me at the farm for Christmas.

'How did you manage to get the time off? Did they mind?' Suddenly the irritation is gone and I'm overwhelmed by this gesture. He gets it. He understands why I need to be here and he's come to support me.

'Mind?' he says.

'Yes, head office. I mean, you're right. Why would they mind?! We haven't had any time off over Christmas in years. You were due to have some, I suppose. This is fantastic! I can't believe you're here. I'll come and meet you.' I grab my bag and sling it over my shoulder, fumbling for my keys in it, with the phone under my ear, gesturing to Mae and Dad that I'll be back.

'Jem, I'm not here for Christmas, for Christ's sake!' he snaps, stopping me in my tracks. 'We've – *you've* got hotels to run.' He emphasizes the words. 'Guests arriving. Christmas parties.'

'Yes.' I'm not quite ready to let my happy little hillock disappear into a pool of disappointment. 'And, by the look and sound of it, it's all going like clockwork. I'm entitled to some time off with my family' – I turn away – 'what with Dad being unwell and things here to sort out.' I pause. 'So, if you've not come to join me for Christmas, why are you here?'

He sighs and tuts. I'd never realized how annoying those sounds could be until now. I don't think I'd noticed it. Or maybe I'd thought it was endearing. It's not endearing now. It's like fingernails down a blackboard, making me wince.

'To take you back, of course.'

'I – I beg your pardon?'

'I've come to pick you up, Jem. If we get back now and in work tomorrow, we may just be able to salvage this mess.'

'Mess?' The happy hillock has evaporated into a miserable puddle as dark as dusk at the farm. 'What mess? I'm here looking after my dad!'

'Head office aren't happy,' he says. 'They love you. They want you to head up the new hotel. Put all your plans in place. But this social-media thing has got them rattled.'

I pause. 'I know. They've just been on the phone.'

'Understandably! You can't be making these posts in your own name and expect them to be happy.'

'Well, they should be. I'm standing up for what's right. For more awareness of what's going on in hospitality and farming in our country!'

And while all the reasons not to rock the boat clatter around my head, I take a deep breath. It may not be right, but it feels right to me. I'm making a stand for small independent businesses. Young people trying to make a living in the countryside. I'm standing up against buy-outs by big business. The likes of Llew Griffiths.

'I can't just let you ruin everything, Jem,' he continues, as if I'm a child. 'Come back to the farm, meet me and get your stuff together. The nurse is here to look after your dad.'

I look at Evie, knitting, finding comfort in something that keeps her in the moment. I've been so busy planning, looking towards the next step on the career ladder, I can't remember when I last lived in the moment. Christmas planning starts in January for the hotels. Bigger and better, at bigger profit! I suddenly think about the sourdough bread I ate for breakfast at the farm. I think about the vegetable plot that's dormant and used to be Dad's pride and joy. And chickens! Wouldn't it be lovely to have more chickens on the farm, like we did when I was young?

'And he'll be able to sell off that bit of land and have some money. You've done your bit. You've done what you always do, gone above and beyond. Just like you will in the new job. You're the boss, babe!'

I listen to what he says about me going above and beyond. And I have: I wanted to do my best and make Dad proud. But I don't think he could be prouder of me than he is now. But maybe Matthew's right. I've done my bit. Dad will be fine with Evie looking after him. And although we don't want the solar panels, it's the only option at the moment.

'I can see that,' I say steadily.

'You have a great career ahead of you. We have

a great future, together. You know I'm planning to propose at Christmas. We're going to have a great adventure in America, you heading up the take-over and me as manager. We're the dream team!' he enthuses, a real change from his earlier tone. He's switched into hospitality mode. It's a front to make the customer feel comfortable, happy . . . and spend more. It's not real. None of life at the hotel chain was real. It was creating an image, a fake world. Here, right now, with these people, is real.

I pause and think about what he's saying. I think about Dad telling people what I'm doing, wanting the best for me. But the chickens keep pecking at my thoughts, along with the ewes. Where will I be when they're lambing if I go with Matthew now? Not in the fields or the lambing shed but looking at the world from the inside out again.

'And take down the posts. Like you said you would. They're not helping.'

All reason is whipped away from me. I take a deep breath and gather the thoughts that are careering around in my head. 'I'm not a child, Matthew. I'm not some young influencer. I'm a nearly forty-year-old woman who has realized she's been backing the wrong horse all these years, climbing to the top of the wrong mountain.'

He lets out another tut and a long sigh. The

fingernails down the blackboard again. 'It's embarrassing, Jem,' he says.

Now I'm enraged! A red mist, like the early morning sunrise over Gramps's field, descends before my eyes.

'Embarrassing? Standing up for what's right?' A flood gate is opening within me. 'For making people aware of where our food comes from, and supporting the people who produce it? People like Dad, and his parents before him. For the young people serving food on zero-hours contracts with no job stability? Why is it that other countries get it and we don't? That's what's embarrassing!'

For a moment, there's silence in the café and at the other end of the phone, until Matthew says, 'They're giving you a chance, Jem, to put this behind you.'

I look around the café at the people gathered here, staring at me. 'They said so on the phone.'

'Good. Okay,' he says. 'And once everything is sorted, we can come back and see your dad, even suggest a visit to Seattle. Give him the best room in the hotel with the best views.'

The best room in the hotel. Seeing life from the inside out. That's what I've been doing all these years. I should have been doing it the other way round.

'Dad already has the best views,' I say, my feet digging in even deeper to where I am right now.

'Jem, I don't want to say this, but either you come

back and we get ready for Christmas at the hotel and New Year in Seattle, or . . .'

'Or what?' I say slowly.

'Well . . . that's it, isn't it?'

I feel my voice drop and an eyebrow lift. 'That's it?' I repeat on a slightly higher volume. 'What about loving me for the person I am, for what I believe in, where I need to be right now?'

'You're different from the woman who left here a few weeks ago. You've roamed off into cowboy country.'

'Cowboy country!' Everyone in the café takes a sharp breath.

'It's like you're living out some childhood fantasy. Roaming around the fields on a quad bike, with dogs, staging sit-ins and ruining the plans of businesses. I thought that was what you believed in too. Getting business done.'

'Yes . . . I did.' I look around the café. 'But this isn't a fantasy. It's real people. Real lives. Real jobs at stake. If we don't support the people making the food, where's it going to come from?'

'I've been in touch with Llew Griffiths. He seems a good bloke. It's a fair offer.'

'I'm sorry, you've done what?'

'I thought I'd google him, after you said about the offer on your dad's field, find out what I could about him.'

'And you contacted him?' I'm incredulous.

'Yes. It all seems like a good idea, makes sense . . . Look, Jem. I'm standing in some run-down barn to get a signal. Are you coming or not?'

This may be the maddest thing I've ever done but . . .

'I'm sorry, Matthew, but I won't be coming back, not now, not in the new year, not ever. My time in corporate hospitality is over. I want to make sourdough. I have a starter to take care of. And I want more chickens. And after Christmas, come the spring, there'll be lambs on the way.'

'You're pulling out? You're not going to Seattle?'

'I'm . . . not coming back, Matthew. Here is where I need to be.'

'Well, I'm not moving here! Jesus, God forsaken! Maybe we're where we both need to be, then,' he says with finality.

'Maybe we are.' I nod, putting the same final full stop to my job and my relationship.

There's a silence. In the background I can hear the dogs barking on the farm.

'You could come back now, put this right.'

'I'm not coming back Matthew. They asked me to decide, there and then, on the phone. I'm not taking the new job. I'm not coming back. I've told them.'

'What did they say?'

'They told me to think about it, but said if I did any

more social media, they'd take that as my decision and sack me.'

'Well, maybe it's for the best. Made the decision for me.'

'What decision?'

'I was wondering if we had a future, if you and I were the real deal, the dream team. It's why I wanted to wait until we got to Seattle to propose, but thought I should do the right thing and speak to your dad. Seems it's a good thing we both know who we really are before it goes too far.'

'And if my standing up for what I believe in and finding out what matters to me made you feel that, it's the right choice. Goodbye, Matthew.' My heart had already let me know we were over.

'Right, well, if that's your decision . . .'

'It's what I need to do.'

'I hope you don't regret it.'

'Bye, Matthew. Happy Christmas.'

'And you, Jem. I hope it's what you want.'

I switch off the phone and look at the people in the café. Right now, I've never been surer of anything. I've made the right choice. I'm not going back. I just don't know how to go forward. But I haven't felt like this in a long time. The sheep, the farm, the people who are working to make it all happen . . . it seems I'd forgotten about them from inside my hotels. Now I'm outside, looking in. It may be cold and wet but at least I can feel something, even if it's just the wind and rain on my face.

'Looks like I'm here for longer than I first thought,' I say, tapping the phone in my palm.

I turn to Dad, sitting by the fire, worry etched on his face.

'Dad . . .' I crouch next to him. 'I know you wanted me to go back, and I wanted to make you proud, but I want to be here.'

His eyes fill with tears. 'The only thing I've ever wanted is for you to find what makes you happy. I didn't want you to feel trapped here, like your mum did. But if here is where you want to be, I couldn't be happier or prouder.'

'It is. It's where I want to be.' With that I put my arms around his neck and we hug, very hard.

'It'll be tough,' he says.

'I know. But that doesn't mean it won't be fun too,' I say, pulling away. Jess jumps up and licks my face and we laugh, but it's okay to laugh when things feel tough.

21

There's a knock at the back door and we all stare at it. There's no time to dwell on the life I've left behind or the one I was going to. I'm not back in the office, overseeing the managers, their Christmas budgets and occupancy rates. I'm not packing to go to Seattle and check out the apartments I could choose from. I'm here, holed up in a café, watching my social-media following rise by the minute and hoping to keep the new owners of this place at bay.

'I'll go,' I say, standing up.

'I'll come with you,' says Owen, close behind me.

I put my ear to the door. 'Hello?'

There's another knock.

'Who's there?' I ask.

'We've come for Mae's jacket potatoes!'

I glance at Owen, then turn back to the door.

'What's the password?' asks Owen.

'Twenty-four days until Christmas.'

Owen and I look at each other, wide-eyed. Then, slowly, I open the back door just a tiny gap and stare at the faces outside. I shut the door. 'There's a queue,' I say excitedly to the group in the café.

'A queue?' says Mae, in disbelief.

'They want jacket potatoes,' I say. 'Your jacket potatoes!'

'How?'

Owen opens the door, wider this time.

'And there's people asking if there's any cawl left. Like the one they saw on the post this morning,' he calls back.

'Who? What people?' asks Evie.

'People who've seen the post! The one I just put up. The live feed. It's like building a community, but online.'

'But we can't just serve food from the back door,' Mae says.

'Can't we?' I say. 'We've come this far. It shows that people are talking. Voting with their feet! Maybe now the new bosses will listen. We can serve them from here, earn you some of the money you're missing out on.'

Evie puts down her knitting. 'I've got a break until my next appointment. I can help.'

'It's just a few jacket potatoes and cawl,' I say. 'Why not? They'll make a donation for it.'

'Shows the owners what they're missing out on. This is the food people want, not plastic burgers and microwave chips. Might change their minds,' Dad joins in.

'Let's get serving then!' Mae says, excited. We open the back door to a line of people and begin to take orders.

We move a table in front of the door and Owen sets up the generator.

We're busy loading jacket potatoes. 'Another beans and cheese!' I call to Mae. Evie is pulling them out of the oven and Dad is cutting them and creating the well. Mae is doing the toppings, I'm taking the orders, and Owen is on lookout for the return of Josh, the corporate guy.

'Last few jackets now,' calls Evie. 'Then we're sold out.'

I look up. Everything inside me leaps like lambs in the field come spring. 'Oh hello. What can I get you?' I say, looking at Llew Griffiths.

'Someone told me about the cawl here. Said it was the best around.'

I take a deep breath and try to calm the lambs in my stomach. 'As long as that's all you want,' I say tersely.

He nods, gazing at me steadily. 'It is.'

'Llew,' says Dad, holding up a hand from his seat behind the counter.

'Edwin.' He raises a hand back. 'Good to see you on your feet, so to speak.'

'I've been meaning to talk to you,' Dad calls from his chair.

I turn to him. 'Not now, Dad. Can't it wait?' Dread washes over me. I know that Dad is going to agree to the solar panels.

'Come in, come in.' Dad waves to Llew, who looks at me. I want to shout, 'No, not yet,' but I let him in through the back door.

'You're not to sign anything without me, Dad!' I call over my shoulder.

'Jem,' calls Owen from the front of the café, 'don't look now, but you've got visitors. Or maybe we should look now.'

A car is pulling up outside the café. 'Quick! Shut the back door!' I shout to Mae.

'Lock it!' Mae says to Evie, tossing her the keys.

'Sorry, we're closed for today,' says Evie, slamming the door, locking it and putting the table in front of it.

'Look, we know this has come as a shock,' says the young man outside the door. He's bending and shouting through the letterbox to Mae. 'We realize that. I mean, the company does.'

'A shock!' Mae shouts back. 'I've got Christmas coming and two kids and my mother to look after. You can't just shut us down with no notice.'

'If you'd just come out and talk to me . . .' he says.

'We're not going anywhere,' I join in.

He shakes his head. And tries again diplomatically. 'You have to come out sometime.'

'Well, it's not going to be now.' Mae slams the letterbox shut, turns and leans against the sideboard.

With that, it all goes quiet and Josh walks back to his car, gets in, shuts the door and pulls out his phone.

'He's telling them they've got a problem,' says Evie, watching through the front window.

'How do you know?' I ask.

'Lip-reading . . . I learnt to do it so that I could work with a deaf patient I had.'

'What's he saying now?' I ask.

'He says there's a problem, and it's called Mae.'

We burst out laughing.

'For someone who never said much at school, you're making yourself heard now,' I tell her.

Her eyes light up and we high-five each other. Then she says, 'It's just, with Rob leaving . . . Owen, you know what it's like.' Owen holds up his hands. 'It suddenly all got to me. All so unfair! On you too, Owen.'

'It is. But you're doing great. Your kids are proud of you, and you should be too, however this turns out,' I say. 'But we're going to have to make sure we stay put, dig in deeper. We can't leave the café empty.'

'Agreed.' Everyone speaks in unison.

We turn back to the man in the car, and it's only then that I remember Llew Griffiths is in the café with us, locked in, sitting with Dad, holding a cup of tea that Evie's made for him, looking very much at home.

Now what?

'We should pull straws to see who stays over with Mae. She can't be here on her own.'

'I'll be fine!' she says, lifting her chin.

'I'm more worried about what you might do to anyone who comes to get you out!' Owen chuckles. And I see Mae allowing herself to soften, just a little.

'We should take it in turns, in pairs,' I say.

'Straws!' Owen grabs a handful and tears off the ends. Then he arranges them in his fist so they all look the same length and holds them out. 'There's two of each length here. All grab one. Those with the short ones, stay.'

'And this way Mae gets to go home to see the kids,' says Evie.

We reach forward to pull out a straw from the hand that Owen is holding out.

I reach in and accidentally touch the tips of Llew's fingers as he reaches in at the same time. It's like an electric shock.

'Sorry!' I say, yanking back my hand. 'You go first. Actually, it's fine. You really don't need to be here. We've got this covered.'

'I know, but, well, I'm here. I may as well make myself useful,' he says.

I wish he would just go, slip out through the back door. But he doesn't make a move. 'After you,' he says.

I take a deep breath and pull a straw. 'It's short,' I say. 'I'll stay tonight, once I've got Dad home and in bed.'

'I can get myself to bed!' Dad says crossly.

'And after I've done the sheep.' I look at Dad. 'And no, Dad. You are not up to checking on the ewes.'

I turn back to the mug and see Llew looking back at me. 'Guess it looks like I'm here too!' he says, holding up his short straw. I have no idea why the lambs are skipping in my stomach again.

'You don't have to! I'll be fine,' I say quickly.

'I'm happy to. Besides, I'm waiting for my car to be fixed and, a bit like Bethlehem, there's no room at the inn. Actually, there's no inn. Not for miles.'

'Ah,' I say. 'Just the pub.'

'And from tonight no rooms. They're closing the B-and-B. Can't get enough cleaning staff apparently. The Polish couple who were working there are going home for December to be with family. So I'm happy to stay. Besides, it would be nice if I could convince you I'm not here to rip off local farmers. I really did think I was doing the right thing.'

'Did?' I raise an eyebrow.

'Let's just say maybe you've made me see things

a little differently. That day we walked the farm, I hadn't thought about the history of the place. Or how important it is that we support our farmers instead of putting them out of business.'

'As long as you keep to your side of the blow-up mattress, you can stay. But only because we need as many people as possible to stop this happening right now.' I sigh. This is a terrible idea! He's the last person I wanted to be matched with. But I can't ask to swap. I don't want everyone to know I'm trying to avoid him, like he's rattled me. I have to play it cool. It'll be fine. I can do this. It's just one night. And we're here to save the café and Mae's job. And stand up to big business buy-outs! That's way more important right now than me having to share the shift with Llew Griffiths.

We spend the afternoon playing cards from a pack Mae had in her bag. And Owen sits at the piano and starts to play. I'd forgotten he could.

'All those years of Young Farmers' Eisteddfods,' I murmur. We sing along to Christmas carols, and I can't help but film it on my phone and share it with followers, with the hashtag #LocalCafeSitIn #Supportlocal.

The local radio station gets in touch and I find myself giving an interview about why we're here, why it's important, how we need to try to save the high streets and remember our farmers. How we need to bring community back to towns like this.

We gather round and listen to the interview go out on the local news, and on the phone-in, many people are talking about the Social Shepherdess getting the online community to vote with its feet. It's been a good day, and by the time darkness falls, I'm exhausted.

I'm about to slip out of the back door to take Dad home when Evie stops me. 'Jem, I can stay at the farm, keep an eye on your dad,' she says quietly.

'I don't need looking after!' Dad barks, looking at me. He stumbles.

Evie is there like a shot, putting an arm out for him to lean on. 'Please,' she said. 'I'd like to. I hate going home to an empty house.'

'In that case,' he says, 'thank you. Maybe a little help would be good. Just until I'm fully back on my feet.' He smiles and so does she.

'It'll be fun,' she says. 'You can teach me how to play cards. Or I can teach you to knit!'

'Maybe,' he says. 'Maybe . . .'

'And I can help, you great oaf!' says Myfanwy. 'I'm only next door.'

'Over a couple of fields! By tractor!'

'Far enough I'd say.'

And they laugh.

It's a big step for Dad, letting someone in to help. A very big step indeed.

At the farmhouse I make up Evie's bed in the room where Llew stayed, with the window overlooking

Gramps's field. I plump up the big pillows and put hot-water bottles into her bed, then Dad's, hoping they'll warm things up for when they climb in, which I shouldn't imagine will be too long. Dad looks tired. Happy but tired.

Then I go out on the quad bike, with the lights on full in the dark night, to check on the stock. I stare up at the sky, like a huge blanket tucking us in for the night. Then I put the dogs inside in front of the range and tell them, with a pat, that I'll be back in the morning. I hear Dad teaching Evie the rules of sevens, sitting in front of the fire, and tell them not to be late to bed with a smile.

At the café, I knock on the back door.

'What's the password?' says Llew, and I roll my eyes.

'It's me. Jem.'

'I know,' he says. 'What's the password?'

'I don't need the password. I made it up,' I say.

'Then you should know it.'

'I . . .' I want to argue. Instead I give in. 'Twenty-four days until Christmas,' I say, resigned.

'Sorry, couldn't hear much Christmas cheer in it,' he says.

'Twenty-four days until Christmas,' I say louder, and I'm laughing as the back door swings open and he's on the other side, laughing too.

'Very good!'

I step inside.

Everyone has left, and it's quiet, just me and Llew. Suddenly I feel rather shy.

There's a blow-up mattress that Mae has brought over, with two sleeping bags from her house. There's Buzz Lightyear and Woody from *Toy Story*, or Paddington.

'Take your pick,' says Llew, pointing to the sleeping bags. 'I'm happy with either.' That makes me smile again.

He's wearing joggers, I notice, and a sweatshirt, a change from his smart shirt and gilet, with smart Redback boots.

'The bathroom's all yours,' he says, pointing to the loo. And I notice he's put candles as bedside lights, and a row of rolled-up towels down the middle of the blow-up mattress, like a bolster.

'Good handiwork!' I say, gesturing to it.

'Wouldn't want you thinking you could take advantage of me,' he says, making me laugh again and grateful he's doing everything to make me feel comfortable.

'Oh, and your dad lent me this, in case it gets cold!' he says, pulling on the pink hat. I still don't know if it was my mother's, or even a tea cosy, and burst out laughing.

'Well, best we get some sleep,' I say. 'Let's hope tomorrow we warrant enough coverage to bring the owners here to reopen the place.'

I use the bathroom, then put on my joggers and sweatshirt, and quietly slip back into the café. I see the outline of Llew on the side of the mattress nearest the door. I slide into the sleeping bag, which I think features Paddington, and lie on my back, listening to the rain on the window, knowing I won't get a wink of sleep.

'So that's it,' he says, as we lie there in the dark. 'You've given up your job. Your dad told me. You don't have to tell me any more if you don't want to.'

I look up at the rose cornice in the middle of the café. 'Yes, I have,' I say, as if I'm confirming it to myself. 'They told me to think about it, but if I did any more social-media posts, they'd sack me.'

'That's brave,' I hear him say.

'Or daft.'

'At least you've got time to work out if it's what you really want.'

'Either way, it feels good. I want to do something real. Something hands-on.'

'I can understand that,' he says quietly. 'Like when I played rugby. It was in the moment. It was doing something I could feel proud of. Something tangible.' And it's as if he's remembering being on that rugby field.

'But not now?' I ask.

'Not so much, no,' he says. 'But it felt like a safe option. I didn't want to put myself out there and take a risk on another dream. This way, I know where I am. I don't have to wonder what would happen if I were to drop a ball, so to speak.' I hear the smile in his voice and it sounds nice. Really nice.

'So you went for a safe sales job?'

'Yes.' He pauses. 'You?'

'Wanted Dad to think I was happy, seeing the world and making a career for myself.'

'Instead of doing what you really wanted, which is riding round the farm on a quad bike. With one headlight out!'

'I must fix that.' I laugh again.

'You certainly look like you're happy here,' he says. 'You've done a lot to inspire others too. If it's any consolation, your bosses' loss is this town's gain.'

A warm glow fills me inside. 'You seem quite happy here too,' I say. 'Looks like farm life suits you!'

And that was it. We lay there, next to each other, near-strangers, lost in our own thoughts, but comfortable enough to let each other do that. I turn my head to the side and see his profile in the streetlight outside, with a small scar under his eye, no doubt a reminder from his rugby days. I keep looking at him: it's a very attractive face.

Daylight creeps in through the drawn blinds as I wake up from a deep sleep. It takes me a moment to remember where I am. Not in the farmhouse or my flat at the hotel but here on a blow-up mattress that Evie has brought, in a sleeping bag, with rain against the window instead of traffic noise outside.

There are no car alarms going off, as there would be at the hotel, no fan-assisted heating kicking in, just the patter of rain on the window and the pavement outside. No rush to the office. I hear gentle snoring beside me. I remember that I'm lying next to Llew Griffiths . . . and my fingers are touching his.

I remain still, listening to his soft snoring. It sounds peaceful. I wonder how to move my hand without waking him.

I actually had the best night's sleep I've had in ages. No worrying about my schedule for the next day, or the new job, just listening to the rain.

The generator starts up and that means coffee – actually, it means tea. A big potful to share.

Llew's eyes ping open, as I whip away my hand and he sees me staring at him. I blush at getting caught out.

'Morning,' he says, smiling.

'Morning.'

'Morning all!' It's Mae with her boys, bounding in through the back door on their way to school. 'You all okay?' she asks. 'How was it? Did you have any problems? We didn't wake you, did we?'

I sit up in my sleeping bag and rub my eyes.

'That's my Paddington sleeping bag,' says one boy.

'No, I was awake,' I say.

'We both were,' says Llew. So he was awake, our fingers just touching in the low morning light.

'I slept very well with Paddington's help,' I say to Mae's youngest, and rub my hand over my hair. It's standing on end.

I reach for my glasses from the chair that's doubling as a bedside table and touch the blown-out candle there, reminding me of our quiet conversation in the dark last night. I put on my glasses and everything comes into vision. It's chilly but luckily the fire is still in the grate from last night, just glowing.

'I'll get some more wood,' says Llew, stepping out of his sleeping bag in his joggers. A far more relaxed Llew than the smartly dressed one who turned up to talk to Dad about the field on my first day. I watch him go to the back door and return with an armful of wood and a bucket of coal . . . I'm seeing him in a very different light this morning. He smiles at me again, as if he's enjoying himself, and I can't help but smile back, as I remember the touch of his little finger against mine. It made me feel excited and nervous all at the same time. The last thing I need to do right now is fall for Llew Griffiths, but on the other hand, maybe I should live in the moment and let myself enjoy it.

22

'Look who I found outside,' says Llew, walking in with Myfanwy, Dad and Evie.

'I've brought some more Welsh cakes,' says Myfanwy, holding Dad's arm. I'm not sure who's supporting whom, him leaning on her or her on him. Either way, it seems to be working. 'Thought they might lift your spirits. And some bacon. Home-grown. By the way, there's a queue already outside the door . . .'

'I had some cawl in the freezer I thought you might like,' says Dad, smiling as he sees Llew already carrying a plastic box from the freezer.

Mae opens the door a little way and peeps out, then shuts it quickly. She turns back to us. 'There's loads of them! I mean a right long queue!'

We all go to the door and she opens it again. We look out.

Mae turns to me. 'What are we going to do?"

'Well,' I say, 'they're here for food and the company . . .'

'They must love your cawl,' says Llew. 'And Mae's jacket potatoes.'

'Myfanwy's Welsh cakes too,' says Evie.

'You can't go wrong with a cuppa and a Welsh cake!' Dad beams at Myfanwy. I notice they're sharing a smile between them, rather than bristling at each other.

'I went to check on him when I got up and he insisted on coming,' says Evie. 'He agreed to take it easy in a chair.'

I go over to kiss his cheek. 'Sit by the fire, Dad. I'll make you some tea.'

'And bring a Welsh cake, please!' he says.

As the kettle boils I can hear the queue outside.

'So, what are we going to do?' Mae says.

I shrug and smile. 'Serve them? Through the back door, takeaway only again,' I say. 'And they have to use the password. Twenty-three days until Christmas!'

And that is what we do. The kitchen is full of festive cheer as jacket potatoes and mugs of cawl go out through the back door. There are bacon butties too, with Myfanwy's sourdough bread. Even Twm Bach comes to join the party. 'Post it on your socials, Jem love. Let the buggers see the queue,' he tells me. 'Let them know Beti's isn't going anywhere! And tell them about Myfanwy's Welsh cakes and sourdough.'

She waves a hand and blushes. 'Well, I suppose the extra income from any orders wouldn't go amiss,' she says bashfully. I know she's struggling too, and the extra income would definitely help.

So I do. There's no going back to my old job now: I post on social media, and the more I post, the more followers I attract, multiplying by the minute with hashtags #saveBetis #shoplocal.

I change my name on my Instagram account to TheSocialShepherdess. That's it: I've left my old world behind and joined a new community online, telling them about life on the farm and here in our small town. It feels scary but good.

'I don't think your new bosses are going to be able to ignore us for much longer,' I tell Mae, then find myself smiling at Llew too. Somehow, here in the café, everything has changed. And I'm even coming to like Llew Griffiths . . . coming to like him very much.

'Okay, Owen and Evie will be staying here tonight,' I say, once the morning and the lunchtime rush are over.

'You get some sleep,' Mae says to me. 'And thank you for everything.'

'No problem. We can't let them win,' I say. We've won the day, I think, but not the war . . . yet.

Something makes me turn to Llew and I hesitate before saying, 'Where will you stay?'

'I'm not sure. The car's not ready. They're waiting on a part from Germany. Could be a little while, with Christmas around the corner. A busy time of year apparently.'

I look at Dad, who seems to know exactly what I'm thinking and nods. 'You're welcome at ours. The room is there. In fact, there's plenty of space!' Upstairs two more rooms haven't been used since my grandparents died.

'Are you sure? Look, maybe it's not a good idea, Jem. I don't want you to think I'm there to try to buy the land.'

'I know you're not, and you're welcome.' I mean it, but he may be offering the only answer we have.

'I'd be happy to pay for bed and breakfast, so to speak. You should think about doing it, if you stay here. It's a fantastic location. And the best night's sleep I've had in a long time.'

I smile at him. 'No payment needed. It's a thank you.'

'A thank you?' He's standing close to me, and I can practically feel the heat from his body and broad chest.

'You know.' I smile. 'It's for helping us . . . that first day when we got in here.'

'Me?' he teases.

'You knew what you were doing when you shut the front door with us inside.'

Now he's smiling widely and it's a very attractive smile; a chip in his front tooth, a scar under his eye, and a slightly crooked nose making him individual, not like Matthew who aimed for perfection, even in his appearance. I wonder what he would think of me now, with bed hair and yesterday's mascara. Strangely, standing beside Llew, I've never felt more attractive, or attracted. There's a fizzing in my stomach, and I feel as if I'm lit up like a Christmas tree.

'Maybe I realized you were right,' he said. 'Maybe it's not one way or the other. Maybe there's a shared way, but there has to be another way.'

'Maybe there is,' I say. 'I don't know what it is, but I do know I have to find one.'

23

The next morning, it's twenty-two days until Christmas. I'm up and feeding the sheep as dawn breaks, a beautiful bright morning as the sun creeps up in the sky, leaving long streaks of pinks and baby blues, like watercolours on a page. I photograph it on my phone, then video my rounds with the sheep, hens and dogs for social media. Dewi is chasing fallen frozen leaves and the three hens, reluctant to get out of bed, are slowly venturing into the yard. I show the field where the ewes are and introduce Bertie and Harriet: she turns her back to the camera and farts.

I head back to the welcoming glow of lights in the farmhouse kitchen. Llew is there, taking up lots of space while making a pot of tea for us all and putting it on the table. This house seems to expand to the number of people in it. It feels full and busy, like it did when Gramps and Nan were here.

'I'm going to make bread, like Myfanwy's, to take to the café, to go with the cawl,' I say.

'I can help,' he says, coming to stand beside me in front of the window. It's starting to get properly light over the cold and frosty yard, as I start to make the sourdough. He's wearing an old rugby shirt instead of a shirt and tie.

'What?' He smiles, and I smile back, excited, even though I've just resigned from my job and checked out of my life as I know it. I have no idea what I'm going to do but I'll have to work something out. Other hotels will take me, I'm sure, perhaps nearer to Dad. Not in the town itself though, there are no other big hotels close to here, otherwise Llew Griffiths wouldn't be standing here next to me.

'You look . . . different,' I say.

'It's the weekend,' he says. 'I don't always wear a shirt and tie. Now, show me what to do.' He looks at the sourdough starter. 'I have a feeling I'm going to be good at this.'

I hesitate. I have to remember this was the man trying to buy our land. He's just staying here, like a B-and-B guest, I remind myself. But helping with sourdough can't hurt, can't it? 'Okay, you can start with this and I'll make the cawl.'

'This is one of the nicest B-and-B's I've stayed in,'

205

says Llew. 'Did you give any thought to my idea? About doing more of it?'

'Not if we've got solar panels on the fields.' I bite my tongue.

He nods. 'Look, take your time thinking about it. You've got until the end of the year to decide. A few more weeks.' He looks at Dad as he comes down the stairs, dressed. 'Discuss it between the pair of you. I know it's a big decision.' He looks out of the window. 'But, honestly, this place could really do well as a B-and-B, if you were looking for other ways of making money. But I promise I won't hassle you. I'll let you come to your own decision. If I haven't heard from you by the end of the year, I'll know you've found a different solution. I promise I'll be happy for you. I won't interfere at all.'

I look at Dad, who doesn't look back at me, and I know what he's thinking. He still doesn't want to influence me in any way. He doesn't want me to feel tied to this place, like Mum before she got her air-hostess job, met her new man and found her wings. I just have to prove to him that this is where I want to be . . . if that is what I want. I know it's right for now, but what about the future? I gaze out at the cold, frosty morning. I just have to prove to him I can make the farm work for both of us . . .

I look at my phone and the images I've just taken. 'Dad, remember the Advent calendar we had?'

He laughs. 'Full of sheep and donkeys. Took you on a journey to Bethlehem. The story of the young couple. Every year you'd stick down the doors and open it the next year, enjoying the story all over again. Nowadays it's all chocolates and face creams,' he says. 'Not sharing a story like it used to be.'

I stare at him.

'What?' he says.

'That's it!' I say.

'What is?'

'Well, I've been thinking about the Instagram posts I put up, how people liked what they saw. But maybe what we need to do is tell the story of Hollybush Farm. Christmas at Hollybush Farm. Like an Advent calendar, I'll post about something every day that makes up a part of this place.' My brain is whirring. 'It's the lead-up to Christmas, and the food everyone will be cooking and eating on Christmas Day.'

'It is.' He nods, letting me talk as I pace around on the flagstone floor. Llew is watching me too.

'Look,' I say, holding out my phone and showing him the pictures and videos I've taken that morning. 'That's the story I should be telling, the life of a farmer in the days before Christmas. The chores on the farm, the work involved every day to make sure that food is produced in this country. How hard it is, but also, how much it means to us and . . . what happens if we cover farmland in solar panels.'

I look at Llew and then at Dad, whose smile is getting broader. 'Take them on a journey. The twelve days before Christmas in a farmer's life!'

'Exactly! Show people how important it is to keep farming going through the cold and dark times. How it affects small businesses.'

'Like the café?'

'Yes. And how providing the potatoes makes a difference to you, and to how we eat.' I'm suddenly very buoyed up.

'It's an excellent idea.' Llew beams.

'Instead of going away from the farm, leaving here to tell people why they should be buying local produce, I should bring people here and show them what we do. I'll take my phone, put together a reel and do a voiceover to tell people what I'm up to. Christmas at Hollybush Farm.'

I gather up my bag and head to the feed shed. After I've put together a reel, with a voiceover, and posted it to music, I add links in my bio to Myfanwy for Welsh cakes and sourdough, and to the farm, for winter vegetables and hogget. I sit, replying to people's questions and comments from the feed shed, and plan all the things I can film and post over the next couple of weeks.

By mid-morning I'm ready to go into town. I nip back to the farmhouse to collect Dad. The Social Shepherdess has a purpose, a plan, a story to tell, including Gramps's field, the vegetable plot, moving the sheep with the dogs and why we move them regularly, testing the ewes for multiple pregnancies and upping their feed when we know which are carrying more than one lamb, Bertie and Harriet and their unbreakable bond, and mending the headlight on the quad bike with the help of YouTube. How you just have to dive in and have a go. I have someone to tell why it means so much that we remember where our food comes from and how it's produced. I want people to see the work that goes on here, but also the fun, and the passion that goes into making sure everything is done to the highest standard.

It's sunny but still cold and the frost has barely thawed as we leave the farmhouse and the dogs settle in the porch.

'Careful, Dad,' I say, as we walk across the yard, carrying the cawl I made last night after dispatching them all to bed and the freshly made bread.

'Yes, yes, no need for fuss,' he says, but I can tell he's somewhat tentative on his feet.

Movement from the field where I put the sheep this morning catches my eye. It's the sheep, the ewes, running and swinging and swirling like a murmuration of swifts, baaing loudly, calling to each other. They seem to be running from something. And then I see it.

'It's her! That woman again, and her dogs! They're in the field! With the ewes!' I point and shout. 'Hey!'

'Ah, our new neighbour,' says Dad. His face darkens. 'Deborah something or other. Staying here, renting and working from home for the month; normally lives in her other home in Cardiff. Works for an upmarket estate agents there apparently.'

'I'll go, Dad. You wait here. Oi!' I shout, but she's too far away to hear me. I set off across the yard. 'Oi!' I shout again, surprising myself at the volume. It's not something I'd usually be shouting. Everything is done by email and in meetings, calm and organized. But I'm furious, just reacting to the moment. It's not planned, or measured.

'Hey! Get your dogs on a lead!' I yell, and point. But she's either not listening or ignoring me, just marching through the field. The dogs are running amok. 'It's not a playground for your pets!' I shout. 'Get your dogs!'

I won't reach her in time, so I do the only thing I can do and film her as I shout again for her to put her dogs on the lead and run down the drive. But I don't make it to her. She's gone and finally the dogs follow her.

I'm puce with rage. How dare she let the dogs scare the ewes like that? This is the farm's livelihood. It's Dad's income, and possibly mine if I stay on. I can't think what to do. Except this!

I lift up my phone. I start to tell anyone who will listen about the dogs that have just cavorted through the flock and the complete disregard of the owner, hoping I've got some signal down here, closer to the road and Gramps's field. 'These animals are the farm's livelihood. They do not deserve to be treated like playthings for pets.' I'm ranting but I'm so angry. 'Keep your dogs on a lead if you can't control them, or if there's livestock around,' I finish, push my phone back into my pocket and stomp back to the Land Rover.

Dad is sitting in the front with the cawl and the freshly baked bread. I'm trying to shake off my frustration as I study the flock, settling down now. I can smell the cawl and the bread, and I'm thinking about cheese. Cheese with the cawl and bread would go well. Could we make sheep's-milk cheese once the ewes start to lamb? I push the thought away. By the time lambing comes round either we'll have sold out to solar panels or I'll be looking for a job somewhere.

I nearly said 'a proper job' to myself. Isn't this what I've been banging on about on social media, that this is one of the hardest, most proper jobs there is? People need to understand that if farmers can't make a living, there's no food to put on their tables or ours. Those turkeys and sprouts have to come from somewhere! And preferably not thousands of miles away when we can produce it all here, on our own land.

I get into the driver's seat of the Land Rover and slam the door.

No one says a word.

I take a deep breath, put the key into the ignition and turn it on.

The Land Rover's engine attempts to turn over but doesn't start.

I squeeze the accelerator. 'Rrr, rr, r . . .' It dies.

'Damn it!' I slap the steering wheel. 'It's no use, it won't go.' I smell petrol fumes and know I've flooded the engine.

'We need to get the cawl delivered somehow,' Dad says. 'We can't let them down. Twm Bach will be wanting his lunch. He doesn't see anyone if he doesn't go to the café. And we can't leave Mae there on her own.'

'What about a cab?' says Llew, pulling out his phone.

'Unlikely. There's only the one and they won't come up the drive,' says Dad.

I look around the yard and an idea springs into my mind. 'Hang on, wait there.'

'As long as you're not going to suggest the quad bike.' Dad chuckles.

I jump out of the Land Rover, my knees jarring on the frozen ground, hurry back into the house and open the drawer of keys on the old wooden dresser. Then I run back into the yard to the old cattle lorry. I open the stiff door and climb into it. In the old days when Dad was going to market, I'd be travelling in the passenger seat, and when I was older I got my licence and drove it myself.

I put the key into the ignition.

'Come on, old girl,' I say, patting the dashboard as I turn the key. Slowly, the lorry lumbers into life, like a big old farm cat woken from a long sleep. Grumpy, slow, creaking at the joints, but stretching out with every forward motion.

'Yes!' I shout, and punch the air. I climb down from the cab and wave Dad and Llew over, all of us smiling like we've won on the scratch cards. It may be a little triumph to some, but it's made everything possible. And small triumphs add up, I think. I can't remember when I last felt like this. When did I punch the air with sheer joy in my last job? When was I last so excited, scared, anxious, happy? This life may be hard, but it's very real. I prop my phone on the dashboard and shut the door.

'We made it!' I high-five Llew, then Dad, the three of us grinning like Cheshire cats as we chug down the high street towards the café and see the queue already forming there.

'Yay!' Dad cheers with me, as I pull up in front of the café, where I see Twm Bach standing first in line. I yank on the handbrake with a crunch.

We all stare at the queue. 'Clearly we're doing something people want,' I say.

'And your social media must be helping,' says Dad, with a proud smile

Llew puts a hand on my shoulder, making my insides leap. 'You're good at this. This is proof that you're getting the word out. People are supporting Mae and there's an appetite for real home-cooked food. You should be proud of yourselves. You've certainly opened my eyes.'

I turn to him and there's a jolt between us. This Llew, in his old rugby shirt, holding a basket of sourdough, is very different from the one who turned up on that first day. I really like this Llew, despite my attempts to resist him.

'Let's get the food in and start serving. I was thinking we should bring some Christmas decorations tomorrow, Dad, get the place a bit festive. Do up the window with lights. Fetch some greenery from the farm and we could have a go at wreaths, like we used to.'

'Good idea!' he agrees. 'We'll get the baubles from the cupboard under the stairs.'

'Don't expect they've seen the light of day for years,' I say.

'Not a lot of point without you here,' he says, and I feel he's letting down the wall he's built, the brave face he's worn, telling me he was fine and wanted me to go, that he liked Christmas on his own.

'Well, I'm here now, and I don't want to go anywhere, Dad. I'm right where I want to be.'

'If you're sure,' he confirms again gently.

'I am! Come on, let's get this food in and start serving. We should put on some Christmas songs too.' I grab my phone and the three of us get out of the truck with our arms full of cawl and freshly baked bread. And I start singing: 'We three kings of Orient are . . .'

Dad and Llew join in. '"Bearing gifts we travel afar . . ."'

'"Field and fountain . . ."' Llew booms in a marvellous tenor.

'I really am seeing a different side to you!'

'Rugby boys can sing, you know!'

'"Moor and mountain, following yonder star."' We're going for the chorus when we spot Mae. Only she's not inside the café. She's outside. On the street. No longer locked in, by the look of it, and two men with a lock-changing van are working on the door. We stop, stand and stare. My heart plummets.

24

'Mae, what's going on? What happened?' She's shivering, her arms wrapped around herself.

She points a finger angrily. 'He happened!'

I feel a drop of icy rain, sleet, falling on my face.

It's the young company man, Josh. He's clearly following orders, making things work, showing leadership. My happy bubble bursts.

'You again!' I glare at the younger version of me. 'I thought they might have sent someone a bit more senior. We're making quite a noise here, you know! People are interested. They want this place to stay open as it is.'

'Look, I'm just doing my job,' he says politely. 'As you know, this place has been sold and the owners, the company I work for, would like to take it over.

They have a schedule to keep so that they can open in the new year.'

I know how he feels, sent in to do a job, but this is about more than his job right now. I bend to put down the cawl. Then, my hands on my hips, I say, 'They want the building, which I'm imagining was a fairly cheap buy, but they don't want the staff whose livelihoods rely on it.'

'They'll be advertising for staff in the new year. Everyone is welcome to apply.' He gives a nice smile. What he has said is straight from the company handbook. The one I've been cantering out for the last God knows how many years, as I climbed up and up the ladder.

'But not now,' I retaliate. I can feel phones being lifted and pointed in my direction. 'Not when they need work. Life doesn't stop for employees while there's a facelift and a new menu. They need to pay their bills. And Christmas is round the corner. Mae has a family. Her life doesn't stop because your company wants to save a few quid by re-advertising her job in the new year.'

My face is hot and angry. Although the schoolgirls are filming me I can't stop. I turn to Mae. 'What happened?'

'I needed to nip to school, to see the concert and pick up the potatoes I'd left cooking at Mum's. The kids would have hated it if I hadn't turned up. I told

Owen and Evie they could go, that you were on your way. I waited for someone to arrive but . . .'

'Oh, God! The Land Rover wouldn't start. I'm so sorry. And then I had to chase off a woman whose dogs were upsetting the ewes. This is my fault.'

'It's not,' she says. Her eyes are red and I don't think she's had any sleep, maybe spent the night crying, worrying about what's going to happen. My heart twists.

'I slipped out. I didn't think anyone had seen me leave. But when I got back, they were waiting for me.' She jerks a thumb at the locksmiths.

'Look . . .' The young man steps forward and I can see Mae is trying not to cry, but tears are slipping down her face onto the tray of foil-wrapped potatoes.

I turn my crossness back onto the young man. 'This is how your business operates, is it? Throwing people out onto the street. Making them jobless and, who knows, homeless before Christmas?'

The tears are now pouring down Mae's face.

'It wasn't like that! I'm sorry. I was just doing what I've been told to do. Besides, you were squatting!'

Mae drops her head. 'He's right,' she says quietly. All the fight has gone out of her. 'I couldn't think what else to do. And now I really have no idea what I'm going to do.'

Josh steps forward. 'I'm really sorry, I am. There was no other way.'

She nods. 'Bet you'll get a Christmas bonus for sorting out their problem called Mae!'

'Ah . . . you got me!'

She gives a little smile, as does he.

He looks back at the long queue of people. 'You've clearly been doing a great job here. People like what you do.'

'You'd be surprised what a difference a jacket potato and a cuppa, or a bowl of cawl and a Welsh cake can make,' says Mae. 'People like home-cooked food. They like the company too, not sitting in their cars at drive-throughs.'

'You're right,' he says. He glances at Dad, holding the bread to him like a newborn baby. 'You know, you have the customers and the food. You don't need a café to serve it from. These people are clearly here because they want to be.'

Llew steps forward, and something in me sparks. 'He's right. Every business has to start somewhere.' He glances at the signwriter already stripping down the old board, proclaiming Beti's Café. If Beti's useless son had been a bit more involved it could have been saved. But clearly people want to be here, and not just for Beti's.

Josh speaks again: 'I can't tell you what to do,

obviously. You just need to work out what you need to make it happen.' He looks at the queue. 'I'm sorry again,' he says, then walks to the signwriter and begins a discussion.

'He's right, Mae,' I say, picking up the pot of cawl and feeling a tickle on my cheeks and nose. The sleet is turning to snow. Tiny flakes. 'Every business has to start somewhere.' It's cold and people are standing around, waiting to see what will happen.

'But where?' she says. 'We can't just serve up on the pavement.'

'Well,' I say slowly, as the problem starts to percolate in my head, 'you have your jacket potatoes.'

She nods at the tray in her hands. 'Loads . . . I thought no one would notice,' she says. 'I don't know what I was thinking of. I couldn't take on a big company. I was being stupid.'

'Not stupid! You were standing up for what's right! Against Beti's useless son, selling you down the river weeks before Christmas!'

Twm Bach is shivering.

'And we're not going to let that stop us now,' I say defiantly. 'You need every penny you can make and you can still do that!'

'How?'

'We have the food.'

'And customers,' says Llew.

We turn towards the cattle lorry. 'Wait there,' I say,

handing Llew the pot of cawl. 'Owen!' I wave, seeing him arrive at the café.

'What's going on?' he says, jogging over to us, looking up at the changing sign.

'We're relocating!' I beam. 'Give us a hand, will you?'

He looks at the café, then the lorry, and smiles. 'Can do!'

Together we pull down the back of the lorry. It's been a long time since it was open but, thankfully, Dad had made me clean it every time we came back from market and had done the same when he was doing the markets on his own. He was a stickler for hygiene, which means it's clean, with fresh straw bales in there.

We walk up the ramp.

'Right . . . seats!' I say, pulling the bales round. 'Let's get Twm Bach out of the cold.' Llew puts down the cawl and we make benches from the bales along both sides of the lorry. It's out of the wind and really quite cosy in there.

Evie arrives and sees what's going on. 'What can I do?' she asks.

'Can you bring Twm Bach in? He could do with warming up.'

'On it,' she says. She gathers him and leads him up the ramp, with Dad, and sits them in the back of the lorry, with blankets she's knitted over their knees.

'Let's get some food going,' I say, aware that people are following us with their phones as we create our makeshift, pop-up food lorry. 'Tell people to bring their own mugs for cawl. They can eat the jacket potatoes out of the foil, like they have been doing. Let's make a table from bales to serve on across here.' I point towards the back of the lorry. 'Leave enough room for us to get behind it.'

I put my phone on one of the little window ledges as we start to move bales. I reach for one at the same time as Llew. Our hands collide and I get that zip of excitement in my stomach. Our eyes meet and we hold each other's gaze in the cattle lorry, with the gentle snow outside.

'You really are something, Jem,' he says, and I blush.

'What? Just thinking on my feet!' I brush off the compliment and we lift the bale together. Suddenly I hear my phone pinging like crazy. I reach for it.

'You're popular!' says Llew.

I look at it and my eyes widen. 'I left my phone on live from when I was at the farm, after shouting about the woman and her dogs! Has all of this been going out live!' I gasp in horror.

Mae pulls out her phone, Llew and Owen too.

'Yes you're live streaming!' says Mae. 'Your camera's still on.'

Bizarrely Mae and I wave at the camera, although

I'm still hoping I'm not really on screen and it's just my left ear.

'It's been seen by thousands! All cheering you on!' says Mae.

'You've got loads of followers! They're all commenting on the jacket potatoes and wondering what's in the cawl,' says Llew, with a grin.

'Everyone's asking where we are, where the lorry is.'

'They want to know, so tell them,' says Llew. 'Be you!'

I stare at him for a moment, then turn to my phone, pick it up and hold it to the lorry while I talk from behind the screen. 'The cawl's made with hogget, which is older lamb, carrots, leeks and stock. We've got jacket potatoes too.'

'Come and see us!' shouts Mae, behind me. 'We'll be here until we run out!' She starts typing and posts the location.

We look at each other and high-five.

'Let's get serving!' I say.

'Leave the live stream on. People clearly like what they see,' says Llew.

Thumbs-ups, waves and hearts come up on my screen.

'Okay. First come, first served. Once we sell out, we'll close. Who's for cawl?' I shout to the line forming at the bottom of the ramp. 'Bring your own mugs!'

'And jacket potatoes.' Mae giggles.

'I've brought Welsh cakes,' says Myfanwy, arriving

out of puff in the lorry. 'Sounds like I've missed all the excitement.' I notice Dad make room for her to sit next to him on the bale.

And I see Mae look up and down the ramp, where Josh is standing. He gives her a discreet thumbs-up. 'Jacket potato, with cheese?' he calls.

'On me,' she says, reaching into her big handbag for a fork, which she passes to Myfanwy with a warm foil parcel to hand to him. 'Thank you for the idea. Just remember to bring your fork back!' She's wearing a cheeky smile. 'I borrowed them from a local café . . .' He grins back, and I get the feeling that, in different circumstances, something might have developed between them.

'I don't think they'll be missed. I'll say they were never there.' He opens the tin foil, letting out the steam, digs in his fork and lifts potato to his mouth, with buttery, stringy cheese. He chews and smiles at her, nodding.

'I'll see if I can find some mugs,' says Llew. 'Maybe the charity shop down the road has some.'

As the queue passes in and out of the lorry, and we're nearly sold out, I say to Mae, 'Maybe we should come back and do it all again tomorrow.'

I hear a cheer from the people outside, eating hot potatoes and cawl while more likes and hearts appear on my phone screen.

Myfanwy is handing round Welsh cakes and telling

people who ask that she's happy to take orders and Dad is telling people to pick them up from the cattle lorry tomorrow.

We've nearly finished serving when Bryn, the local community police officer, appears.

'What can I get you, Bryn? Looks like you could do with warming up! But there's not much left.'

'I could . . . but the thing is, I can't let you park here.'

'Oh, come on, Bryn! It's just a couple of people trying to make a living,' I say.

'I know, I know . . .' Bryn holds up his hands, then takes a mug of cawl from me. 'This is delicious! Reminds me of your nan's cawl. There was always a pot of it on the go up at the farm.' He takes another big mouthful, enjoying it, but frowning. 'But I can't let you park here . . .'

I sigh. Mae, Llew and I look at each other.

'But,' he smiles, turning away from the phone. 'There's always the old cattle market. I know it's up for sale, now the mart's closed there, but people are using it to park on all the time. The owners seem to be turning a blind eye.'

We turn to each other and clink mugs of tea that feature *Gavin & Stacey*'s Pam and Mick, which Llew bought from the charity shop and the hairdresser filled for us. 'Cattle market tomorrow then!' I say.

25

The next morning we're up early. Llew is in the kitchen making tea when I come down. He hands me a mug and has one for himself. 'Could you do with a helper?'

I take the mug, smiling. 'What – outside?' I nod towards the yard.

'Yes, it's felt good to be outside recently. Better than life inside a smart car. And I think I did okay with the fences and the gate.'

'You did! And if you think you're up for it, that would be great, thank you.'

With head torches on, we head out with the dogs into the yard. There's a layer of snow over the fields and even the sheep's backs. We load the feed and hay onto the quad bike. I start its engine. One headlight is still not as bright as the other but better than before.

'Climb on, then!' I say. Llew straddles the bike, me sitting at the front with him behind and around me. I drive us to the field with the feed and a mallet to smash any ice on the water butts. Llew starts on the ice while I feed and count the ewes. They seem happy and content, unaffected by yesterday's visitors careering through the flock. Unaffected from what I can see, but I'll have to keep a close eye on them.

Back in the kitchen we get ready to go back into town with the cattle lorry. I don't want to let Mae down this time. I gather some greenery from the yard, holly, fir and eucalyptus, and pile it into the back of the lorry, then hurry round to the cab.

Once again it lumbers into life, like Bagpuss waking from his slumbers. I get the heaters blowing, then scrape the windscreen clear of snow.

Dad appears in the porch, dressed warmly. He's even found a Santa hat to wear, and a light-up jumper. The box of Christmas decorations is at his feet.

We drive into town, the cab filling with the smell of the eucalyptus and fir, blown around by the heater, reminding me of Christmases with a real tree in the living room. I can't remember the presents, but I do remember the smell of the tree, and homemade hogget stock on the range. Nan would be prepping vegetables grown by Gramps.

We arrive at the old cattle market and pull up. Dad is looking around, memories flooding back to him, and even a sentimental tear in his eye. 'Good to be here, eh, Dad?'

He nods. 'Very good to see the place being used again.'

Llew jumps out of the cab, opens the gate and secures it, waving me in. I roll down the window and call, 'You look like you've done that before,' as he waves us onto the yard, leaving tyre marks in the snow, and points to the perfect place for the lorry: we can be seen from the road, but will be sheltered from the cold wind whipping through. It's like a ghost market: you can picture the farmers leaning on the pens, inspecting the livestock, the air full of expectation and conversation. But with the market gone, it's like the town and community went with it.

We open the back of the lorry, let the ramp down and set up straw bales for seating. Owen arrives in his truck, with Jess poking her head out of the passenger window. 'Brought the generator. Thought it could help with lighting.'

'Brilliant!' I say, coming down the ramp.

'Like we used to do at Young Farmers' camps.' He smiles. 'And I've brought the old oil-drum barbecue!

It was still in the shed there, round the back.' He points to the old building where we used to have our weekly Young Farmers get-togethers, overgrown and barely used now.

'I knew doing those events would come in handy.' I laugh.

'You used to love being in charge of them.' He laughs too. 'Getting us all organized, sorting out what we were eating . . .'

'Mostly undercooked sausages and vodka shots.'

'They were good days,' says Owen.

'They were,' I agree.

'Brilliant! A barbecue!' says Llew, appearing from the back of the lorry. 'Hey, Owen!'

'Hi.' He holds up a hand. 'Fancy helping me to get this going?'

'And, Dad, can you help me with some fairy lights in here? We can put up some greenery and weave fairy lights through it, around the entrance.'

'On it,' he calls back. 'This feels so good. As Owen says, like old times.'

We hang multicoloured fairy lights across the ceiling of the lorry and round the door, and put up a cork board Evie has made, listing what we serve: jacket potatoes with various fillings, cawl and bread.

'I suppose I'd better let people know where we are. Anyone seen Mae?'

We shake our heads.

'You don't think she's got cold feet, do you?' Evie asks.

I check my phone to see if she's messaged, just as Mae arrives, out of breath and red in the face. 'I don't believe it!' she pants. 'Sorry, had to stop at the school to take in PE kit that Corey forgot. But you're not going to believe what I saw on the way here! How did you get in?'

'The gate was open. Llew just pushed it back.' I smile at him. 'Have you got the jacket spuds?' I ask.

'Yup, here.' This time she's carrying them in a washing basket with a Thomas the Tank Engine duvet.

'Great!' I say, then frown. 'So what's got you hot under the collar?'

'Look.' She pulls out her phone and shows me the screen. I frown some more.

'That's Beti's Café!'

'Yes!' she says. 'Now part of the Coffi Poeth group.'

'Ah . . .' I muse. 'I know them. They're popping up everywhere. Well, it's looking smart, I'll say that.' The new signage is much like that in their other stores. 'Looks like Beti's Formica is out.'

'But their prices. So expensive! And they're going to do specials . . . jacket potatoes and Welsh specialities. They've stolen our ideas.'

I screw up my eyes and try to read the story on Instagram.

'What?'

' "New additions to our menu!" '

Llew is reading it over my shoulder and, despite the seriousness of what Mae's saying, I'm enjoying the closeness of him being there. 'Stealing your idea and rolling it out as their own. Looks like you've got competition,' says Llew.

I take a huge breath.

'Well, we'll see about that,' Mae says. She shoves her phone into her pocket and puts down the washing basket of potatoes in the lorry.

'Where are you going?' I ask. 'We should get ready to open.'

'I'm not going to be made an idiot of any more!' She marches out of the cattle market towards the high street and the café.

'No, Mae,' I call after her, into the sharp wind. 'Let's just show them we were here first!' But she's not listening and is set on confronting them.

Josh is there, talking to people carrying in new furniture from a big truck. It's exactly the same as the furniture in their other shops.

'Hey!' she calls. 'Hey!' Owen, Evie, Llew and I are all behind her, at a distance, with no idea how to help.

'Is that it? You just wanted to talk to me to find out what sells well? Try the potatoes and see how much people like them. Is that why you got us to open the lorry outside the café? Were we product-testing for you? You thought you'd see how much business we

could rustle up, then steal our ideas and customers!' she shouts, as she stalks up to him, ignoring
the driver trying to get a signature for safe delivery
of goods. He sensibly steps two paces back from Mae
and her wrath.

'No.' Josh holds up his hands. 'It was quite the
opposite. I was trying to tell my bosses what a great
job you'd been doing here. I told them about you
and how they needed to keep you on. I showed the
pictures of the queues the two of you had rustled up
and how people were talking about your food on
social media. I didn't mean any of this to happen.'

Mae looks at the menu on the door of the café.
'New specials coming to Coffi Poeth, jacket potatoes
with a variety of fillings.' She turns back to him. 'Well,
all you've done is nicked my idea.'

'I'm sorry. Your idea was excellent, to serve a brilliant fast food that's healthier, more filling and easy
to make. I was trying to bring some ideas to the table.
Stand out a bit, I suppose.'

'And? Did you?' Mae asks crossly.

He hesitates. 'Well, they were impressed. They
think it's a big thing. They saw the social-media feed.'

'And?'

'And' – he swallows – 'they want to roll it out in
their other cafés.'

'So, I've been thrown out of my job. You encouraged
me to showcase what I've been selling out here on

the street and now your bosses want a piece of the action. I suppose you got a nice Christmas bonus for suggesting it!'

He bites his bottom lip. 'I'm sorry. I didn't mean for any of this to happen. I really didn't. I thought if I told them how well you were doing, they'd want to keep you on and not lose you. I was impressed. I wanted to help.'

'But you didn't, did you?' She puts her hands higher on her hips.

He slowly shakes his head.

'They like the idea.' He meets her gaze. 'But say they can save a lot by not employing anyone until they're ready to open in the new year.'

For a moment Mae drops her eyes and says nothing, then slowly raises her head and her chin. Her face is furious. None of us moves.

'*Urghhhh!*' She lets out a roar of frustration, leans forward and stamps on his toe. 'Not sorry!' she says, and storms past us towards the old cattle market.

I stand, mouth open. Definitely not Mousy Mae any more. 'Mae, wait,' I call, and catch her up. 'You okay?'

'No, I'm furious!'

I hurry to keep up with her. 'There's not a lot we can do about them.'

'Well, we'll just have to sell more than they do!' she shouts. 'And make sure no one wants to go there when they open.'

'Mae!' I say, trying to keep up with her.

'We need to make sure that we sell shedloads. Let everyone know where we are, and that we were here first!' she says.

'I agree. Bigger and better. Festive too. Let's do it!' I say. I'm a little excited and sad at the same time: what I thought might be the start of a lovely friendship, or even more than that, for Mae has been blown out of the water.

26

We're in Christmas hats from the supermarket, and Llew has been out to get more fairy lights. With the lorry lit up like Santa's grotto and Christmas music playing from my phone, we look at each other, Llew, Dad, Myfanwy, with her Welsh-cake orders on a small table she's brought from her hallway, Owen, Mae, Evie and me.

'Ready, everyone?'

They nod. I take a deep breath and lift my phone. I know what I'm doing. My employers made it very clear that if I didn't stop there would be no turning back. They'd withdraw the new job offer and terminate my employment. But, call it mid-life madness or whatever you like, I can't stand by and watch big companies swallowing little ones any more. The independents are trying to make a living, trying to pay their bills, and this is the only way I know how to help. I press 'live'.

'Hi, everyone. Just to let you know we're still selling jacket potatoes and cawl, and we're here in the lorry on the cattle market for today. Come and see us and say hi! Give us a wave, a thumbs-up or a share, and the first person here today to see us gets a free meal,' I say, checking Mae, who nods.

'Anything you like!' she shouts.

I put down the phone. We don't have to wait too long.

The schoolgirls are the first in line, and this time they've brought friends. Twm Bach is there, smiling and chatting on one of the straw bales next to Dad, the pair of them remembering when the cattle market was the place to be and when they were young men growing up, learning, waiting to take over the family farms. But every now and again I see Dad catch Myfanwy's eye. He's holding her notebook and taking down more orders for Welsh cakes, bread and bara brith from a steady stream of customers collecting orders.

Jess lets out a bark of excitement as the queue at the lorry grows. The air is full of Christmas cheer, with the smell of wood burning on the barbecue, and people standing round it with cups of tea and Evie handing out more of Myfanwy's Welsh cakes to waiting customers.

'Let Jess out of the truck, Owen,' I suggest. 'She's welcome to lunch too.'

The queue grows and by the end of lunchtime, when the kids have gone back to school, some teachers too, the mother-and-toddler group, and some white-van drivers who have heard about us on social media have left, we're sold out.

'That's the last potato.'

'And the last of the cawl,' I say to Mae.

We turn to each other and high-five.

'That was brilliant,' says Evie. 'I'd better get off to my next client. But I'll be back tomorrow.'

'We'll have to make more for tomorrow,' I say to Mae.

She smiles and nods. 'Same time, same place?'

'Think I'll add shepherd's pie to the menu. We have plenty of hogget. I could do shepherd's pies in foil parcels, like little boats.'

'Good idea!' says Mae. 'I'll add sour cream to my menu and maybe sliced mushrooms.'

'I'm thinking of doing a hogget curry at some point. A real winter warmer.'

'Good idea!' Mae agrees.

And the ideas, like our enthusiasm for the lorry, keep coming.

At home, with the fire lit, Llew out on the quad bike checking the ewes and their feed, I experiment with a shepherd's pie recipe, carrots and onions, browning the meat. I season it, stir in some flour, add stock and Worcestershire sauce, then top it with a thick layer of buttery mash and slide it into the oven.

By the time it's ready, Llew is back, showered and changed, and Dad has found a bottle of red wine he's been keeping for a special occasion.

'And this is a special occasion. It was wonderful to be back at the cattle mart today,' he says. 'Proper community. Haven't seen that many people since . . . since it closed down. It felt like a celebration,' he says, as he pulls the cork from the bottle. At the same time I take the shepherd's pie from the oven. Golden crispy mashed potato on the top, with dark brown peaks, the gravy bubbling up at the edges, giving us a hint of the soft, seasoned meat and vegetables below.

I take it to the table, where Llew is pouring the wine. 'That looks fantastic!' he says. 'Honestly, you could serve hot meals if you ran a B-and-B.'

'But is it a goer for the cattle lorry? We've got under three weeks until Christmas to get people out and mixing with friends and family. Is this going to pull them in?'

'Well, it's got me hooked. Shall I take a picture for your socials?' says Llew.

I start to serve, dipping the big spoon into the crunchy crust, scooping it with the dark brown gravy onto a plate and handing it to Dad.

'The reason they made shepherd's pie like this was because no one knew when a shepherd would be in, so the potato kept the pie filling hot for whenever they were ready to eat,' says Dad, tucking in. 'Well, that's what my mother told me.'

I put another plate in front of Llew, the aroma of savoury pie rushing up to greet us.

As we sit and eat in the kitchen, there is nowhere I'd rather be . . . and no one I'd rather be with.

I put my fork into the potato, with golden crunchy bits, and a sprinkling of cheese, then dive into the meat.

'It's just like your nan's,' says Dad. 'You didn't need to follow a recipe, just remember what you loved about it. How it made you feel. That's all we can do in life, isn't it? Follow our instincts. Go with what's in our hearts.'

I couldn't agree more. The rich gravy sits with the sweet carrots and caramelized onions and clings to the buttery mash. It's just how I remember it in this kitchen when my grandparents were still here.

'This is . . .'

'Fantastic,' finishes Llew.

'Blooming marvellous,' says Dad. 'Just like we used to have.'

We sit and eat in silence, enjoying the comfort of the food and the here and now in the soft light over the table.

When we finish, I look at our empty plates.

'So? Do we think people would like it? Would they buy it? *Mamgu*'s shepherd's pie?'

'Absolutely!' they chorus, and I have another dish to take to the lorry tomorrow.

'Any news on your car?' I ask Llew, as we're washing up, then wishing I hadn't: once his car is done, his time here will be up too. I berate myself and wish I hadn't said anything. 'Not that I'm pushing you out!'

'Sure?' He laughs, and the room feels warm, safe and very cosy.

'The body parts firm is still waiting for something to come in. But, seriously, if I'm in the way . . .'

'Not at all,' say Dad and I simultaneously.

'It's been lovely having you here,' says Dad, and I don't need to tell Llew that I feel the same. With no other thoughts about what we're going to do in the new year to save the farm, it's lovely to be right here, right now.

The next morning, the weather has taken a turn for the worse. There's a cold, icy wind. Llew meets me again in the kitchen, handing me tea in a mug.

'I thought you'd have run a mile by now,' I say. 'I mean, you're the smart country businessman who never gets his boots dirty. Aren't you desperate to get home?' I take the hot tea and sip.

'Maybe I'm beginning to like it around here.' Then

he introduces the elephant in the room. 'Besides, I still have business, remember?'

I don't want to talk about it. I want things to stay just like this, without having to think about the blooming solar panels. 'Not on my watch!' I turn away from him to the coat rack.

'Jem,' he says gently, 'I know I said I wouldn't say anything, and I'm not talking as Llew from Solar Panels now. I'm talking as your friend, I hope. Just . . . you know you can't put it off for ever, don't you? Your dad needs to do something to stay on the farm. And this way you can still graze the sheep around the solar panels.'

I throw my head back. 'I know. I just wish it wasn't like this.'

'I'm sorry. I promised not to discuss it. But I will try to get the best deal I can for him. But you two need to decide by the end of the month. My office has been on the phone, reminding me that you've got until the end of December to sign the contract.'

I look around the kitchen, so cosy with the lights on. If only there was another way of making a living. Of making the farm pay properly. The pop-up is bringing in a bit of money. Mae insists we share anything we make, but it's not enough to turn down the solar panels. I wish it was.

I nod. 'I know. It needs to be done.'

*

241

At the cattle market, we park in the same place as we did yesterday. Mae is waiting for us. She's made twice the amount of jacket potatoes.

'*Bore da!* Morning,' she says. She's wearing a pair of flashing Christmas earrings.

'Morning, Mae!'

I wish I could feel cheerier, but I'm still thinking about Llew and the solar panels. I slide out of the driver's cab followed by Llew, who takes a tray of shepherd's pies from me, our fingers just touching and sending a bolt of electricity around me.

I stop and stare at him. 'What am I doing here, Llew? Why am I here in a cattle lorry selling home-made shepherd's pies? I'm just putting off the inevitable, avoiding what really needs to be done, burying my head in shepherd's pie and cawl so I don't have to face the facts. Maybe' – I take a deep breath – 'I should talk to Dad, and we'll just sign the paperwork. Agree to the solar panels. Get it over and done with. I mean, me selling this from the lorry . . . it's not going to make enough money, is it, to turn down the solar panels?'

'No, but you want people to understand where the food is coming from. Not from the mega-farms in America. Because it matters. Farmers should be able to make a living from what they produce.'

We hold each other's gaze.

'Or maybe I should fall on my sword, tell my

bosses it was a moment of madness, and beg them to reconsider and take me back on in some role. At least I could try to raise a loan then, buy us more time, for Dad to stay on the farm.'

'Is that what you want? Just to buy time? Or are you trying to make a difference here? To do something you believe in?'

I nod slowly.

'Well, then, you've already got me questioning what I'm doing. Why I'm buying up land for solar panels, or to use as building plots, looking at other options for farmland. But you've taught me that's not what we should be doing. We should be looking at how farmers can make a living. Teaching people to know where food comes from, how to cook, how to eat better.'

'But when? After Christmas, in the new year? When everyone goes back to how they were? When Coffi Poeth opens? What then?'

He shakes his head. 'I don't know. I really don't know.'

'Me neither,' I say, but I like having him around and I don't want this to end. I know it has to. When his car is ready, he'll be going back to wherever his home is. And the only memory of his time here will be row upon row of solar panels. If only I could tell him how I feel. But with Matthew only just becoming a thing of the past, that would be totally foolish.

27

As we pull down the ramp and start to set up, the queue is already massive.

'Looks like we're in for a busy time,' I say to Mae, and we get to it, setting out the food we've brought with us, and letting people know where we are on social media.

We're cramped behind the table as we lay out the food we've brought with us. In no time at all, jacket potatoes and shepherd's pies are flying out of the lorry.

'I need to reach over you,' Mae says, grabbing some napkins. As she does, a load of them fly up into the air and whip away on the wind, landing in a puddle. The light snow has been replaced by rain, and the mood is a little more sombre.

The rain pours down on the roof, melting the

remnants of the snow that was there yesterday, drowning the Christmas tunes as we work around each other to serve as many people as possible and get home to the warm and dry. Myfanwy and Dad are squashed together, handing out her Welsh cakes from a corner and taking more orders that Dad writes down. It's pretty packed in here.

Outside, I hear a bark and a shout.

'Hey!'

I look out of the lorry. A woman is holding two Labradors pulling at their leads and straining to get at Jess. She's cowering from the dogs and the woman.

'That dog should be on a lead!' she snaps. 'I could report you for unsettling my dogs.'

Evie stands up from where she's sitting in the lorry, talking to a couple more of the farmers there, and offering to check their blood pressure. She sees the woman.

'I mean it! That dog needs to be on a lead!' I recognize her as the dog-walker in Dad's field and plan to have a word with her. But Evie reaches forward before Owen has time to answer. She fishes her newly finished scarf from her knitting bag and ties it around Jess's neck.

'She is now!' says Evie, defiantly.

Owen turns to her and I see the spark land between them, taking them and me by surprise. I watch them smile, which makes me smile too. There is hope everywhere, I think.

'Excuse me, are you selling those?' asks another woman. 'I'd love a scarf for my dog for Christmas.'

'Er, no, but I could,' replies Evie.

'You could bring more down, sell them here,' says Owen, smiling at her.

I turn back to the queue. We're nearing its end now. A woman seems to be hanging back. 'We've still got a little left,' I call to her, and beckon her forward. She walks up the ramp, into the brightly lit, festive lorry. 'Hi, what can I get you? We've got a final shepherd's pie. Mae? Jacket potatoes?'

'Just with butter and cheese now,' says Mae, clearing away around me.

'Actually, I just wanted to . . .' The woman swallows '. . . I wanted to speak to you.'

Her tone is serious.

'Look, if it's about us parking here, we didn't think it would be a problem . . . I know we should probably have applied for a licence. If you tell us what we need to do . . .'

'No, no,' she says, waving a gloved hand at me, cutting me off, and I can see she's plucking up courage to say something. 'It's not that. It's your social-media posts,' she says.

'Oh. I know the company weren't happy and I know they said they'd withdraw the offer of a new job if I did another. And I agreed to that and left. I'm not with them any more. I didn't think they'd send someone down. But I'm not reconsidering. I realized my dad needed me. And he still does. And . . . if I'm honest, I need to be here. Seattle was me running away, trying to prove I could get to the top of the ladder. Probably to my mum, proving to her I was someone and she shouldn't have abandoned me. But anyway . . .' I'm waffling, as if someone has turned on a tap that has been tightly closed for years and now won't stop flowing. I take a deep breath. 'I don't need to prove myself any more. I need to be me. I'm happy here. Not working for a big company. I was running away, trying to find my happy place, when it was here all along. I'd lost sight of what was important, where food came from, and how hard farmers are working. Big companies should be supporting them, not just chasing profit and getting food for the lowest price.'

'I agree,' she says.

'You agree?' I'm confused. 'I thought you'd come here to tell me to take down my posts. Or persuade me back . . . Are you a journalist?'

She shakes her head. 'I don't know anything about your company. Or any of that. I'm certainly not a journalist.' She pauses, as if gathering her thoughts. 'I just want to tell you to keep doing what you're doing. My name is Janet. I follow you on social media.' She takes a deep breath. 'So does my son. He's been working on a farm. He's had a . . . hard time. It's been a tough year for all of us. But your posts have helped him, sharing what daily life is like on the farm, how you have to adapt, learn, try to find your way, and letting other farmers know they're not alone. You've created a community, a supportive one. I just wanted to say thank you.'

I'm stopped in my tracks. There are tears in her eyes.

'You made him understand he wasn't on his own.' She lets out a little hiccup, trying to keep the tears back.

'Oh.' I don't know what else to say, so I step out from behind the table and hug the woman. 'Is he okay?' I ask, letting her go.

She nods and sniffs, and Evie hands her a tissue. 'He's going to get some help too, find someone to talk to about his dark thoughts.'

'I can recommend some places,' says Evie, gently, standing beside us, her hand on the woman's back, the three of us in a triangle.

She wipes her tears. 'That would be kind. Thank you.'

We've done something good here, I think. And it suddenly feels worthwhile.

'Thank you again, for what you're doing,' she says.

I hug her once more and wish her well. 'We need to be there for each other,' I say. 'We're stronger together.'

'We are,' she says. 'You're doing something valuable.'

'Looks like we'll be back here tomorrow,' I say to Mae.

'We will!' says Mae, and I look at Llew.

He turns away from his phone. He takes a deep breath. 'It's my car. The garage. It's ready. They're looking for me,' he says, staring at me, just as his car comes into the cattle market, delivered back to him: the scars from the crash and the time we've spent together might never have happened.

I can't step away from where I am now, beside the woman who has taken so much strength from connecting with us on social media. I look up at Llew. I can't tell him how I feel. That I want him to stay. Or can I?

I wonder what he's feeling right now. But I can't just walk away from this conversation. I raise a hand and wish him well. He raises his, and with that, awkwardly, he turns to leave.

'Happy Christmas,' I call after him. And I mean it.

I just wish he was spending Christmas here with me.

28

Over the next two weeks, the wind picks up even more, biting at my extremities, and the temperature drops, freezing me to the bone. It seems to be punishing me for imagining I could stick this out on my own. It's freezing in the field every morning when I move the ewes, feed and count them. Afterwards Dad and I drive to the cattle market. It's bitter, and my mood is darker by the day.

Each day, about mid-morning, we set up the lorry and turn on the fairy lights. My mood isn't helped by WhatsApp messages from Matthew, telling me he's been offered the Seattle job, my job, to take up the area manager post there, instead of just hotel manager. It's a step up, overseeing the hotel and others they hope to acquire. He hopes I don't mind. He's moving seamlessly into the post I created, with the frameworks I put in place, filling the gap I left behind, like a footprint in the mud that is filled with water and no longer there at all. I had tried to make my mark, only for it to be erased and filled in by someone I thought I'd have as my wingman. Turns out he was more interested in taking the pilot's position. He didn't want me, the real me, just the potential I could give him, the life he wanted. Well, he got it, and I gave him the leg up to get him there.

But it's not Matthew on my mind. It's Llew Griffiths. I'm wondering if he's mulling over his time on the farm or if his comfy office is where he wants to be. He's been gone for ten days with no contact, keeping to his word that he wouldn't contact me about the solar panels but would let me and Dad make our own decision.

Despite the weather, the queue outside the lorry is growing. A line of people is holding up cameras, photographing us and posting. Then three things happen.

Mae and I can barely move around each other. She has more dishes of fillings and I've doubled up on shepherd's pies and made a hogget curry, which Nan used to make, and brought that with me, thinking it could work with the jacket potatoes.

'It's no good, you'll have to move up a bit!' she says, as we juggle everything on the table at the back of the lorry, with us behind it. 'I'm going to need more space.'

'I can't,' I reply tetchily. 'I need that space there too.'

Our tempers are fraying.

The wind whips up and into the lorry, and the atmosphere feels as frosty as the bite from the icy air outside. It doesn't stop there. As the wind whooshes, the lorry even starts to sway.

'Let's just get going,' I say to Mae, keen for the lunchtime rush to be over and to get back to the farmhouse. The wind is making everything hard, including keeping the food warm.

'I need the generator so that I can warm up the beans on the hotplate,' says Mae.

'I'll have to heat the curry too,' I reply, wrapping my hands around the cooling pot.

Outside people are getting impatient, standing in the wind and rain. The generator noisily does its best to keep up with the portable stove we've got there, and the lights and speakers for the music.

I lift my phone to tell people we're here, what's on the menu, and that Myfanwy is taking orders for Welsh cakes and sourdough.

'It's not like it is on social media,' I hear someone in the queue say. And I listen. 'They don't seem nearly as friendly.'

'I heard their portions aren't as big as they make out,' says another.

'I heard there's a big chain behind them and it's all a publicity stunt.'

I'm about to go out and tell them that's rubbish, that we're just trying to do what we can to make a living and keep local business and farming going, when there's a *bang*.

With that, the generator gives up and everything switches off with an exhausted sigh.

'Excuse me, are you in charge here?'

'Yes? Me and my friend,' I say, looking out into the windswept cattle market at the bottom of the ramp to see a familiar and unwelcome face.

'I'm Deborah Atkins, from the estate agents who are selling this site.' She's the dog-walker from the cottage at the end of the farm drive.

'I know you,' I say. 'You're the woman staying in the cottage near Hollybush Farm.'

'God, the place with the vicious ram and horse!'

'He's not vicious, and she's a pony.'

She narrows her eyes at me. 'Do I know you?'

'I'm the owner's daughter. And you're the woman with the out-of-control dogs you walk in our fields, terrorizing the flock.'

She sniffs. 'I'm afraid I have to shut down this little hobby of yours. The owners have asked if you could move your lorry. They have an interested buyer for the site and I've been sent to arrange for the locks to be changed on the gate.'

29

'That's it, then,' says Mae, as we push up the ramp of the lorry and close the doors for the last time.

I'm feeling wretched, but what had I expected? It was never going to be a long-term solution. I just got carried away, with more and more likes on social media, getting the word out there. 'Looks like it,' I reply.

'I'm sorry I got a bit tetchy in there,' says Mae.

'Don't worry. Me too,' I say, but neither of us has our heart in the apology. I'm cold, tired, deflated and beaten by a woman who seems determined to destroy everything that matters to me. Deborah bloody Atkins. But no matter how angry I'm feeling, I'm sad that this is the end. I have no idea what else I can do. I'm shivering.

'Will you be okay?' I ask Mae.

She looks down at the washing basket of unsold

jacket potatoes. 'Looks like we'll be having jacket potatoes for a few days.' She tries to smile. But we don't laugh like we'd usually do.

'Yes,' I reply, feeling I've let her down.

We fall into silence and then she asks, 'Any news from Llew?'

'He said he won't call. It's up to us if we want to call him to sell the land. What about you and the Coffi Poeth man? I thought you were getting on.'

'Until I stamped on his foot!'

And finally we laugh.

'Not my finest hour.'

We fall silent again.

'Sorry I couldn't do more, Mae. I wanted this to work.'

'Me too,' she says.

'Well, in a way, it did. We were victims of our own success! If we hadn't got such a following on social media we might have been able to keep going a bit longer.'

'At least we know people liked what we were doing,' she says.

I hug her. 'Will you be okay, for money?'

'Yeah. Like I say, we've got jacket potatoes for now. Just need to work out how to pay my rent this month. It's rent or Christmas this year.'

'If I could have thought of any other way . . .'

'What about you?' she asks. 'Will you sell the land?'

I look at Dad sitting in the lorry's cab. 'I expect so. I can't see any other way. At least the money will come through fairly quickly, and Dad won't have to sell the farm just yet.'

Myfanwy has loaded her little car with her table and Dad hands her her order book. 'Don't be a stranger,' he half mumbles to her.

'Don't have any more funny turns without letting me know,' she tries to joke. But I can see that this little project has brought us all closer together, but now things will go back to how they were.

Owen has put the generator into his truck and Jess is sitting in the passenger seat wearing her red and green scarf, with Evie at her side. At least something good has come of all this, I think. So good to see Owen and Evie together and them both smiling shyly, like they're at the start of a whole new adventure together.

I turn away from Mae. 'Bye, then.'

'Bye,' she says, and I climb into the cab and start the lorry. It lumbers into life and I leave the cattle market, with Deborah Atkins holding open the gate for us and shutting it firmly behind us.

Dad is fast asleep in the seat next to me as we make our way back to the farm. As we head up the drive, I stop off to check on the sheep, then walk over Gramps's field, still wondering what he would say if he was here now and saw what was about to happen.

Is it a good thing? Is it progress, helping the environment? Or is it the thin end of the wedge when farming will be lost for ever? Then I think again of the mother I met, her son struggling after a tough year on the farm. If others can't make ends meet, how do I think my being here can help Dad? Maybe selling the land is the only option we have left. I turn away from the field, climb back into the lorry and Dad wakes up.

'Nearly home, Dad.'

'It was fun, wasn't it?' he says. 'Shame we couldn't keep doing it.'

'It is, Dad. And, yes, it was fun.'

'That's why I loved this job. Always different, and at the end of the day, putting a smile on people's faces. Good food, produced well. It's something to be proud of. *You*'ve made me very proud,' he says, and tears tickle the back of my eyes.

Three long lonely days later, with just a week to go until Christmas Eve, I've uploaded my Christmas-on-the-farm Advent posts and I'm back in the kitchen on my own, hating the way I left things with Mae. I'm heating curry for me and Dad from the big pot on the stove when there's a knock at the door.

The dogs bark as I open it to see Mae, Evie, Myfanwy, Owen and Mae's boys. Mae is clutching a pile of foil-wrapped jacket potatoes.

' "Silent night, holy night . . ." ' they sing, recreating

the jolliness of us arriving at the café when the lock-smiths moved in until we realized that meant she was out.

I smile and open the door wide so Dad can hear them and let them carry on singing until they peter out.

'No point in having all this food left and not sharing it,' Mae says, with an apologetic smile. 'I felt dreadful the way we left things in the cattle market. You did so much to try to help me. I really am sorry we argued.'

'Quite right about the food,' I say, 'and no need to apologize. Like I said, we were victims of our own success! If I hadn't done the posts, drawing so much attention to us, then been excited by the response and the long queues, we might have been able to keep going a bit longer, at least until the other side of Christmas. I'm sorry.' I hug her, even though she can't hug me back.

'So not only have we brought dinner,' says Owen, 'we picked Myfanwy up on her way over too.'

'I brought Welsh cakes.' She hands me the tin. 'Once I started baking I couldn't stop. That woman at the market was a right piece of work.'

'Come in, the fire's lit. Dad, we've got company!' I call to him in the living room. 'Go on through.' I shut the front door and usher them in towards the fire.

'Drinks,' says Dad, delighted to see everyone. 'What about that whisky you brought me for Christmas,

Jem? Now seems as good a time as any to break it out!'

Everyone pulls off their coats and their cheeks glow in the light from the fire blazing in the little hearth. Even Dolly the Jack Russell perks up at company. She jumps onto Myfanwy's lap and settles in for a cuddle.

I see Dad and Myfanwy share a smile. 'Good to see you here again,' he says quietly.

'Good to be here, Edwin.'

The boys sit on the floor and play with Dewi and a leaf he's chasing, filling the room with fun and laughter.

I go to the kitchen, open the whisky and pour it into glasses, with a bowl of ice on a tray and a little jug of water, then take it into the living room. 'I'm just heating some curry. Would you like some?'

'Yes, please,' they all say.

'With jacket potatoes!' says Owen.

'Do you want to bring Jess in?' I ask Owen.

'She won't come. She's happy in the truck or in the field. She'll be watching the ewes.'

'Would you boys like milk to drink?' I ask.

'Please!' they say.

'Perfect.' I trot into the kitchen to put the potatoes into the range to warm.

Just as I'm back from handing out two glasses of milk and starting to set the table, there's another knock at the door. I can't think who would have come up here in this vile weather, and hope it isn't someone to tell me that Bertie and Harriet have broken down the fence and are out running wild again.

I pull back the door and stare. 'It's you!' I finally say.

'Yes, me.' His nose is red from the cold and his hands are shoved into his pockets.

'I thought you'd gone back to Cardiff.'

'Er . . . so did I. I was out, driving, and found myself heading this way.'

'I see. Look, if it's about the contract . . .'

He holds up his hands. 'I told you, I won't ask. I'm not here because of that. I just couldn't stay away.' He looks over my shoulder into the kitchen. 'I just wanted to tell you that what you did at the cattle market was great.'

I tilt my head to one side. 'Thank you.'

'I heard you got closed down there,' he says, moving from one foot to the other, clearly cold.

'We did. How did you know?'

'Social media, of course!' He smiles, making my insides zip and twist and twirl.

'Been checking out my feed, have you?'

'I have. I heard what happened.'

'It was sad, but kind of inevitable. It wasn't our land. We just went with it for as long as we could.' I remember the woman who came to thank me. 'But I think we did some good while we were there. I heard they've got a buyer interested.' I look hard at him. 'It's not you, is it?!'

He shakes his head. 'Although now you mention it . . .'

We laugh.

'You could take it on,' he says. 'Raise the money to
lease it. That's what I really came to say.'

'I need to get another job. Getting fired wasn't the
best Christmas present to give myself. And losing my
biggest promotion to date to my ex was not in the
game plan.'

'Neither was doing what you've done. Helping
raise awareness of where food comes from, young
farmers, and young people in the hospitality industry. You should be proud of yourself.'

'Actually . . . I am. And what about you? Have you
really not come for a decision on the land?'

'I told you, I'm not going to mention it.' He takes a
deep breath. 'You're not the only one thinking about
where they're going in life. I'm handing in my notice.
I need to do something a bit more worthwhile.'

'But . . . Really?' The cogs whir in my head. 'Does
that mean the offer is off the table? We haven't made
a decision yet!'

'I know. And it makes no difference to me now.
This is a copy of the contract. It's valid until the end
of the month, like I said. It'll still stand. I've made
sure of that. But now that I don't have an interest
in the company, you can make up your own minds
about what's best.' He holds out a brown envelope

to me. 'I know you wanted to save the farm and keep it how it was. I thought solar panels might be the way. But maybe there's a different way. Think about the cattle market. It was good while it lasted. I really admire what you've done, standing up for what you believe in. Maybe you could try to raise the money for the lease.'

'I wish we could. It would be perfect. Bringing back the old cattle market would be amazing. It would mean so much to so many people. Bring the community back together again. Stop so many people feeling alone. And help people understand there's more to eating than going to the nearest drive-through.' I wish I could make an offer on the cattle market. 'While I've been here, on the farm and at the café, I've realized I spent so much time telling people how enticing food should look and bringing in customers . . . Now I know that what matters is where the food comes from, how it tastes. Keeping it simple is far better than filling the pockets of people who don't care about the food chain.'

'It made me see it's time for a new chapter for me too. I don't have to do a job I'm not a hundred per cent invested in.'

He hands me a bag with two bottles of wine inside it, as laughter filters through to us from the warmth of the living room.

'What's this?'

'Call it a leaving present. Something for you to share this evening with everyone. A little thank-you for having me and helping me see I need to do something that has meaning for me . . . I'm scared of, well, failing again.'

I reach out and take the bottles. 'You didn't fail in rugby. You got injured,' I tell him. 'But it doesn't mean it wasn't part of the journey.'

He nods. 'I'm thinking about other sportspeople who have had injuries or setbacks, and getting them outside, like being here on the farm. It's as good as any gym, and in the outdoors. Win-win.'

I look out onto the yard. 'It is! I'm finding muscles I'd forgotten I had!'

'Persuading people to work together, mending fences and shifting straw,' he says, as the idea grows, 'is good for the body and the mind.'

'Great!' I say. 'You could offer week-long boot camps, working out on a farm.'

'Maybe one day,' he says. 'Maybe I should take a leaf out of your book and go for it. Well, I'll be on my way.'

'Thank you.' The hospitality habit in me jumps into action. 'Won't you come in, stay?' It's actually the farmer in me who wants him to stay. I pull the door so it's almost closed behind me.

He shakes his head. And I notice the snow starting to fall, heavier than before, and settle on his hair.

Suddenly I want to tell him everything I've been desperate to say since before he left. And for someone who usually knows what needs to be said, I'm at a loss. I have no idea how to put what I'm feeling about him into a coherent sentence. He looks at me and I try to work out what he's thinking. What if I make a complete fool of myself? What if he doesn't feel the same? We stand and stare at each other as the flakes of snow fall around him.

He gives a little cough. 'Happy Christmas, Jem. I hope it's everything you wish for.'

I open my mouth, but nothing comes out. There must be something I could say to make him want to come in. But this was closure for him. He doesn't need to be here or come back again. And then I say the only thing I can think of. It's not like I know him well. I can't just tell him how I feel about him, that I think about him all the time, keep wishing he was in the kitchen when I get up in the morning. Wishing he was joining us now, around the little fire, to eat hogget curry and baked potatoes. I just can't risk it, can I?

'And you, Llew,' I say, and watch as he walks away, his car lighting up with a bleep. I'm thinking about him leaving, but also his words: could we really try to raise the money for the lease on the cattle market? Could we make it something more permanent for all of us?

30

The range is keeping us warm in the kitchen and I've found Christmas candles in the old box of decorations to put on the table. The room is warm with the smell of the spices in the curry and the jacket potatoes in the oven. Owen pours the wine into small water glasses I've found in the cupboard. Evie is finishing laying the table.

'Shall I put this somewhere?' She holds up the brown envelope Llew has left.

I take it from her and see on the back a handwritten note with a phone number, clearly in Llew's handwriting. For the cattle-market lease, a name and number. I put the envelope on the shelf above the table and call through to everyone. 'Dinner's ready.'

The kitchen fills with warmth as we sip the wine and eat.

'A perfect marriage!' says Myfanwy.

'We should make more of these. Maybe do a twist on them,' says Mae. 'Meat and veggie fillings.'

'Using seasonal ingredients,' I agree.

'We'd need to find a supplier,' she says.

'We have all the room you'd need to grow stuff here,' Dad joins in. 'The kitchen garden is full to bursting,' he says, clearly loving the company. 'My father used to grow plenty for us. I have more than I need in the shed.'

'Your father and my father,' says Myfanwy, 'would swap vegetables. Like a barter system.'

'More like an arguing system.' Dad laughs and so does she.

'Silly old fool!' They smile at each other warmly, which makes me feel warm too. Outside the snow is falling steadily, and I wish Llew was here with us, instead of on his way out of town for good.

'If only we could have found a way to make the lorry more permanent,' I say.

'If only we could've found somewhere to park it, make it a regular feature,' says Mae.

'It's a week until Christmas Eve,' says Evie, thoughtfully.

I sigh, thinking about Llew and the cattle market. It's not too late. They haven't sold the lease yet. 'What if . . .'

'Yes?'

'What if we could raise the money to buy the lease for the cattle market? Secure it for a year.'

They're staring at me.

'A full-time food-truck market, where we rent space to other providers. We make different things. People can eat what they want. Sit at tables together.'

'We'd need separate food trucks!' Mae laughs, making me laugh too.

'We would. But imagine, we get more food trucks to help make it profitable and a permanent feature in the town.'

'But how?' Mae asks.

'Llew suggested it.'

'Llew?' they all say.

'Is he here?' Mae wonders.

'He brought the wine. He's decided to leave his company.' Dad looks concerned. 'It's okay, the offer still stands, Dad. He brought the signed documents. We have until the end of the year to decide.'

'Shame he didn't come in. Nice fellow,' says Dad. 'I like him.'

I can't help but think that I totally agree. I take a deep breath. Looks like the one good thing, right under my nose, was the one I let get away. I wish with all my heart I'd said what I wanted to say. But I can still feel him here, supporting the idea of the food market, telling me to go for it. Telling me how I'd inspired him go for something he believes in. All the time I'm considering the food-truck market, a little bit of him is still here, I think, taking some comfort from that. 'He said he thought we should try to make a go of it.'

'What? The cattle market?' says Mae.

I nod.

'But how would we get that kind of money?'

'Well, I did have one idea. I've seen it done before when people want to raise money for the community.' All eyes are on me. 'What about a GoFundMe page?'

'A what?' asks Dad.

'A GoFundMe page online. We ask people to contribute, like a collection, and give them something in return.'

'Like what?' asks Mae.

'I'm not sure . . . free pies, or something.'

'A Christmas event, for the community,' says Myfanwy. 'Give them a little Christmas spirit. It's what this place has been lacking for a year, ever since the out-of-town stores moved in and people stopped seeing each other.'

'Something like that, but we haven't got long. There's someone interested in the cattle market already, as we know. But' – I turn to Dad – 'it would mean, if we could make it into a profitable business, we wouldn't have to sell Gramps's field. We could run the cattle market and turn it into a full-time business.'

Dad gazes at me. Part of me wonders if he'll tell me that selling off the land is the sensible option. I hold my breath.

Then, suddenly, he smiles. 'We'd be daft not to try,' he says, his eyes twinkly. ' "Faint heart never won fair maiden!" '

'But how?' says Mae. 'How would we do it?'

'Well, we could do a food-truck fair somewhere else, show people what we're trying to do.'

'Yes,' they all agree. 'But where?'

None of us comes up with an answer. My phone pings and I look down at it.

Missing the cattle lorry. Best jacket potatoes around! someone has messaged.

Loved the shepherd's pies! says another.

I pick up my phone and read out the messages. 'We could speak to the cattle-market owners, see if they'll let us do one night. A Christmas food-truck fair there!' I feel a growing excitement. 'A gesture of goodwill. We ask local food producers to join us there for one evening. Ask for a donation for the pitch and explain we're trying to make it a regular feature. A go-to destination for local food . . .'

We all look at each other, waiting for someone to say why it's not a good idea.

No one speaks.

The tinsel and fairy lights glitter.

'A Christmas fair on the cattle market to raise enough to get the lease . . .'

'Before anyone else does! Or buys it!'

'Or smothers it in solar panels,' says Owen.

'Affordable good food!' says Mae.

'A proper town Christmas fair,' says Owen.

'Perfect!' says Dad, and smiles at Myfanwy. 'But we haven't got long. We need to get the word out, get the community behind us.'

'What about . . . a tractor run?' says Owen.

'Oh, yes!' say Myfanwy and Dad, beaming.

'A what?' Mae laughs.

I'm still scrolling through the pictures on my phone of the lunches in the cattle lorry at the market. I loved it.

'All the farmers put lights on their tractors and drive through the villages and into the town and end up somewhere where there's music and food. They carry buckets and raise money on the way,' says Myfanwy. 'We used to do it every Christmas. End up back at one of the farms. They were great fun!'

'And think of the content for the socials,' I say, still scrolling. 'It would really get people talking about what we're trying to do. But we do a GoFundMe page too, to raise the money and try to get the deposit together to buy the lease.'

'Post your videos about why it's important.' Mae waggles a finger at my phone, making me laugh.

'It's brilliant,' says Evie to Owen, leaning in and kissing him, him kissing her back. And we give a little cheer at the love these two have found in each other, and the glow in their cheeks.

And I can't help but wish I'd found someone to share that spark with, and think I may have done. He just isn't here to share this moment with us. I wish I'd been brave enough to tell him how I feel. I wasn't being brave with Matthew. I was playing it safe, like I have in my job all these years. It's time to throw caution to the snowy wind and see which way it takes me.

'Just one thing. How are we going to get Deborah Atkins to agree to this?' asks Dad.

The mood around the table dips.

'He's right. She was the one who threw us out. She's not going to agree to us going back. She just wants to get the new clients to buy it.'

I look down at my phone. 'I think,' I say slowly, as the idea dawns on me, 'I may just have a solution. Like you say, social media isn't all bad.'

31

'She said yes!' I punch the air. The others, gathered around the kitchen table with a pot of tea, are staring at me standing in the doorway.

'No way!'

'Way!'

'The agent selling the cattle-market lease said yes?' Mae wants confirmation. It's as if no one has been home. Last night they left, but they're back this morning, with the snow settling on the fields overnight, sitting around the table waiting for news.

'But how?' asks Mae. 'She wanted us off the site. They've changed the locks on the gate.'

'Well.' I lean in and pour myself a cup of tea. 'It looks like she's changed her mind,' I say, holding up the shiny new key.

Mae gasps. 'Tell us!' she says, excited. She's keeping

an eye on her boys through the kitchen window. They're having a snowball fight and playing with Dewi, who clearly thinks he's having the best fun.

'I recognized her when she turned up with her dogs. Actually, it was the dogs I recognized first when she was there at the market and said Jess needed to be on a lead. It took me a while to place her. Deborah Atkins is Dad's new temporary neighbour, renting the cottage at the end of the drive for December. Her dogs were being a nuisance in Gramps's field.'

'And?' says Mae, holding her cup to her chest.

'The dogs I filmed the day we were late to meet you at the café and the locksmiths came in.'

'And?' says Mae.

'Well, I suggested that maybe her bosses wouldn't want to see footage of her and her dogs in our field when they were trying to build a high-end clientele here. I also suggested she needed to build some good relations around here. Take it from me, I know how social media can ruin your career.' I feel as if a weight has been lifted off my shoulders now that I know I'm not going back to the hotel or to Seattle. I'm here for as long as I can be, and I have to try to make this work.

'So you blackmailed her?' says Myfanwy.

'Well, I wouldn't say . . . Actually, yes, I did. I said if she didn't let us do one last night on the cattle market I'd post this to her bosses' social-media feeds and let everyone know who she was.'

'Bloody genius!' says Dad, proudly.

'And we're on?' asks Mae.

'We're on!'

'*Eekkkkk!*' she shrieks. 'So when?' She comes to sit at the table.

'Well, we're close to Christmas now,' I say. 'Shall we do it after Christmas in the lull before New Year?'

'Or a New Year's Eve food event?' says Evie, taking Dad's blood pressure at the same time.

Faint heart. I hear Dad's words. *I admire how brave you are.* Llew's voice is in my head again. I take a moment to look around the table. 'Or . . . do we just go for it and make it a Christmas Eve feast? A place for families and friends to meet before the big day. Eat together, swap presents . . .'

'Sing carols!' says Dad, clearly feeling his old self.

'It's very short notice,' says Mae, looking unsure. 'How do we know people will come? Don't we need a bit more run-up time? People are busy getting ready for their own Christmases right now.'

'Could be just what we need around here, a bit of Christmas cheer! The town hasn't had any of that for a while,' says Evie.

'That's the thing about social media,' I say. 'We're living in the now. It's immediate. Look what happened when we did the live feed. People came, wanting to be a part of it.'

'I'm in!' says Mae, banging her mug onto the table.

'I'm happy to help,' says Owen. 'It'll stop me thinking about another Christmas without the girls.' Evie stretches out a hand and touches his arm.

'Anything I can do,' says Myfanwy, looking at Dad, and I can see a growing affection between the two of them.

'And me!' says Dad. 'It'll be a proper town get-together! Can't wait! Best Christmas in a long time!' He beams, and I couldn't agree more. If only Llew was here to see it.

'So we get it out on social media . . . a tractor run and food-truck festival! Christmas Eve at the cattle market.' I'm making a list. 'And we get in touch with the local producers, anyone who wants to come and set up a stand.'

Evie packs away her blood-pressure kit. 'Hot dogs would be good!' she says.

'I could do the barbecue again,' says Owen. 'All those years of Young Farmers parties have come in useful after all.' He smiles. 'And camping with the girls! I'll suggest it for the holidays, maybe Easter. I'll talk to their mum.'

Evie smiles. 'Good plan. I know they'd love that just as much as Disneyland.'

'They could come here,' I say, 'if that's all right, Dad?'

'Brilliant idea!' He gives a thumbs-up.

'They could come and see the lambs, help feed them,' I say. 'Get them involved on the farm.'

'I could do some knitting with them too. Make blankets for the lambs that need warming up,' says Evie.

'That would be great. Now the heifers have gone, my girls don't really get outdoors. It's all computer games,' says Owen, regretfully.

'Time we got young people back on the farm and helping,' I say.

'Thanks, Jem.'

'I can't wait to see tents on the field! Like we did as kids,' I recall.

'And the smell of bacon cooking in the early morning, dew on the ground,' Owen puts in. 'Best bacon butties ever!'

'Hear, hear!' says Dad.

'I'll do cakes,' says Myfanwy, 'for the food market.'

'Great,' I say, adding it to the list.

'I'll bring a table,' Myfanwy goes on, 'which means I'll have a proper pitch and will pay for it. Might make some mince pies too.'

'Okay if I bring some dog scarves to sell, last-minute present ideas?' asks Evie.

'Of course!' I say. 'Great idea!'

'I'll bring the generator for lights and music,' says Owen.

'So that's it! We're going to do it!'

'Yes!' we all say.

'Let's get it on social media, then.' I pick up my phone and set off for the feed shed. 'We have a farm to save here,' I say, over my shoulder. 'And not just one farm. We all need to make a living. This might be the way to save us all from selling up or out.'

32

Christmas Eve

The farmhouse kitchen is full of the smell of cawl, shepherd's pie and spicy hogget curry, just like it was when Nan was here, cooking up a storm. It feels like she's right here with me, Gramps too.

'Looks like we're all set, Dad,' I say to him. He's wearing an elf's hat with large pink pointed ears. 'Let's just hope word has spread, the tractors turn out, and plenty of people.'

'I'm sure they will, love. You've done so well, telling everyone about it.'

I open the computer. 'A quick look at the GoFundMe page before we go.' It's become something of an obsession, watching the figures mount up and reading the good-luck messages, saying what a good idea it is and how more communities should do it. 'Loads of people have got behind the idea!' I smile.

'It's great, love. Really proud of you.' And Dad drops a kiss on the top of my head. 'Following your heart is always the best option,' he says. 'That and remembering there's always hope.'

'You could remember that too,' I say.

'What do you mean?'

'You and Myfanwy.' I grin. 'Maybe you should tell her . . . you like her.'

I wait for him to say something jokey, to tell me they're too old for that kind of thing, but he doesn't. Instead he pats my shoulder and turns away. 'Maybe I should. Or maybe she'll just laugh at me and I'll be making a complete fool of myself, thinking I could have another chance at finding someone.'

At the cattle market, Deborah Atkins is looking as if someone has stolen her Christmas turkey. Neither of her dogs is in sight.

'Just make sure you're out of here by midnight,' she says. 'It's a one-off.'

'Thank you for the opportunity,' I say politely.

'I didn't have much choice. Just have your party and I can close the deal on this place in the new year.'

'But you agreed to give us first refusal,' I say firmly, slipping into business mode.

'Yes,' she says, as she rolls her eyes. 'But I really

can't see that happening, can you? A few hot dogs and Welsh cakes? You'll have to sell an awful lot of cups of tea and jacket potatoes to raise the money to secure this place.'

'We are,' I agree, with a smile. 'And I think that's exactly what we're going to do.'

She sniffs. 'I have friends coming for Christmas, so I need to get off.'

'You not joining us, then, Deborah?' I ask, with my best difficult-customer hospitality smile. The sort they can't help but respond to although underneath it says, 'I want to throttle you!'

'No. It's really not my thing,' she says.

'I thought I saw you last time we were here. My mistake.'

'We have a hamper from Harrods,' she says quickly. 'Brought it with us. I like to know where my food comes from.'

And that, I think, is an argument for another day. Today, Christmas Eve, is about celebrating those who are here and want to be a part of this, with home-reared food, and spend time with friends, neighbours and family. We've done it. We're here, and it feels great.

The market is already a hive of activity. Owen is guiding the trucks into position, creating a horseshoe shape. 'Saved your space for you!' he calls up to me, in the cab of the lorry, and directs me to where we pitched before.

'Wouldn't it be great, Owen, if we could make this work and get the lease?'

He chuckles. 'You'd need a site manager I'm thinking.'

'We certainly would! Know anyone?'

'I think I do . . .' He beams, and it's lovely to see the old Owen back, with those dancing eyes. Evie might have something to do with that.

I park and go to the back of the lorry to drop the ramp down.

'Hi, are you, Jem?' I hear, just as I'm lowering it. I turn to see a woman with a bicycle, but not just any old bicycle. 'The Social Shepherdess? I recognized you from your post the other day.'

'Yes,' I say. 'I am.'

'I've been following you on social media. You're great. I'm Beca and these are my boys. We live over the mountain at Ty Mawr. We have a *gelato* business. Milk from our cows.'

'I know your *gelato*! And I remember your grandparents' ice-cream parlour. It's great to have you.'

'Here. The price of my pitch.' She holds out an envelope.

'Thank you so much,' I say, taking the envelope. 'I hope you sell out. *Gelato* would be perfect with Christmas pudding.'

'Actually, we have mince-pie-flavoured *gelato*, and Christmas pudding.'

'It's got brandy and raisins in it,' says the younger man with her.

'It sounds delicious. Save me a pot,' I say. 'I'll pick it up later.'

He takes out a pad from his rucksack, makes a note, and Beca looks on with pride.

'I love the bicycle,' I say, gesturing at the big freezer compartment at the front.

'It's like the one Beca's grandfather had before they opened the ice-cream café,' he tells me, and the slightly older young man smiles at his brother.

'It looks fantastically festive,' I say. It's decorated with fairy lights and tinsel and pride is beaming off the three proprietors.

'They're our own recipes. Well, I say ours, but Blake is our recipe creator.' She waves at him. 'It'd be great if this could become a regular thing. Keep going!' she says.

'We will, thank you.'

As I begin to set up the lorry, with fairy lights, the straw for seating and our table, I'm looking out for Mae, who isn't here yet.

More and more trucks arrive and start setting up. There's a toasted-sandwich van, selling golden, crispy sandwiches with a choice of fillings, a pulled-pork-baps stall and another selling macaroni cheese, made with soft, stringy local cheese and pasta from a trailer, and Pizza on the Hoof in an old horsebox, with the chef and owner in a black bowler hat wearing Italian and Welsh scarves around his neck.

Dad and Myfanwy have found their way into the old auctioneer's booth and have been testing the microphone with lots of 'Hello? Hello?' I wonder if he'll tell her how he feels, or if it's just too much of a risk for him. Christmas music is playing over the Tannoy now, carols, Frank Sinatra and Neil Diamond, clearly a favourite with them both. Everyone is smiling, snow is falling steadily and the air is filling with the most amazing smells of barbecuing sausages, wood-fired ovens and the spices from my curry. But there's still no sign of Mae and I'm worried. I pull out my phone to see if she's messaged me.

Where are you? All okay? I ask.

I'm here! I look up and around but still can't see her – and then I do! She's waving manically at me from another horsebox, decorated with homemade bunting and paper chains. The kids are there too.

I run down the ramp. 'Where . . .' I'm lost for words in the excitement of it all. 'Where did you get it?'

'Owen knew someone. Said he was happy it was being used. I'm just borrowing it. We scrubbed it, me and the boys.'

'Best time ever!' they chirp.

The other is finishing writing on a chalkboard: 'Hot potatoes, with cheese, beans and veggie chilli'.

'We're calling it the Spud Family,' says Mae. 'Even Mum's come to join us.' She points to her mother, sitting in the back of the trailer on a camping chair.

'I'm so happy! This is brilliant! And from the way the crowdfunding is going, there's a chance this could happen,' I say. 'Have you checked the page?' On my phone I show her how we're doing, and we let out squeals of excitement and hug.

'This would never have happened without you,' Mae says.

'It wouldn't have happened without you!' I tell her. 'You're the one who staged the sit-in and made us all realize we needed to see what was important around here.'

'But you're the one who made it happen.'

'Not yet I haven't. But maybe, fingers crossed, by the end of the night. Best I put something up on social media and let people know we're here.'

'Get posting!' Mae instructs, with a pointed finger.

'Considering I was the one hiding behind the corporate suit, who would have thought I'd end up being the Social Shepherdess?' I put up a picture telling everyone where we are, that they should like and share the post.

There's music playing but I haven't seen Dad or Myfanwy for some time.

'Everything okay?' Mae asks.

'I'm a bit worried about Dad. He said he'd meet

me back here, but I'm not sure where he is. I haven't seen him since they set up the Tannoy and got the music going. That was quite a while ago.'

Mae looks around. 'Okay, we'll keep an eye out for him. And let others know if need be.'

I head back to the lorry and spark up the tea lights in a muffin tray, a little kitchen hack I saw on social media, and put the cawl and curry on to keep warm. I stand back and feel proud of how I've created these dishes, using instinct and memories. No books or measurements, just what I can remember. As Dad said, I've followed my heart.

'Smells amazing!' says Evie, poking her head into the back of the lorry. 'Okay if I put my easy-up tent out here?' She indicates the side of the ramp.

'Fine, let me give you a hand,' I say, going down the ramp into the lightly falling snow. Together we put up the easy-up and she settles herself in a chair. Owen comes over, kisses her and lights a fire in an upside down bin lid, on a circle of stones. 'Will you be warm enough?' he asks.

'I will.'

'Owen, have you seen Dad?'

He shakes his head. 'I'll keep an eye out for him,' he says, and returns to his big barbecue with a spring in his step and Jess at his side in her Christmas scarf, which has had holly and mistletoe added to it.

'It's so good to see the two of you together,' I say,

trying to push any what-might-have-beens with Llew to the back of my mind.

'It took me by surprise,' she says, picking up her knitting. 'I didn't think I was ever going to feel anything for another man. But that night we spent in the café, just talking, we understood each other, the hurt, the loss, but also made each other smile. I don't feel guilty, though I thought I would. I know he would be happy for me that I've found Owen.'

'I do too,' I say. I look up at the snowy sky and wonder where Llew is and if he'll have the Christmas he hoped for.

At five o'clock, Owen opens the gates and the queue starts to pour in.

By six there's still no sign of Dad and I'm really worried. What if he's collapsed somewhere? Or what if he decided to tell Myfanwy and she doesn't feel the same way? I shouldn't have pushed him into it. What if he's upset? Despite the money box being full, and there being lots of people around, I won't relax until I know where Dad is and that he's okay. I turn away and pull off my apron.

'Shepherd's pie, please. I hear it's one of the best around, like the shepherd who made it.'

'I'm sorry, I'm not serving right now . . .' I stop in my tracks, my insides jolting, and slowly turn, staring at the familiar face, as if there's nobody else around.

He smiles.

'You're back.'

He inclines his head.

'For a decision on the field?'

'I told you, that's not my business any more.'

I frown. 'Then' – I swallow – 'why?'

He stares at me. 'Because I couldn't stay away.'

'Why?' I say again, needing to hear it.

'Because there was somewhere else, with someone else, I would far rather be.'

I go to step forward when I hear a shout. 'Jem! Quick!' It's Owen, calling to me from the barbecue at the front gate.

'Oh, what? Is it Dad?!' I run to the ramp. 'Owen? Where is he?'

I turn to Llew. 'Look, there's all sorts of things I want to say.' Words and feelings canter around my head, meeting my worry about Dad head on. 'But right now, could you look after the stall?' I toss the apron to him.

'Of course. You go.' He moves seamlessly around and behind the table. 'We have plenty of time to say what we need to say,' he says, making me feel like home is within touching distance. 'Go and find your dad!' Owen bounds up the ramp, like the young Labrador he always reminded me of.

'Hey, you're looking happy!' says Llew.

'I am. It's what finding love again can do for you, mate! Good to see you back!'

Llew looks between me and Owen. Just for a moment I say nothing, then: 'Owen and Evie are an item. They got together over knitted dog scarves and leads!'

'We've found your dad!' says Owen, with a smile.

'Is he okay?'

'More than okay, I'd say!' He points.

I look at Llew. 'I'll be back. I need to see Dad.'

'Go!' he instructs.

And with that there is a loud *parp* on a horn, followed by others. And there, rolling into the cattle market, is the first of many brightly coloured tractors.

'Parp!' the front one sounds again, an old Massey Ferguson, and there driving it is Myfanwy, Dad at her side, his arm around her, waving and smiling with a Christmas hat on and delivering a little Christmas kiss to her cheek. Happy tears spring to my eyes.

'There's always hope,' I say, and turn my face up to the snowflakes, wondering if Gramps is looking down.

I hold up my phone and film the tractors coming into the market, one after another, all lit up and playing Christmas music. The people in the market are clapping as they rattle buckets of coins, ringing in their arrival. As I'm filming, my mother messages me from Australia. It's her standard Christmas greeting. *Hope you get what you want for Christmas. Happy Christmas, Love Mum x*

I reply, wishing her a happy Christmas and sending her a clip of the tractor rally, knowing it would be anathema to her. She's happy sitting on the beach in Australia with her new husband and other family. It's fine. I'm glad she found her happy place. I'm happy being back in mine.

'Hope is exactly what I wanted . . .' I gaze at Llew, who smiles at me, making it impossible for me to ignore how he makes me feel and hoping he feels the same. After all, he's here, isn't he? Llew Griffiths is here, on his own, wanting shepherd's pie and wearing an apron in the back of an old cattle lorry. A far cry from the smartly dressed country-gent outfit he arrived in.

He serves the next customer. My insides light up and settle into place: they are now exactly where they should be. I join him behind the table to serve shepherd's pie while he dishes out curry and flatbreads.

The music is blaring out from the speakers and the tractors are all parked, adding extra light and excitement as the snow falls even heavier. Owen arrives in the back of the lorry but this time his face is not so cheery. 'Jem, one of the boys on the tractors says there's dog-walkers with dogs off the lead, heading towards your land. Thought you should know.'

'Oh, no! Not again! I suppose she thinks we're all here so she can let her dogs off the leads to worry the sheep. It's not on!' I slam down my spatula and run down the ramp. 'We'll have to close up if I'm to get back up there.'

'Don't worry, I can go,' says Owen. 'My truck's out

front. One of the tractor boys can take over on the sausages. I'll make sure those people know to put their dogs on leads around the flock. Don't worry.'

'Are you sure?' I ask.

'Sure I'm sure.' He looks between me and Llew and smiles. 'Just save me some dinner before you run out.'

'Okay.' I smile back. 'Will do!'

He disappears down the ramp, kissing Evie, and Jess jumps into the passenger seat of his truck beside him.

I watch him leave and look over to where Mae is standing outside her horsebox. Another familiar figure is there. 'Evie, what's going on?' I call, gesturing to Mae, who is talking with the young man, Josh, from Coffi Poeth. 'What's he doing here? And on Christmas Eve?'

Evie comes to stand next to me. 'Looks like . . .' She pauses to lip-read. '. . . He's offering her a job.'

'*What?*'

'She can't believe it,' Evie interprets.

'What kind of job?' I say impatiently.

' "If you want it," he's saying.'

'But what *kind* of job?' I ask again.

'Manager of the café . . . and she gets to choose her own menu,' says Evie.

'Yes!'

I see the chain's manager nodding. I look at Mae's face.

' "And I get to test new menus and you'll roll them out in your other cafés?" ' says Evie. ' "Yes, you know what works," he's telling her.'

' "I do. I know what people can afford to spend too. How to make our shopping go further. And ready meals that don't cost the earth. Jacket spuds that people can heat up at home." ' Evie continues to translate.

' "The bosses really do want to know more. Nutritious, affordable takeaways. They realize what's going on here. People want good, home-cooked food. They've seen the social-media feeds." '

Mae narrows her eyes. 'What's the catch?' she asks.

' "What's the catch?" Mae's asking,' Evie relays to me.

' "No catch" he's saying to her "other than it's Christmas and I thought you'd like to hear the news now." ' Evie takes a sharp intake of breath. 'He said he'd resign if they didn't agree!'

We both look at them staring at each other.

Then watch as Mae drops her eyes. He's watching her. She slowly lifts her head.

'What's she saying?' I ask Evie anxiously.

'She's saying, "I don't think I can. I'm sorry. Thanks for trying. But I can't go back. Not after we've come this far. I want to find somewhere I can carry on selling my own food. Like here. If this works tonight, I'll have a regular pitch." ' Evie smiles as she translates, "she says she loves it." '

He stares at her. ' "I understand. And, if it's of any

consolation, I think you're doing exactly the right thing. What you're doing here is brilliant. You and Jem. I can't wait for this to turn into something more permanent. I'll suggest they put the jacket potatoes on hold. Too much local competition. But . . ."'

She looks at him.

'"I did get them to agree to a bonus. Call it a payment in lieu of notice. A goodwill gesture."' He hands her an envelope. She opens it, stares into it, then throws her arms around him.

Evie and I hurry over to hug her, and her boys join in. She looks up at Josh. 'This is my rent sorted. Thank you. Now I can have Christmas and pay the rent. Look, it won't be much, but how about Christmas at ours? The boys are going to be made up when I explain they can have a present each from the sales. This is Jacob and this is Luke, by the way.'

'Only if you promise to let me take you and the boys out for Christmas lunch . . .'

'Really?'

'Really. My way of saying sorry for all of this. You shouldn't have had to do what you did to get them to see how badly you were being treated or for them to give you notice.'

'I'm sorry, too. I shouldn't have stamped on your foot like that.'

They look at each other and laugh.

'So, you'll let me take you to lunch tomorrow?

There's a hotel, out of town, but they have a table. I have it on hold. I was hoping you'd say yes. Your mum too. Like I say, my way of saying sorry.'

She looks down at the boys. 'We'd love that.'

'Christmas for one is never much fun,' he says.

'No,' she says quietly. 'I'm Mae, by the way.'

'I know!' He laughs.

'And now it looks like I might be your problem.'

'I'm Josh.'

'Happy Christmas, Josh. And thank you.' She looks up at the mistletoe over the door of the horsebox and I have a feeling I know where this is going as the boys cover their eyes and giggle.

'Jem,' I hear, as we turn away from Mae, who is kissing Josh under the mistletoe. It's Bryn, the community policeman.

'Shepherd's pie, Bryn?' I say, walking towards the lorry ramp.

He's not smiling. 'You'd better come. There's been an accident.'

'An accident?'

'Is it Owen?' Evie looks like she's seen a ghost.

He shakes his head.

The words catch in my throat but I manage to say, 'What's happened?'

'It's Jess.'

33

We pile into the police car and Llew's, leave the lively hubbub of the market and head into the snowy lane towards the farm. No one is speaking. All we can hear is the swish of the windscreen wipers batting away the snowflakes that are falling heavily now.

We pull off the road and up the track and see a figure in the field of ewes. It's Owen. He's hunched over. Llew pulls up beside him and we jump out. Evie is by his side in a flash, through the gate and running across the snowy grass. Owen is hunched over Jess and he's cradling her in his arms, tears rolling down his face. He's taken off his jacket to put over her. He looks up at Evie, and then at me following close behind her. 'She was protecting the flock, like she's always done. Following her instincts,' he chokes out, through the tears pouring down his face.

Llew takes off his coat, places it around Owen and puts a hand on his shoulder. Evie is crouched beside Owen, sliding her hand into his.

Another car pulls up and it's Mae, with Josh. I watch them get out and walk slowly towards us.

'Is she okay?' asks Mae.

I give a little shake of the head. 'We should get her to the vet. I'll ring the emergency number,' I say.

'I've rung them already,' says Bryn. 'They're waiting for you, Owen. You just have to get her there.'

Owen shakes his head. 'There were dogs, loose in the field. More than two. A group of holidaymakers, I think, with dogs off the leads. It was chaos. There was one dog, kept chasing the sheep, wouldn't leave them alone. I tried to shoo him away. The owner had no control whatsoever! Jess jumped out of the truck and' – a big sob – 'that dog went for her instead!'

'Like I say, I've let the vet know, and I'm on my way to see the owners now. Get her to the vet, lad,' says Bryn.

Owen shakes his head again. 'I . . . can't . . .'

'Owen, the quicker we get her there, the better.'

'I can't. I don't have the money. Cancelled my insurance.' He lays his head on Jess's coat.

I look at Mae, who nods. 'We've got that covered,' I say. 'There's plenty in the buckets from the fundraising this evening.'

295

He looks up at me, eyes red and swollen. 'You can take the truck,' he says. 'It's all I've got, but it's yours.'

'Owen, I don't want your truck! It would probably cost me more to keep it on the road. I just want Jess to get to the vet. Go now!'

He gives a little sniff. 'You're right. Yes. Thank you.' He gets to his feet, Jess in his arms. Llew steps in to help. Evie tucks the coat around the dog and Owen's shoulders, keeping her arm around them all the way to the truck.

'Text us as soon as you know anything,' I call after them.

Evie turns back to me, tears rolling down her cheeks. 'We will. Thank you.'

We watch them as the truck heads towards the main road and the veterinary surgery, tyres leaving tracks on the snowy drive.

'I'll be going,' says Bryn, as upset as the rest of us. 'Good job one of the tractor boys called me. And I had a call from the walkers, about a farmer antagonizing their dog,' he says.

'What? They rang the police to complain about Owen?'

'Yup!'

'Unbelievable,' says Mae.

'Out-of-control dogs harming livestock! A farm isn't some playground!' I'm enraged. 'People's livelihoods are at risk. And the animals' wellbeing!

Oooffff!' I say and cover my face with my hands. 'And now Jess. Owen loves that dog.'

'When he's been at rock bottom, she's been there for him.'

'Like he is for her now.' I feel two arms wrap around me and pull me close. I can smell him, like pine and woodsmoke, and something close to hope.

I lift my head see the snowflakes in his hair and on his cheeks. 'You didn't expect this when you turned up here this evening.'

'The thing about being around you, Jem, is that I've come to expect the unexpected.' He smiles. 'And I think I quite like it.'

I smile back. 'I need to check the flock,' I say to Mae. 'Can you finish up at the food market?'

'Sure.'

'We'll meet you back here with the keys.'

'Leave the lorry, I'll get it tomorrow.'

'What about Mrs "You Need To Be Out At Midnight"?'

'Stuff her!' I say. 'There are more important things to worry about tonight. And I'll be letting them know that on social media. This might be the season of goodwill. It might be Christmas Eve. But that means treating others as you'd want to be treated. It's about looking out for others.'

I reach into my pocket, pull out my head torch and put it on. Llew turns on his phone torch.

The ewes are cowering under the big oak tree.

'You don't have to stay,' I tell him. 'I can manage.'

'I want to,' he says. 'I told you. I'm beginning to like the unexpected.'

And despite the misery of the night, the cold and the snow, my heart swells, and I know there is nowhere I would rather be than on the farm, and no one I'd rather be with.

34

When we finish checking the flock, we return to the farmhouse.

'I'm going to check messages.' I hold up my phone.

'I'll put the kettle on, shall I?'

In the feed shed I sit on a bale and look through the window. In any other circumstances this would be the picture-perfect Christmas setting, I think, looking out over the fields on Christmas Eve with the dogs at my feet. I check my messages but there's nothing from Evie or Owen yet about Jess.

Then I check the crowdfunding page and my mouth falls open.

There are small donations and messages on social media from people saying how much they appreciate what I've been doing. People who have visited and holidayed here want to help, as do van drivers who have visited the food trucks and the biker community, who came tonight to celebrate Christmas Eve together and raved about the shepherd's pie. There are big donations from companies based in the area, the largest from Coffi Poeth. Maybe guilt money, I think, but we'll take it anyway.

My phone rings with the news I've been waiting for.

I walk back to the farmhouse. The windows are full of warmth from the orange glow inside. The dogs run ahead and wait at the door. I let them in and peel off my scarf and hat. An old Massey Ferguson tractor is parked on the yard next to Llew's car, topped with snow.

Dad and Myfanwy are sitting at the table. Dad has the whisky bottle out. Myfanwy is getting out mugs.

'Is that your tractor, Myfanwy?'

'Hadn't driven one on the roads in years. Felt like we were a proper community again tonight. But what news on Jess?'

There's a knock at the door.

I open it. It's Mae, holding the keys.

I beckon her in. 'Jess needs an operation . . . as soon as possible.'

'The crowdfunding?' says Mae.

I nod. 'If we need to get more, we'll find a way to do it. I've explained on the GoFundMe page what's happened, that this fundraiser was all about community, and right now one of our community needs the money. Anyone who isn't happy with us spending it can ask for their donation back, but no one has. It's the right thing to do.'

The clock slides round to midnight. 'Let's have a toast,' says Dad, pouring whisky into the mugs. Myfanwy is handing them round. 'To family and friends, old' – he looks at Myfanwy, who laughs – 'and new.'

'And to Jess,' I say. 'If I had a Christmas wish it would be for her to get well and go home.'

'To community,' says Llew. 'And remembering what's important.'

We raise our glasses.

And that night, when the others have left, Dad accompanies Myfanwy back to her farm on the tractor to make sure she's home safe and sound, and tells me he'll be back in the morning. As we watch them go across the field, with the fairy lights sparkling, we shut the door and I look at Llew, then do something I have been wanting to do for what seems like a very long time. I lean towards him as he leans towards me and feel his lips on mine, soft at first and then becoming more urgent, as I lead him up the stairs to my big brass bed and fall onto the thick eiderdown.

And later that night, as I lie in his arms, gazing out at the falling snow, I realize that hope is always with us: we just have to look for her.

35

Christmas Day is quiet and sombre as we wait for news of Jess's operation with the emergency vet. Llew and I check the ewes again.

'One here is worrying me a bit,' I say. 'I think I'll take her up to the barn, keep an eye on her.'

'Okay.'

'Let's go and get the cattle lorry. I'll move her in that.'

Llew goes to get his car keys and we head to the cattle market. The gate is shut and I unlock it. The only evidence of last night's food-truck festival is the cattle lorry with its lights, bunting and the oil-drum barbecue, clearly too hot to move last night, and a piece of tinsel hanging from the speakers on a pole. The bins have been emptied and the festoon lighting put away. Everything is as it was, just covered with a layer of snow.

I think of what this place could have been if we'd managed to get the lease. But it wasn't to be. There are more important things than potential. There's living for the here and now. And right now Jess is being prepped for her operation.

I climb up into the lorry's cab, put the key in and the radio bursts into life with 'In the Bleak Midwinter': '. . . if I were a shepherd, I would bring a lamb'. Tears spring to my eyes.

Llew follows the truck as we leave the cattle market, lock the gate and drive towards home. I pull up at the cottage where Deborah, the estate agent, was staying. It's all in darkness. No lights, no dogs, no festive cheer.

'It looks like life in the countryside at Christmas isn't for everyone,' I say to Llew.

'Certainly isn't without its ups and downs,' he says, and kisses me. Right now, I'd like to take him back to bed and stay there, under the eiderdown.

I climb back into the cab and drive to get the ewe that seems under the weather. We guide her into the back of the lorry and take her up to the barn. I make a pen for her there with plenty of fresh straw and water.

'We'll be back to check on you soon,' I say, as we

walk towards the farmhouse. The tractor is in the yard; Dad and Myfanwy are in the kitchen.

'Happy Christmas, love,' says Dad. 'Although it won't be a happy one until we hear news from Owen on Jess,' he says, saying exactly what we're all feeling.

'Happy Christmas, Dad,' I say, holding him tightly, feeling grateful to be with him, on the farm. 'Why did I ever want to leave? What on earth did I think I'd find in Seattle that I haven't got here?'

'Christmas trees!' says Dad, laughing.

'Ah, talking of trees . . .' Llew disappears outside and comes back with a small, misshapen object, holding it in one hand. We all burst out laughing.

'Where did you get that?'

'At the petrol station at the end of town. Open for two hours for last-minute essentials and gifts, it said on the door. He was just closing. This was the last one.'

'I'm not surprised!'

'Ah, don't say that, you'll hurt his feelings!'

'It's a he?'

'Yup! He's called Stewart . . . Stewart Little. Loved that film!' says Llew.

'And how did you bring it here?'

'In my car!'

'In your car? The clean and tidy one?'

'Not any more,' he says. 'Mud and pine needles all over it, but it smells nice.'

'Well, I think that little tree's adorable,' says Myfanwy. 'You going to put him up?'

'Yes! Will you help?' I ask.

'I will, but then I should leave you to your Christmas Day.'

'Absolutely not!' Dad and I say at the same time.

'You're not going back to an empty house. We're all here together and that's how it should be,' he says firmly.

'Absolutely!' I say.

She looks at Dad. 'I don't want to be in the way. This was your mum's home, Jem. I don't want to step on any toes.'

'No toes to be stepped on, Myfanwy. Mum made her decision to leave a long time ago. I wish it hadn't taken me so long to remember this is where I belong. We can all choose where we want to be and who we want to be with. Leaving has shown me how much I want to be here. And how happy I am seeing Dad so happy. If it's my blessing you want, Myfanwy, you have it.'

'I want you here, Myfanwy, because I can't remember the last time I enjoyed myself as much as I have, spending time with you of late,' says Dad. 'And if it's all the same to you, I'd like to keep doing that. Last night wasn't just a one-off for me.'

My cheeks burn as I blush.

At first she says nothing, then breaks into a smile.

'Oh, you silly old fool! Someone's got to keep an eye on you. And, no, it wasn't a one-off for me either.'

I give a little cough and try not to let my imagination go there. I'm just glad that they're happy.

'Besides, I'm not sure I can remember how to cook a roast dinner. Might need some help.'

'We'll all help. We'll be fine!' She gives Dad a special smile.

'Oh, I got you this, love,' says Dad, handing me a little box. 'For Christmas.'

'How? You haven't been out,' I say, looking down at the box he's handed me.

'I was going to give it to you last night, when it looked like the food-truck market was going to take off.'

I'm intrigued. The box is an old egg box he's cut and Sellotaped together. Inside, there is a key.

'It's a key for the front door of this place. The farm's yours, Jem love, but only if you want it.'

'I . . .' I don't know what to say.

'You've got way more ideas than me on what to do with it. But I'll understand if you don't want it now.'

'You're giving me the farm?'

'Like I say, I want you to make the decisions for what you think is best for the farm. Your farm. It's your time. You have ideas aplenty. Not just for this farm, but others too, trying to think of new ways to earn a living. Look at Myfanwy's order book. It's bursting!'

Myfanwy agrees, sitting beside Dad and taking his hand.

'Plenty of ideas,' I muse, recalling what Llew was saying about it becoming a B-and-B. But it needs work. 'Just not the money.' The brown envelope with the contract for solar panels catches my eye on the shelf.

'You can keep it, sell some of it, or all of it. I'll agree with whatever you decide.'

'Well, I got you a scarf, from Evie, and one each for the dogs.'

'Perfect!' he says, pulling his from the bag and wrapping it around his neck.

'You two go and sort out the tree,' I say to Dad and Myfanwy. 'I'll start on the veg.'

I stare out of the window. The snow has stopped falling and is freezing now. It's still and silent. I wish I could feel happy about the farm, but all the joy has gone out of the day as I stand at the sink, peeling potatoes, listening to Anneka Rice on Radio 2. Not even the song about Ernie, with the fastest milk cart in the west, can raise a smile, like it usually would between Dad and me. Llew is next to me. The bottles of fizz he bought from the shop where he got the tree are still in the fridge.

'What's your thinking about your dad giving you

the farm? You don't have to say but I'm not here for any reason except to listen.'

I sigh. 'Maybe you and Dad were right all along. The only way is to sell Gramps's field. The solar panels.'

'Surely there's another possibility.'

I shrug sadly. 'The food market might have worked, but now we don't have the money for that, and the deadline has passed. The solar panels are the only other solution. It might give me enough to do this place up, set up a B-and-B like you suggested. It won't make a fortune but it will supplement things.'

'What if there was another way?' he says, standing beside me, peeling carrots.

'Then I'm all ears!' I say.

'It's just I was thinking . . .'

Suddenly we see the light blue truck coming up the drive. 'It's Owen!'

'That was quick!' says Llew.

'Please let it be good news!' I say, as we run to the door and fling it open. Owen gets out, head down. There is no Jess following him. It seems strange to see him without her. It's cold, really cold.

Evie gets out of the front passenger seat, pulling her coat around her, looking out on the frozen fields around us.

Owen walks over to me, standing in the open

porch. 'She's in surgery now. They said to ring at five. Just wondered if we could spend the day here with you, rather than waiting at home.'

'Of course!' I say, and fling my arms around him. 'Come in, both of you.'

'Hey,' says Llew. 'I'd say happy Christmas, but it doesn't seem right.'

'No, but happy Christmas anyway!'

We all stand and watch the sky darken out of the window.

Dad comes into the kitchen wearing his scarf and a new hat Myfanwy has given him, with the label still on. 'Well, being together is what counts,' he says. 'Let's have that glass of something to warm us up.'

'Agreed. Don't want to ruin your day. But, like I say, we couldn't think of anywhere else we'd rather be,' says Owen, as Llew opens the fridge and hands the bottles to him.

The meat is cooking and the radio is on. It may not be traditional to have hogget for Christmas dinner, but it is in this house. We're a farm and we eat what we produce. I shudder to think of how *cwtch* hotels are serving standard lunches, weighed, portioned and priced to bring in the biggest profit, forgetting what this meal is all about. It's about being grateful for what we have.

Owen is making a fuss of the dogs in front of the fire when there's a knock at the door.

I open it. 'Twm Bach? Come in, you must be freezing!'

I guide him into the little living room that, once again, seems to expand to embrace the amount of people in it.

'Went out for a walk,' he says, 'and found myself coming this way, so I thought I'd see if there's any news.'

Owen shakes his head. 'I have to ring at five. But *diolch*, Twm. The thought is very much appreciated.'

'Have a drink,' I say. 'And happy Christmas. Why aren't you with the family?'

'They invited me. But I couldn't face the journey in this weather. Think it's going to close in again.' He looks around at the sky. 'Brought you some sprouts. Had them growing in the garden. Shame for them to go to waste.'

'Well, take off your coat and sit by the fire. Some-one pour this man a drink,' I say. 'And lay another place at the table.'

Llew smiles at me, making my insides melt and reminding me of last night . . .

He pours Twm Bach a glass of fizz, hands it to him and shows him to a seat by the fire with Dad and Myfanwy. He's not like Matthew, who liked to show off his hospitality skills. He's just one man, caring for the others he's with. And we all seem content to be in each other's company, waiting for news of Jess on Christmas Day.

Lunch is a quiet affair. Llew helps me in the kitchen as we serve up slow-roasted hogget, soft, flaking and full of flavour, with rosemary and lots of thick dark gravy. There are roast potatoes, crispy on the outside, soft and fluffy within. The Brussels sprouts from Twm Bach have been steamed and tossed in melted butter with some of Myfanwy's bacon, peas from Dad's freezer and roasted carrots. Not your traditional Christmas dinner, but so full of flavour and grown right here on the land. Despite the delicious food, no one really has much appetite today.

It's snowing again. 'Good job you stayed put, Twm, and you, Myfanwy,' says Dad.

'I could smell the snow in the air,' says Twm.

'It's good to have you here,' says Dad to Myfanwy, and they clink glasses gently.

We're just finishing lunch, putting the plates on the side and Myfanwy's Christmas cake in the middle of the table, with a pot of tea for those who want it, when a car I don't recognize comes up the drive. It pulls up close to Owen's truck, and out gets Mae, with the boys, opening their mouths to catch snowflakes on their tongues. She hurries to the front door.

'Any news?' she says, flinging it open.

Owen repeats he's ringing the surgery at five.

Josh is joining in with the boys, catching snowflakes.

Something strikes me. 'Wait a minute, I thought you and Josh – I thought you were out for a posh lunch.'

'We were, and it was incredible. I'm really grateful to him. But I couldn't get hold of anyone, so we finished pud and came straight here after dropping Mum off at her flat. She had a lovely time, but was ready for a nap. So, this is Josh, everyone,' she says, officially introducing him to us as he stands in the doorway covered with melting snowflakes.

'Hope we're not intruding,' he says shyly, stepping in through the kitchen door. 'I brought some wine.'

'Not intruding at all!' I say. 'Come on in. You're very welcome.'

'I know things haven't been easy, what with the café closing.' He turns to Owen. 'And I'm sorry to hear about your dog. I have everything crossed for her.'

Owen looks up at him. 'Thanks, mate,' he says.

'How about a game of cards while we wait?' says Dad, gently. 'Game of sevens!'

'Yes!' say the boys. And then one says, 'I hope Jess is going to be okay. I like her.' He gets something out of his pocket, wrapped in a paper napkin. 'I saved her my sausage and bacon from lunch,' he says, holding out the parcel to Owen, who looks as if he might weep all over again.

'She'll love that, thank you,' says Owen, with a crack

in his voice, taking it. 'I'll tell her you saved it for her.' I know he wants to say, 'If she makes it home . . .' but doesn't. Instead he says, 'Right, let's set up the cards.'

We cut the cake, which is dark and full of fruit, and has a hint of brandy under the layers of soft yellow marzipan and sweet white icing.

'I make one every year. No idea why. No one to share it with, and I'm still eating it at Easter.'

'It's habit . . . tradition,' says Dad. 'It's hard to let go of the past,' he says, his eyes on me.

'It is,' she says. 'Stubbornness,' and they both laugh.

'Sometimes you have to find a way to make new ones. New memories.'

They're staring at each other and I'm thinking this may be the start of a very different new year.

I consider what Dad said about letting go of the past.

'Well, I'm hoping you'll be sharing this cake with me again next year,' says Dad, and Myfanwy beams.

I can feel Llew next to me, smell the pine of Christmas-tree sap on him and feel the closeness of his strong body. 'You okay?' he murmurs into my ear, making my insides melt like chocolate.

'Just thinking about the past, the future, what to do for the best for the farm,' I say. 'Wondering what the new year will bring.' I glance up at the envelope on the shelf. Is Gramps's field one of the things I have to let go of? The traditions of the past, the sheep in the field, grazing. And let the solar panels go ahead to save the future of the farm. I wish some sort of sign would tell me I'm doing the right thing in agreeing to them. I look at Llew, wondering if he will be a part of the new year and my new future.

I pour more wine, and tea for Owen, who doesn't want a drink until he knows how Jess is, in case he has to go to the vet straight away, while Dad deals the cards. We play hand after hand with one eye on the clock, laughter finding its way into the unusual Christmas Day.

At five to five, it's dark outside. We've been watching the clock slowly tick around the last hour. Owen stands up at the table. 'I'll go to the shed and make the call,' he says. He puts his hand on Evie's shoulder and she puts her hand on his and looks up at him. We watch him pulling on his coat and leaving through the front door, with his phone as a torch, Ffion and Dewi at his feet, as if they're not used to seeing him without a dog. A cold snowy blast pushes its way into the kitchen, flicking up cards and reordering them as they land.

We deal the cards again, but no one is really concentrating on playing.

He's gone a long half-hour. We look at each other and everyone is thinking it must be bad news if he's away so long. I haven't put up today's Instagram post but what can I say? How can I end it on a cheery note when Jess may not make it? The tension in the kitchen is rising and I'm at the sink putting all my frustration into scrubbing the pans from lunch until, finally, the wooden door to the farmhouse opens and Owen is there, hair covered with snow, eyes wide.

We wait for him to speak.

'She's going to be okay,' he says. A tear escapes, a hiccup too. 'She'll need meds and I don't know yet how I'll get the money, but I will.'

Evie is the first on her feet, hugging him. 'I'll make more dog leads and scarves, that'll help! Maybe dog hats too.'

'And we can do another food-truck night,' says Mae. I see the worry on her face; having turned down the job at the café, what will she do now?

'We can give the Amazon vouchers we got for Christmas from Josh,' says one of the boys.

Owen throws his head back and laughs. 'Thank you, *diolch*, all of you. For today and everything. Happy Christmas!' He leans forward and picks up his untouched glass of wine. 'I can bring her home tomorrow.'

'Well, best you stay here for the night,' I say. 'Looks like we could all do with staying put! I'll find more blankets and pillows.' I'm in my comfort zone, sorting out bedrooms and makeshift beds for the night as the snow falls heavier outside.

The cards are dealt once again, this time with much more ambition, rivalry and laughter. With the make-shift beds organised, I head to the back door. 'I'm going to check the sheep,' I say, winding my new scarf from Evie around my neck.

I pick up the keyring that Llew bought me from the shop where he found the tree. It's a little Land Rover, with a Christmas tree on top. I feed the key Dad has given me onto it and hold it up. 'Best present ever,' I say, wishing there was another way to keep the farm and I could stay here for ever.

'I'll come with you,' says Llew, pulling a hat off the hooks. Yup, could be my mother's old one again, pink with the bow. 'Actually, I have another present for you in the car.'

'Best Christmas ever,' I hear one of the boys saying, as we step out into the snow and I look back at the golden glow of the lights in the kitchen.

'Oh, Jem, might be an idea to look in at the ewe in the shed,' calls Owen. 'Shout if you need me.'

'Okay,' I call back, stepping into the cold, wintry evening.

In the shed, where the ewe is, I spot it immediately. 'She's not due yet! Too soon!' I say, watching the ewe as she lies down.

'She's going to give birth?' says Llew.

'Yup, clearly the lamb has its own ideas . . . Bertie,' I add, 'you and your break-outs to the girls' field.'

'Do you want me to get Owen?' says Llew, pointing back towards the farmhouse.

'I think we can probably manage between the two of us and Mum,' I say, gesturing at the ewe and stripping off my coat. 'It's not like I haven't done this before.' It all comes flooding back, my days of lambing beside Dad in this shed. Happy days.

'I'd certainly like to think we can,' he says, and together we kneel in the straw and help the lamb into the world.

Llew opens the kitchen door and the boys look at me as I walk in, carrying the lamb, wrapped in an old blanket, their eyes agog.

'This one needs a bit of help getting warmed up by the range,' I say, and the room sighs with happiness.

'Is she going to be okay?' asks one of the boys.

'I hope so. With a bit of warmth and some milk. I'll make a bottle and you can feed her, if you like.'

I make up the mixture and the lamb starts feeding from the bottle.

'Looks like this one's a fighter,' says Dad.

'What are we going to call her?' asks one of the boys.

'I don't know,' I say, watching them take turns to hold the bottle as the lamb tugs on the teat.

'What about Mary?' says Luke.

'Or Angel?' says Owen.

'Gabriel is nice,' says Mae. 'Or Josh?'

'That's because she fancies him,' says Luke to me. 'I can see she's happy. I like it when Mum's happy!'

'Me too,' I tell the pair. 'And she likes seeing you happy as well!'

'Today has been very happy,' says Jacob. 'Can we come back for my birthday?'

'And feed lambs!'

I laugh. 'Well, yes, that would be lovely,' I say, not adding, 'If we're still here, me and the flock.' I think of how lovely it would be to hold children's parties on Gramps's field in the spring and summer, with a barbecue going, like last night at the cattle market, but with good weather.

'What about Hope?' says Llew, watching the children.

I turn to him. I want to have this man in my life not just for Christmas but for a long time after. 'I think Hope is a very good name.' I look around the group. Dad is wearing his napkin on his head like a pirate's hat, as if it was the most normal thing in the world. 'Hope is what we all need.'

We move from the kitchen to the living room and I put the lamb, full and sleepy, in front of the fire there and sit on the arm of the sofa. Llew hands me a drink and sits next to me. The others follow us in and the boys sit on the floor next to the lamb. I take a picture of her, and introduce her to my followers on Instagram.

'Everyone, this is Hope. And hope is what I'm wishing for you all this Christmas,' I say, into the microphone and post it.

'So, we were talking while you were bringing a new lamb into the world,' says Mae, sharing an armchair with Josh.

'Hope,' corrects Luke.

'Hope,' says Mae. She takes a deep breath. 'We want to do another food night. Keep doing what we started, keep the idea of the market going.'

'Well, that sounds good,' I say, sitting on the arm of the squashy sofa sipping the spicy red wine.

'But where? We haven't got the money to buy the lease on the cattle market and I don't think that woman would agree to us doing another fundraiser. In fact, I'm not sure we'll see her around here again.'

They look at Dad, then at me.

'It was your dad's idea,' says Mae.

He beams.

'Well?' I ask.

'Here!' he says.

'Here?' I frown.

'Yes! On the farm. Or, more precisely, in Gramps's field.'

'But the solar panels? I can't see another way. We're going to have to agree to sell it.'

'But it's not agreed yet,' says Llew. 'Not until the new year. You have until twelve o'clock on New Year's Eve, the last day of the year, to agree . . . or not.'

I think about the contract on the shelf, waiting to be signed.

'And if it goes well . . .' says Mae.

'. . . we could do more!' My eyes widen. 'Easter-egg hunts, summer parties for children! Bring in more and more local producers to sell food, hot and cold. Like a food hub. You could have the lorry beside Gramps's bench and run a daily café there! You could keep going with the jacket potatoes and I could make the cawl and curry to sell. Get people to come to the farm for lunch, serving local produce. It could be brilliant! It's the perfect spot for the lorry.'

'I think so,' says Mae. 'And, of course, we'd get the right paperwork and consents and make it all above board.'

'Gramps's Field Café!' I say. 'You run it and I'll supply the potatoes and cawl.'

She grins. 'It could be perfect!'

'And,' says Evie, 'use the barns for producers, like me. A barn to make my dog leads in.'

'We could do them up!" I say, excited. 'A proper farmers' and producers' food-stall market.'

'And rent the barns to other food producers, once they're done up.'

'But if we use Gramps's field, where will everyone park?'

'I've got room,' says Myfanwy. 'You can use the connecting field at mine.'

'Yes!' exclaims Dad. 'And you can do more of your baking and sell it there. It'll be delivered straight from your farmhouse to the market.'

'But!' I say, and they all look at me.

'But what?' Llew asks.

'But what if no one comes?' I say, and the room falls flat again.

'But what if they do?' says Llew. 'We'll get it on social media. Explain what's going on and what people can expect. What they can get out of coming.'

'People want to feel connected and that's what you did,' says Mae.

'It's a risk,' I say, 'trying something new. The solar panels would be a safer bet.' I look at Dad.

'Maybe this farm has been playing it safe for too many years. Like Myfanwy says, we're set in our ways, me and her. We're so used to our farms being next to each other and being rivals over the ram, we wouldn't try something new, like getting along. It took a bout of sepsis to change that! And the threat of losing the farm! Who'd have thought you talking into your phone and telling everyone about what it's like on the farm could have made such a difference and touch people's lives?' He gazes at me so proudly. 'Got to be worth a shot, love,' he says.

'But we've so much to lose,' I say, and look round the room. 'But so much to gain if it works.'

They wait with bated breath.

'A weekly food-stall market . . . events here, at the farm.'

'Bringing farmers back together,' says Owen.

'And the people living here,' says Mae. 'Getting them eating better food. Knowing where it comes from.' She turns to Josh. 'It's what people want these days.'

'And comfort food,' I say. 'Food that makes them feel good, in a place they can spend time with family and friends that isn't a brightly coloured fast-food outlet.'

'Or, worse, a drive-through,' says Mae.

'Maybe you could run some rugby workshops, in the summer . . . get people working out on the farm,' says Llew, making me smile. 'You don't need an indoor gym to stay fit. And it's so good for the mind too.'

'Imagine if Gramps could see it. The barns full of people who want to make local produce. The field full of food trucks. We could even do allotments and rent them to people,' I say, my mind galloping ahead.

'Get people coming here, instead of heading out of town.' I look around. 'It has to be worth a try. I can't promise they'll come, but there's only one way to find out.'

'When?' says Mae.

I smile. 'A New Year's Eve street-food festival here at the farm!'

And with that Hope, the premature lamb, gives a little bleat of encouragement and we laugh.

'We need some Christmas Hope!' says Dad.

'Got any more sprouts, Twm?' I ask.

'Loads!'

'Thought we could sell them in paper cones, salted, with butter and a bit of bacon!'

'That sounds lovely!' He chortles. 'I'll be there for those!'

And Dewi runs in with bits of ripped-up paper in his mouth, tossing it around.

'What's that?' asks Dad.

'Looks like the solar-panels contract,' I say. 'Must have blown down from the shelf when we came in from the barn.'

'Well, then,' says Dad, not attempting to get the envelope back from Dewi. 'Looks like this has to work now.'

36

'A taste of Wales,' I say into the camera. 'Any food producers, get in touch. We want you to come along. Let people taste your food and tell them where it's come from.'

'Now all we have to do is hope,' I say in the shed, the next morning, after Llew has filmed me talking about our new year food festival. 'Hope the producers turn up and people come to eat the food.'

I can't bear to think what will happen if this doesn't work. The farm will definitely have to be sold. We're out of options.

Llew puts down the phone and walks over to join me.

'Hope,' he says, looking at the lamb: she has been reunited with her mum, wearing a warm jumper Evie knitted.

'What will you do now?' I ask. 'When do you have to go back?'

'I'm not sure,' he says. 'What about you?'

'If this doesn't work? Look for another job.'

'What about the B-and-B idea? People would love to stay here. I know I do.'

'It could work with something else, but not on its own. If the street-food festival took off, and the barns, it could be part of it.'

'Stronger together?' he asks.

I nod.

'I get it. A bit like the people I've met since I've been here,' he says. 'You, Mae, Owen, Evie, your dad and Myfanwy, you've all rallied around Owen and Jess.'

'I don't want to sell. I'm staying here and I'm going to make this work! I can't do it on my own. You're right, we're all stronger together. I thought I was a lone wolf when I worked at the hotel, didn't need any help, but it wasn't a team. People worked for me. Here, we've got to work together.'

I look at him as he pulls me close. 'Same when I gave in my notice. I realized I didn't care about what I was doing. I wasn't helping people. I thought I was, but it was about getting the deal. Competing with my colleagues. Seeing who could seal the most deals. It didn't mean anything.'

I stare at him, suddenly terrified of saying what's on my mind.

37

New Year's Eve

It's pitch black, as Llew and I check and feed the ewes. The last day of the year. And what a year! I would never have expected to end up back at the farm, with a man I've only just met, but with whom I may be falling very much in love. I glance at him as we lay fresh straw in the pen for the ewe and her lamb, still wearing one of Evie's unique jumpers.

I remember how I managed to tell Llew how I was feeling. Took the leap of faith. It took me two years and three months to admit to Matthew how I thought I felt about him, and look how wrong I got that. Turned out I was just part of his plan for the perfect couple on his Facebook page. The power couple, about to start their new life in Seattle. 'Living the dream'. Well, I know now it wasn't my dream. My dream is here . . . What he wanted was my job. The life in Seattle, come what may! The corporate couple. We never discussed having a family: it wasn't on the cards. And now more than anything I want to stay here, and build on the little family we have. Dad and Myfanwy. Mae, the boys and Josh. Owen, Evie and Jess. And I may be taking a leap of faith, but I've never felt so happy, relaxed or myself. Just being me, where I want to be, with the person I want to be with.

Back in the kitchen, the lights are on, warm and welcoming. Owen and Evie are already there, Jess wearing her cone around her neck, with a festive scarf from Evie. Dad and Myfanwy arrive from her farmhouse across Gramps's field, the fairy lights still lit up, and join us in the kitchen. As tea and toast are made, the kitchen fills with the scent of caramelizing bread. Between us we fill the toast rack and keep the toast coming from on top of the range. There's butter in a dish on the worn pine table, which has more stories to tell than I care to think about, from the chew marks left by different puppies, the paint stains from when I was a child and the burn from the pot of chilli I made on my eighteenth birthday. It's like all my past is here . . . and possibly my future.

'Right. The weather. It looks like it'll be cold and clear,' says Owen. 'The ground's hard, but that'll work in our favour with the trucks.'

'If they come.' I feel a wave of uncertainty.

'All the people from the Christmas Eve feast have said they're coming.'

'So it's just the customers we need,' I say, feeling anxious. 'What if no one comes?'

And none of us has an answer to that. We just have to do our best and hope.

Later that morning we head to Gramps's field. Evie is putting up signs with arrows from the road to the car park at Myfanwy's. The lorry is by Gramps's bench. Owen is organizing generators and the festoon lighting from the yard to the field and to Myfanwy's. He and Llew have their heads together, planning where each food truck should set up and where they can feed off the electricity. Josh and the boys are collecting wood for a firepit in the middle of the yard. Myfanwy is running up bunting and stringing it around the place.

I pick up my phone and start filming the activity in the yard and on Gramps's field. Bertie, Harriet and the ewes are watching with interest. Ffion and Jess wander the yard together, like the sisters they are, taking comfort from each other's company.

'We should ask everyone coming to bring a lantern

to help with lighting,' I say suddenly, imagining how this place will look all lit up.

'Great idea,' says Llew. 'Put it on social media!' I kiss him quickly and hurry up to the shed, where I put together a little reel and tell people that the trucks will be open from five and to bring lanterns and torches. The video gets loads of likes and reposts and I hope that means this will work, for Jess's sake, and the farm's.

This could be the start of bringing back the community to the area and starting a whole new future.

At four o'clock the first of the trucks arrives, checked off the list by Llew and directed into place by Owen. It's a beautifully decorated horsebox, with fake flowers and lights, selling homemade cakes and honeycomb.

'Hi, welcome to Hope Food Festival,' I say, to the young woman. 'I love your truck.'

'Thanks. I'm just starting out, so I wasn't sure if I'd be the right fit here.'

'You'll be perfect! We're here for all the comfort food.' I smile. 'If you need anything, just ask us. And thank you for coming,' I say, as she hands me her pitch fee.

She's followed by the boys from the tractor run. They're going to do hot dogs again, on Gramps's field, on the big oil-drum barbecue. And others follow, the macaroni-cheese truck, crêpes sold by members of the Young Farmers with their parents. The kids are test-running the chocolate spread and seem to have it all over their faces. The lorry is set up to serve shepherd's pies, hogget curry and cawl, with homemade bread; the trailer next to it, with Mae's jacket potatoes, boasts pots of grated cheese, beans, tuna and a vegetarian chilli.

At twenty to five, the firepit is lit. The festoon lighting from Gramps's field to the yard is turned on. All the food trucks have battery-operated fairy lights and smoke is spiralling upwards from the fire. The barbecue and the sweet crêpes smell amazing. The scene looks and feels fantastic.

'Something you created,' Llew says. 'It's amazing.'

'What if it's not enough? What if no one comes?'

He pulls me close. 'Then you will at least have tried.' He kisses me. 'One last thing to do,' he says, and disappears towards the field where the cars are parked. I can see him and Myfanwy in conversation.

Later I do a mental check that everything is set. Now all we need is customers. I take a deep breath and look around for Llew. He went off about half an hour ago with Myfanwy.

'Jem!' I hear a shout. It's Mae. She's standing on the edge of the yard, looking over the field towards the end of the drive. Like fireflies in the night, there are lanterns and torches flickering at the bottom of the drive. I can hear the chug of a tractor.

'It's Llew and Myfanwy. They took the tractor and trailer to town to pick up people from outside Coffi Poeth,' she shouts, coming towards me. 'Myfanwy's driving! Llew put it online! A tractor ride to the farm!'

'But he hates all that online stuff!'

She beams. 'Looks like he realized maybe it's not such a bad thing after all.'

And there, coming up the drive, is the tractor with lights all over it, and a group of young revellers flourishing phone torches, riding in the trailer with Llew pointing out where everything is and the parking in Myfanwy's field to the left. Cars are backed up behind the tractor.

'They came,' I say, quietly at first, then look at Mae. 'THEY CAME!' we shout.

'It's like the Three Wise Men, a bit late, but they've followed the star and made it.' She throws her head back and laughs.

Llew is standing in the trailer, holding up a lantern and waving at me. The tractor stops in Gramps's field and Llew jumps down, helping people off the trailer and pointing them towards the festoon lighting that is showing the path up to the firepit in the yard where there are straw bales to sit on, at a suitable distance from the fire. It has a pen around it, organized by Owen. People start to wander up towards the yard, some stopping at the barbecue for their range of hot dogs: chilli dogs, hot dogs with cheese, and even a veggie dog.

Music is playing and it's crisp and cold.

'Hello, you!' says Llew, pulling me close to him.

'Thank you!' I say, feeling choked. Now. I should tell him now. Tell him I want him to stay here, with me. Make this work one way or another. Run a farmer's market every month, maybe a farm shop from one of the barns, sell our produce and other local farmers', with Mae running a café here.

'Llew, I . . .' I lift my face to look at his. I know this is what I want. I want to tell him, right now. I lean in closer to be nearer his face and his lips. I want to ask him to stay. Tell him I've never felt more certain about anything.

'You've got a queue,' he says. 'Need a hand?'

I turn to see people waiting by the cattle lorry. 'Yes!' I say, and we hurry up the ramp and start serving under the dark but glorious starry night. The very last of the year.

As the queue quietens, I pull out my phone and look at all the pictures shared, loved and liked on social media of the Hope Food Festival. I look around for Llew. I need to tell him what's on my mind.

'Excuse me?' says a young man, holding up a

lantern. 'Is it true you're going to rent out studio space in your barn?'

I give a little laugh. 'Word travels fast,' I say. 'I'm certainly thinking about it.'

'I'd be interested. I make chopping boards from wood. I'm with the cake lady,' he says, pointing to the pretty horsebox. 'I've been looking for somewhere to set up, but I can't find anything I can afford.'

'Well, give me your number and, if all goes well, hopefully, we'll make these events a regular thing and find some space for young entrepreneurs like yourself.'

'I could do workshops too. Oh, and I do IT for a big company, if that helps.'

'It does,' I say. 'We all share our skills, so I think we could make this work.'

As we're swapping numbers I hear the laughter first, then a voice I recognize. I freeze.

'You wouldn't think this was the same place, honestly. When I first came here it was like something from Cold Comfort Farm!'

My mouth drops open in surprise. I close it and collect myself. 'Matthew!' I say. 'What are you doing here?'

38

'Jem!' He holds his arms wide. 'I was just saying how you've changed this place.'

I clear my throat. 'Yes, I heard.'

He walks towards me and kisses me on both cheeks, leaving me feeling cold. 'Happy New Year!' he says, smiling.

I have no idea what he's doing here. 'Shouldn't you be getting ready for Seattle? You leave tomorrow, don't you?'

'Yes! But we had to take a run out here first. This place has gone mad on social media. Hope Food Festival.' He looks around. 'It's what people want! Good home-grown, affordable food.'

'Yes, we like it,' I say stiffly, not needing his endorsement for what he referred to as Cold Comfort Farm.

'I'm impressed,' says a man with him.

'Jem, this is Paul Henry, a new member to the board at Cwtch Hotels, in charge of diversity, new ideas,' says Matthew. 'With you gone, we need to come up with some fresh strategies of our own. I've shown him what you've been up to here.'

The irony of this being my idea isn't lost on me.

'Had to come and see it for myself,' he says, wearing the same smile as Matthew. 'Before Matthew shoots off to the States. Not sure I could have found my way on my own.' He gives a ridiculous loud laugh.

'Maybe I should have kept it secret.' I frown, remembering what it was like working for the hotel chain, never being at home for Christmas or New Year. Never imagining there was a different way of living. 'So you came here on New Year's Eve? Drove all the way to see our food festival?'

'We did!' he says, as if I should be impressed. 'As I say, you have a very persuasive way of selling this place and being on a farm on your social-media feed. It's impressive marketing.'

I want to laugh at Cwtch Hotels following my feed and finding it 'impressive'. But it's not that that's bothering me.

'Don't you have family you want to be with this evening? Friends you want to share a drink with? Don't you find it odd that you're out working on New Year's Eve and not taking time to enjoy a local pub or restaurant, encourage and support the industry? Actually enjoy being in the world you work in?'

He shakes his head. 'Not for me. Taking the early flight with Matthew to go through new ideas for the Seattle hotel. I must say, though, this is very impressive,' he says, looking around at the busy yard, people eating and drinking – there's a fishing boat on a trailer, selling local beer, and the barmen are singing sea shanties: a late but very welcome addition to the party who heard about us from the pizza truck. They had a cancellation so asked if they could join us here.

'You know,' Matthew says, into my ear, 'you could still be part of the team over there. I know they'd have you back if you asked. I could put in a word. And this place will have done you loads of favours. What you've pulled off here is incredible.'

'If I asked to go back? Begged, you mean,' I say, feeling my festive spirit dissipating into the starry sky.

'Or . . . there is another option,' says Mr Diversity, as Llew comes to stand beside me. I see Matthew eye him suspiciously.

'What's that?' I wish I didn't want to know.

'This place?' he says.

I look at him. 'What? The farm?'

He nods.

'Everyone wants to get into farms these days! Ever since Jeremy Clarkson and Kaleb. Look at the crowd you've pulled in. We could help be a part of it.'

'You'd want to invest?' An injection of cash to help us on our way is appealing.

'No, we'd buy it.'

'Sorry?' I lean in, as if I haven't heard him correctly.

'We'd buy the farm, and you could do what you do best. Turn it into a boutique hotel. Farmhouse B-and-B.'

I repeat his offer back to him. 'You want to buy the farm and turn it into a B-and-B.'

He nods.

Llew drops his head and walks away. I want to go after him. Ask him what he thinks.

'With food festivals every week on the car park or yard. We roll out the design and formula to other farms that are struggling, buy them and make them boutique B-and-Bs with street food.'

I stand open-mouthed.

Just as I hear, 'Ten, nine, eight . . .' I check the time on my phone, trying to get a picture of the field to post . . . It's nearly midnight and my shaking hands fumble over the video button.

'It could be the start of a big business,' I hear him saying, as I struggle to get a snapshot of what we've created here.

'. . . seven, six, five . . .'

I glance around again, clutching my new phone, which Llew insisted on buying me for Christmas and which connects to a network that works from the farm, which will help with the social media. People are holding up their lanterns and drinks and counting. Dad and Myfanwy are holding each other in their arms, beaming. Mae is holding hands with Josh, thinking no one can see them.

Evie is stroking Jess, and Owen is by her side. It's just Llew who's missing, and I'm trying to see where he went, wondering if he's gone before I had the chance to tell him exactly how I feel and what I want here at Hope Food Festival.

'. . . four, three, two . . .'

My eyes fill with tears. He's not here. I look back at Matthew and hope to God he's not going to lean in for a . . .

'. . . one! Happy new year!'

Matthew leans towards me as I put up a hand. 'I think we're way past new-year kisses,' I say. 'I wish you well, Matthew, but no, I don't want Seattle, and this farm is certainly not for sale,' I say to both men. Suddenly the air is full of happiness and joy. No bangs or whistles from fireworks, just families and friends wishing each other luck for the new year and celebrating their friendship and love around a huge, glowing firepit, radiating warmth and happiness.

It's the sign I needed, if I needed one at all. I pull out my phone and press the button to film, and as I do, I set off, following the festoon lighting, towards the car park where Llew has the boot of his car open.

I have to stop him leaving. Tell him how I feel and that I'm not going to sell out to big business.

Suddenly, I can't help myself, I break into a run, and when I reach him, I throw my arms around him and hug him hard. 'I loved this! Thank you! Actually, I love you! Oh, I didn't plan for it to come out like that! Actually, I don't really have a plan. But I love you, and I'm hoping I haven't scared you off, and I just want to know if you'll stay here, with me, at the farm.'

'What about Matthew and his companion?'

I turn to look at the drive. 'If I'm not very much mistaken, Matthew and his companion are leaving now.'

He looks at me. 'And you, are you going with them?'

'No, I'm not going anywhere! Corporate life is out of mine for good! This dream is not for sale! This is about all of us building this place together.' I stop smiling. 'I thought you'd left.'

'I thought you might leave.'

'But you didn't.'

'Nor did you!'

I laugh.

'What?' he asks, and laughs back.

'That idea, about the outside gym, healthy bodies and minds, here on the farm,' I say. 'You could . . .' I swallow and take a deep breath '. . . you could always stay here. If it worked,' I say quickly. 'If you wanted to. I mean, if . . . you, me . . . if you thought . . .' I'm rarely tongue-tied, and I think I've got my words out, roughly in the right order. 'You could run your boot camps from here. Have people to stay at the farm and get them working out here.'

'I thought you'd never ask!' he says. 'I don't have a lot to offer. But I promise you, I'll put my whole heart into getting the food market off the ground. I'll help you.'

'The pay's not great, but there's always a cuppa and a Welsh cake, and a pot of cawl on the go.' I smile. 'And there's this place, the barn,' I say looking around. 'Thought I'd make it into a classroom, teach local businesses about social media, how it can help them. Creating a community. And, of course, we'd need Owen back working here, as farm manager.'

'Definitely. And you could do all sorts of classes too, wreath-making at Christmas, knitting classes with Evie.'

'It'll need doing up.'

'Looks like I'll have to roll up my sleeves.'

'Sounds perfect to me.'

'If we can make this work, if we can all work together, create our own little village, here at the farm, we could all benefit from it.'

'Let's hope we do.'

'I like the sound of that, Hope food trucks in the fields . . . maybe a farm shop and workshops.'

'Let's hope this goes well, then!'

'Looks like we should probably stay here together.'

'I think we should. We've got a lamb to look after between us.'

'Yes, the custody battle could've been messy.'

'Think you might have to change your car.'

'You're right.'

'I just came to the car to fetch these for you,' he says, closing the boot and handing me a box.

'What is it?'

'I told you I had something for you in the car. A present. It's just been so busy, I kept forgetting to give it to you. Until Matthew arrived.'

'But you left when they were making their offer. I thought you were leaving.'

'I knew you'd make the right decision. You didn't need my input.'

I open the box and see a brand new pair of pink, flowered wellington boots, just like my old ones, but without the cracks.

'I love them!' I say, hugging him.

'You'll need them if you're going to be a full-time farmer now. Got myself some too.' I look down at his muddy boots.

'I can take them back and get you plain ones, if you like,' he says, suddenly serious.

'Now, where would be the fun in being the same as everyone else? We're all different. They're perfect! Thank you!'

I smile, then lean in to kiss him. Finally, when we break apart, I say, 'Happy New Year.'

'Happy New Year.'

'Come on, I think we deserve a drink. I'll go with Myfanwy to take the tractor-ride customers back and you open a bottle. I'll meet you in the kitchen.'

We walk back to the yard, hand in hand, looking up at the starry night.

'I think Gramps would approve,' I say.

And in the background I can hear a clock ticking . . . in my head, in my heart, in the pit of my stomach, as if something has woken up in me. Something a lot like feeling I'm where I belong, with the people, and one person in particular, I love. And maybe this isn't the end of a mixed-up year but the beginning of a whole new one.

'I wonder where we'll be this time next year,' I say.

'Here, together, a family . . .' he says, and kisses me all over again. Already I'm looking forward to the spring, summer and autumn, not from the inside of a hotel lobby, but from out here, where it all begins, where everything feels real.

We walk up towards the yard where the others are standing, smiling and clapping. Mae, Evie, Dad, Myfanwy and Owen. 'Finally!' they cheer.

And I blush.

'What?' I try to bluff my way through their enthusiasm.

'You left your phone on live again!'

'Everyone on your socials is wishing you all the best and can't wait to see what happens to the pair of you and Hope Food Festival in the new year!'

'We've got nearly a million likes!'

I look up at the stars, scattered across the clear dark night, each of them twinkling, but one in particular sparkles particularly brightly over Gramps's field. I know who that is. He always said when I was away, starting my career, that if I was ever homesick I should look up at the sky, find the brightest star and know that he would be looking at the same one. And now we're all together looking up at the same special star.

'Hear that, Gramps? A million!'

I don't know whether to laugh or cry. But I know I'm happy. I'm at home and I may not know what this year will bring, but with Llew beside me, my family and friends, between us we have hope.

ACKNOWLEDGEMENTS

I am surrounded by a lot of young farmers where I live in West Wales. And it's these young people I have to thank for inspiring this book. It's a hard job, physically and emotionally. It can be long hours for not a lot of pay. But for them it is a way of life. And I love their dedication to the profession.

My daughter went to work for a charity, the DPJ foundation, a mental health farming charity. The foundation was set up by Emma Picton-Jones following the death of her husband, Daniel. He was a husband and father to young children and was suffering from poor mental health. He was an agricultural contractor, a part of the industry that has one of the highest suicide rates. The foundation was set up in 2016. Emma's vision was to support those in the agricultural sector. The charity was set up in Pembrokeshire and has grown and now covers the whole of Wales working with organizations like NFU Cymru, FUW, Young Farmers Clubs and Vets to help get the support to people working in the industry that they may not know how to get. Their motto is 'share the load', because it's sometimes easier to talk to a stranger than it is to those close to you. The DPJ foundation offers support with counsellors and therapists and awareness of mental health within communities. To date they have helped over 1200 families in Wales.

It was Emma's story that inspired me. And the volunteers who work with Emma. You must look out for the Hywel Davies Lorry at agricultural events. It's a converted lorry, complete with lights made out of milking parlour equipment, where people can pop in for basic health checks, a cup of tea, a chat and if you're lucky one of Ceri's welsh cakes. You can see where the idea for the converted lorry came from in this book. There's Sian making teas and Emma the nurse who drives the lorry and will give you a quick once over, doing blood pressure and other checks that people working in rural communities may not be able to get around to easily.

They offer grief and bereavement support and are there to listen and share the load. Please do look up their website and follow them on social media. They are doing wonderful work. And this is what made me want to write this book. This, and to raise a glass to the young entrepreneurs that I see here in my part of Pembrokeshire. Young people setting up businesses, in hospitality, tourism, diversifying on the farms and in our food sector. I really believe there is a new wave of awareness happening, where people are starting to pay attention to where their food is produced and

Acknowledgements

how far it has travelled to make it to their tables and these young farmers are behind that.

www.thedpjfoundation.co.uk
Instagram @thedpjfoundation
Facebook: thedpjfoundation

Happy Christmas all and remember to share the load.

With Love

Jo
x

*Read on for some delicious
recipes and to discover
more of Jo's uplifting and
heart-warming books . . .*

Traditional Welsh Cawl

Cawl is a hearty Welsh stew typically made with lamb and root vegetables. It's simple, warming, and full of flavour.

Serves 4–6

Ingredients:

1 tbsp vegetable oil or beef dripping
800g lamb neck or shoulder (bone-in preferred), chopped into chunks
2 large onions, peeled and chopped
1.5 litres water
1 beef or lamb stock cube (optional, for richer flavour)
3 carrots, peeled and sliced
2 parsnips, peeled and chopped (optional)
½ small swede (about 300g), peeled and chopped
3 medium potatoes, peeled and quartered
1 small leek, cleaned and sliced
Salt and freshly ground black pepper
Fresh parsley, chopped (to garnish)
Crusty bread to serve

Method:

1. Heat the oil or dripping in a large saucepan or stockpot over medium heat. Add the chunks of lamb and brown on all sides. Remove the lamb and set aside.
2. Add the chopped onions to the same pan and cook gently for 5 minutes until softened. Return the lamb to the pan, cover with water (about 1.5 litres or enough to cover it entirely), and bring to a boil.
3. Reduce the temperature to a simmer, and skim off any scum that rises to the surface of the water. Add the

stock cube and stir, then cover and leave to simmer gently for 1 and a half to 2 hours.

4. Add the carrots, parsnips, swede and potatoes, then simmer for a further 30 minutes until vegetables are tender.

5. Stir in the sliced leeks and let the stew continue to cook for a further 10 to 15 minutes. Season with salt and pepper to taste.

6. Serve with chunks of crusty bread and enjoy!

Shepherd's Pie

There's nothing quite like a shepherd's pie for dinner – simple and comforting, this is the perfect recipe to warm up with on a chilly winter's evening.

Serves 4-6

Ingredients:

For the filling:

1 tbsp olive oil
1 onion, finely chopped
2 carrots, diced
2 garlic cloves, crushed
500g lamb mince
1 tbsp tomato purée
1 tbsp plain flour
300ml lamb or beef stock
1 tsp Worcestershire sauce
1 tsp fresh thyme leaves (or ½ tsp dried thyme)
Salt and freshly ground black pepper
A handful of frozen peas

For the topping:

900g floury potatoes (e.g. Maris Piper or King Edward), peeled and chopped
50g butter
50ml milk (more if needed)
Salt and white pepper
50g mature cheddar cheese, grated (for topping)

Method:

1. Heat the oil in a large frying pan or saucepan over medium heat. Add the onion and carrots, and cook for 5–8 minutes until softened. Stir in the garlic and cook for a minute or two longer, until fragrant.

2. Add the lamb mince and cook until browned, breaking it up as it cooks. Add in the tomato purée and flour and stir for 2 minutes, then add the stock, Worcestershire sauce, thyme, salt, and pepper. Stir well.

3. Simmer uncovered for 20–25 minutes, until the sauce has thickened. Stir in the peas and cook for a further 5 minutes, then set aside.

4. Preheat the oven to 180°C (160°C fan) / 350°F / Gas mark 4.

5. While the filling is simmering, boil the potatoes in salted water for about 15–20 minutes until tender. Drain well and mash with butter and milk until smooth and fluffy, and season to taste.

6. Spoon the lamb mixture into an ovenproof dish (around 25cm square), and spread the mashed potato over the top, starting from the edges to seal in the filling. Use a fork to rough up the surface and sprinkle the cheese over the top.

7. Bake for 20-25 minutes until the top has started to colour and the filling is bubbling up around the edges. Leave to stand for 5 minutes, and serve!

Hogget Curry

A hearty yet mild curry, this is a British-Indian fusion dish with a rich and fragrant sauce that perfectly complements the robust taste of mature lamb, also known as hogget!

Serves 4

Ingredients:

800g diced hogget (shoulder or leg), trimmed of excess fat
2 tbsp vegetable oil
1 cinnamon stick
4 green cardamom pods
4 cloves
1 tsp cumin seeds
2 onions, finely sliced
4 garlic cloves, crushed
1 tbsp fresh ginger, grated
1–2 green chillies, finely chopped (adjust to taste)
2 tsp ground cumin
2 tsp ground coriander
1 tsp turmeric
1–1½ tsp chilli powder (to taste)
1 tsp garam masala
1 tbsp tomato purée
1 tin (400g) chopped tomatoes
150ml natural yoghurt (or 200ml coconut milk for a creamier version)
300ml water or lamb stock
Salt to taste
Fresh coriander (to serve)

Method:

1. Heat 1 tbsp of oil in a large, heavy-based pan over medium-high heat. Brown the hogget in batches, then set aside.

2. Heat the remaining 1 tbsp oil, and fry the cinnamon stick, cardamom pods, cloves and cumin seeds until fragrant. Be sure not to fry these for too long, or else they'll burn!

3. Add the sliced onions and cook gently for 10–15 minutes until soft and golden. Stir in garlic, ginger, and green chilli, and let these cook for a further 2 minutes.

4. Stir in the ground cumin, coriander, turmeric, chilli powder and garam masala, followed by the tomato puree, and fry for a minute or two, until aromatic.

5. Add the chopped tomatoes and cook for 5–10 minutes until the sauce thickens and darkens slightly.

6. Return the browned meat to the pan and stir well to coat in the sauce. Add the yoghurt (or coconut milk), followed by the stock or water. Stir to combine.

7. Bring to a simmer, cover with a lid, and cook very gently for 2–2½ hours (either on the hob or in the oven at 150°C (130°C fan)/ 300°F / Gas mark 2 until the meat is tender and the sauce has thickened.

8. Let rest for 10–15 minutes before serving for deeper flavour. Serve over rice or with naan bread, and garnish with fresh coriander.

Welsh Cakes

Deliciously soft and crumbly, these small scone-like cakes are the perfect sweet treat with a large mug of tea!

Makes 12-16 cakes

Ingredients:

225g self-raising flour
½ tsp mixed spice
85g caster sugar (plus extra for dusting)
Pinch of salt
110g unsalted butter (cold), cut into cubes
50g currants or sultanas
1 egg, beaten
Splash of milk (if needed)

Method:

1. Tip the flour, mixed spice, sugar and a pinch of salt into a mixing bowl, then add the butter. Rub the cubes with your fingertips until the mixture resembles fine breadcrumbs.
2. Stir in the currants or sultanas.
3. Then, add the beaten egg and work it into the mixture until it has formed a soft (but not sticky!) dough. If the dough is too dry, add a splash of milk. It should have the consistency of shortcrust pastry.
4. Lightly flour a work surface and roll the dough out to about 5–7mm thick, then cut into rounds using a fluted or plain cutter.
5. Heat a flat griddle, heavy frying pan, or bakestone over medium heat. Lightly grease it with a little butter or oil.

6. Cook the Welsh cakes in batches for about 3 minutes on each side, or until golden brown and cooked through. Be sure not to overcrowd the pan or your cakes won't cook evenly.
7. While still warm, dust with a little caster sugar, and enjoy!

Take one woman longing for the perfect Christmas . . .

All Clara has ever wanted is Christmas surrounded by loved ones, full of warmth and delicious food. So when her new boyfriend asks her to move to Switzerland, she can't help but say yes! After all, what could be more perfect than Christmas in the Alps?

Add a dash of surprise

She quickly signs up for a tempting chocolate-making class, but it turns out to be chocolate-making bootcamp! And her boyfriend isn't all he seemed either . . .

And enjoy a magical festive treat!

Despite it all, Clara begins to make friends – including the aloof yet intriguing Gabriel. With all of the ingredients at her fingertips, will she finally be able to whisk up her Christmas dream?

Could one big surprise save Chloe's Christmas?

Chloe can't wait for Christmas . . . to be over! Her son Ruben is staying with his dad and Chloe is planning to ignore the holidays all together. Her only festive touch is her son's advent calendar, to help count down the days till he's home again.

But a surprise call changes everything. Chloe might be the unexpected owner of some land in Canada! Surely, it's a scam. Or could it be just the escape she needs right now? Ruben's latest note in the advent calendar tells her to 'say yes!'

In a flash, Chloe's new countdown to Christmas involves a log cabin in the middle of a snowy forest, a community that's worried for its future, a gruff lumberjack who gives her butterflies and a *lot* of pancakes with maple syrup . . .

One Icelandic Christmas holiday. One snowstorm. An adventure they'll never forget!

Twenty-five years ago, Freya and her three best friends created a bucket list. The future seemed bright and full of hope . . . But now they are travelling to Iceland in memory of the friend they've lost, determined to fulfil her dream of seeing the Northern Lights at Christmas.

They didn't count on an avalanche leaving them stranded! Handsome local, Pétur, comes to the rescue, showing them how the community survives the hard winter. With Christmas approaching, Freya and her friends throw themselves into the festivities, decorating and cooking for the villagers using delicious local ingredients.

But will they manage to see the Northern Lights? And can Freya's own dreams come true, this Christmas?